CURSED SHARDS

Tales of Dark Folklore

EDITED BY

LEANBH PEARSON

Cursed Shards: Tales of Dark Folklore

ISBN-13: 978-1-922856-48-7

V1.0

Printed in Palatino Linotype and Black Heat.

IFWG Publishing International
Gold Coast

www.ifwgpublishing.com

Table of Contents

Foreword

Kirstyn McDermott

To break a mirror, the superstitious among us would say, is to bring seven years' bad luck upon yourself. To dispel this, you will want to get rid of the broken shards. Perhaps bury them deep in old dirt by the light of a full moon, or simply wrap them in newspaper and throw them into the wheelie bin, drag it out to the street and hope for the best. But don't keep a single piece, not matter how prettily it glitters on your palm. Bad luck. Seven years. And that's just ordinary glass!

What of a mirror made from darkest magic, a mirror that imprisons tortured souls within its depths, souls belonging to the Fae? What happens if you break such a thing as that? Would the resulting shards be cursed, or blessed? You might throw them away as quickly as you can, send them to all corners of the world, not quite knowing whose paths they will cross and what luck might be wrought from their will. Or you might be tempted to keep one, or two, or more, fashion them into magical artefacts, tools, weapons. You might think a curse could, in worthy hands, become a blessing.

Perhaps you would be right.

Then again, we all know how unwise it is to trust the Fae.

Bear such speculations in mind as you step into the realm of *Cursed Shards*. A shared-world anthology is a curious beast, a circle of trust and faith in which the authors link hands and warm their collective imagination around a single flame. Such a book calls to mind witches and bonfires, their spells sung to the sky, their bodies spinning faster, growing giddy and sweat-slicked. Or the fat white mushrooms of a fairy circle, springing up overnight from almost nothing, their caps bedecked with dew drops, inviting you so beguilingly to step into their centre and kneel. The stories in *this* anthology take their cue from the titular tale by editor Leannbh Pearson, each holding somewhere at its heart a single piece of the cursed mirror—at times remarkably, unexpectedly transformed—each expanding the shared world, adding history and filling in detail with their own unique flourishes. While darkness certainly dwells here, as the subtitle would suggest, the authors also bring love and triumph and a liberal dose of humour at its most wicked.

On your travels, you will stumble across many things that catch at your skirts, that feel oddly familiar while wearing strange new garb. These are not retold fairy tales so much as stories under the influence of faerie, folklore and legend, stories that weave themselves into the rich and time-worn tapestry that is the Fantasy genre. Some references are specific—Pinnochio, Bluebeard and even Robin Hood wander across the stage—although often only making themselves known once the tale is well under way and propelling the narrative in surprising directions. For the most part, though, the familiarity is organic, revealing itself in the fabric of the world, in the beats of the story. Here you will find dangerous quests and courageous, albeit reluctant, adventurers. Impossible tasks and befuddling riddles. Beast-infested forests and cottages that seem bigger within than without. Wizards and witches and wraiths, oh my!

And curses, of course. So many dark and delicious curses.

Showcasing a mix of emerging and established voices, *Cursed Shards* is an ambitious anthology that seeks resonance in more than simply theme or subject matter. The eclectic tales have much to offer readers of contemporary fantasy, fairy tales and folklore, many of whom will no doubt be delighted to discover a favourite new author or two among their pages. But take heed before following the winding path through the ill-lit forest: you are entering the realm of the Fae and things will not be as they seem, so trust your heart more than your eyes. If you make a promise, keep it honourably. If you are asked a question, answer it truthfully. Above all, mind your manners. The Fae cannot abide rudeness and, believe me, you do not want to land on their bad side.

Oh, and that intriguing shard of glass you've found? If you know what's good for you—or even if you don't—you'll cast it to the ground and walk away. It's keen of edge, that thing, and so very cruel.

And your blood, dear reader, is the very least of its desires.

Introduction

Leanbh Pearson

Be careful what you wish for…

We've all heard childhood fairy tales and hearthside stories passed from generation to generation warning us of unseen dangers lurking in the dark forest, the glimpse of a future in watery reflections, and to be wary of objects and people offering impossible gifts. The Fae are ageless beings dwelling between light and shadow, stalking the moonlit nights and wielding powerful gifts and curses.

Welcome to *Cursed Shards,* a collection of dark fantasy stories inspired by folklore, legends, fairy tales and mythology. Ten authors spin ten different tales ranging from deserts, icy mountains and dark forests to legendary warriors and to the mythical Fae.

A realm where the landscape is as volatile as its rulers and an ancient cursed mirror, a once-powerful magical artefact created with blood magic, was shattered before it could be used against the realm. A cursed mirror broken but never destroyed. Ten shards remain: now disguised and repurposed into ordinary items that are traded, stolen, and sold between rulers, common folk and the Fae. Whenever a shard re-appears its curse influences the decisions of all who come within reach, threatening Fae and mortal kingdoms alike.

Here, the ancient adage 'be careful what you wish for' is true.

The Cursed Hunt

Leanbh Pearson

The Black Tower was a labyrinth of twisting tunnels and hidden chambers. Without our guide, it would have been impossible to navigate. In this solitary keep, the Dark Mage had enslaved Jorn—a coblynau—who could work with all metals, including iron, earning them mistrust from the other fey. Against his will, Jorn had forged the Cursed Mirror but not before his body had been bent and broken for his efforts. He hobbled in front of us, willingly leading my mercenary band through the underground passages and into the heart of the Black Tower. If the powerful Snow Queen and the five mortal kings were right, the Dark Mage had no knowledge we were coming.

I squinted in the dimness of the tunnels, the shadows still dense despite the torches Jorn had lit for us. Was this the effect of the foul magic here? Did the darkness eat the light?

Behind me, my brother Fergal paused mid-step. "If the Dark Mage bound thirteen fae souls to the mirror, can they escape when it's broken?"

I looked at Fergal. Tall and broad-chested, blonde hair in warrior braids, he wasn't one to ever fear anything. But his eyes darted around the tunnels, and his hand never left his sword hilt.

"We're told to suspect it, which is why that young mage is with us. He's apparently the most skilled in the kingdoms. Even so, be wary, Fergal."

"Fiana," I called to the lithe female archer behind us. "Be ready when we enter the main chamber."

She nodded, taking several arrows from her quiver.

Fergal grabbed my arm. "You owe me a drink after this, Herne."

I grinned. "I owe you several, if I recall."

He grinned wolfishly. "You do."

We climbed worn steps that soon changed to staircases showing signs of recent habitation. Fergal moved silently for a big man, his broad shoulders blocking the rest of the warriors from attack as we climbed the narrow staircase. Fergal's wife Fiana moved with deadly grace, arrows trained on the space between me and my brother.

Jorn stood at the top of the spiral stairs, the coblynau waiting with his hand on the door knocker. I studied Jorn in the light of the brighter torches up here. He wasn't pale skinned like dwarves or goblins who dwelled deep beneath the earth. I knew their kind avoided the coblynau, driving these rare fae metal workers deeper below the mountains. Scars traversed what was visible of Jorn's body, deep red scars following his veins where the damage of iron had scarred his dark skin.

"Pray you haven't betrayed us, Jorn."

He turned lava red eyes on me and scowled. "I owe no allegiance to the Dark Mage. He thought breaking my body was equivalent to breaking my will, and now he's sadly mistaken. I'll dance merrily over his corpse."

I pivoted on my heel to regard my small band of mercenaries and the young mage at the rear. Silently, I gestured to Fergal and Fiana, and they checked their weapons as did their men. I gave a swift nod to Jorn and he swung the door open.

I charged into the vast chamber, my sight adjusting to the bright light provided by many sconces lining the walls. Sword drawn, I moved carefully onto the sunken floor, glancing up at the high glass dome above. Moonlight poured in from the sky, contorting the torchlight and twisting the shadows that slid along the tiled floor to the platform. A robed figure stood in the shadows on the platform, a massive glass window behind him. I whistled to my band of warriors and hoped Fergal and Fiana could pierce the glamour cast by the Dark Mage too.

Several doors on the opposing side of the chamber burst open, and the Dark Mage's warriors rushed into the room. Arrows shot through the air and swords met shields. I ignored it all. Slipping around fighting warriors and dancing between arrows, I kept my focus on the Dark Mage and the glamour he used to try to hide himself. This was my only task. I was here for him.

He turned to me; face hidden in the depths of his cowl. I climbed the steps to the raised platform, my heart thudding with dread. He was a not to be underestimated.

He laughed. "The Snow Queen sends a mortal warrior?"

I moved one more step towards him, body sidelong to his, sword raised to protect my torso and keep him in sight.

"Do you know the tale of your Snow Queen? To avoid the complications of emotions, she buried her heart in the depths of the glaciers. She's no protector of mortals. She's cold and cruel, without loyalty to anyone but herself."

I knew the legend of the Snow Queen, how Holda had become a feared leader among the Fae. But I knew he tried to weaken my resolve with doubt, the five mortal kings had joined Holda to rid the land of the Dark Mage's spreading evil. I hoped the wiry, skilled mage could destroy the Cursed Mirror as promised once I killed the Dark Mage.

The shadows at the Dark Mage's feet rippled, and I finally saw a splinter in his glamour. Swift and without hesitation, I threw my knife, aiming for the break in his glamour that exposed his left side. The blade hit true, burying to the hilt in the tender flesh beneath the ribs. The Mage dropped his hands, breaking the illusions of his magic as he clutched at the wound. The cowl fell back and I saw the face of the deadliest man in the kingdoms. Young and handsome, full of pride, he could have been the son of any lord at court. He stared at me, pale with shock and confusion. I couldn't lower my guard.

He dropped to one knee. "Fool," he snarled.

I stared at his long fingered hands, but could already feel his potent magic leaking across the platform with his lifeblood.

The clamour of battle stilled surrounded us. I spread my feet, shoulder's width apart and lifted my broadsword. The dying mage knelt before me, impassive as he waited for the fatal blow. Quick footsteps ran lightly up the steps on the platform and I jerked my attention to the left. Jorn walked to stand up beside me, staring at the man who had imprisoned and tortured him. The coblynau wore an expression I couldn't read. Fast as lightning, Jorn darted forward and grasped the knife hilt buried in the mage's side. He wrenched the blade free with enough savagery to open a fist-sized wound. Dark blood spilled across the tiled platform, pooling around Jorn's boots and soaking my own. I couldn't blame him for his hatred, but such a brutal death was an ugly way to kill. The Dark Mage coughed, spraying blood across the platform, his breathing a choking rattle as he struggled for air. He coughed again, dropping to his hands and knees before rolling onto his back. I didn't move, forcing myself to stand with sword ready until I was certain of his death, until his vacant eyes stared sightlessly up at the domed chamber ceiling.

Hidden in the safety of the shadows, Fergal stepped aside and the wiry mage in our band hurried towards the platform. He ignored the Mage's bloody corpse, and unlike others in the chamber, his gaze was on the glass window overlooking the ruins. He walked straight to the window and turned aside, hands outstretched as he plucked at the air. The mirror materialised where it had been hidden by the Mage's glamour even after his death.

It was a huge, free-standing mirror, the metal frame curved with arching wings that spread from its back like a bird. I watched the young mage study the strange glass, the peculiar silver-grey, which was shadowy and dull rather than a reflective surface. The dark energy of the Mage's power still pulsed from it, raising the hairs on my arms and neck.

"I need to destroy it. There's a terrible perversion to the magic, the corruption of death, and the torture of imprisoned souls."

"Do whatever you can. That's why you're with us."

He nodded and lifted his hands high towards the night sky. The sleeves of his robe fell back revealing tattoos covering the length of his arms. Whispered invocations slipped from his lips, and as his summons grew louder, voice echoing eerily off the walls, I held my position on the platform, guarding our mage even while the Dark Mage's blood still cooled at our feet. All the warriors in the room shifted uneasily as magic coiled around them, while Fergal tapped his ringed fingers against the hilt of his broadsword. I'd not seen him so anxious since our first days on battlefields.

I gasped as the mirror rose into the air, the impossibly heavy structure lifted upwards by an invisible force. I glanced at our mage, noticed the strain on his features to control what was happening. His hands shook with the effort to lift the mirror higher. I peered into the shadows of the glamour drenching the chamber, and saw spectral hands clawing from the mirror's surface, fingers gripping at its edge, holding it as they carried upwards. Sweat ran freely down our mage's face as the mirror continued towards the domed arch of the ceiling.

"Are those the cursed souls?" Fiana asked.

I glanced at her. "I'm not sure but it seems likely. Be ready for anything that might happen. I'm not sure the souls bear as good or ill will."

The mirror hovered unsteadily in the air, its dull surface now reflecting the chamber and those standing here back at us. But what it revealed was a distortion. Darkness pooled where Fergal's shadow should be, the impossibly long form reaching across the floor and away from my brother. My reflection was a twisted parody of myself, the blade in my hand dripping dark scarlet to the tiles.

"Run!" the mage called, shattered the spell and the silence.

Thirteen pairs of ghostly hands gripped the mirror's edge and suspending it in the air. The chamber seemed to wait, and then those thirteen pairs of hands released it. The massive metal wings on either side of the mirror clanged against the stone tiles, and glass of the shadowy surface shattered into slivers, shards, and thumb-sized pieces. Darkness rolled through the chamber, dimming the torches in the sconces, and even obscuring the moonlight. The men and women who'd been warriors or slaves within Black Keep raced towards the broken mirror as if it were made of coin or flour.

I whistled to my band, and Fergal and Fiana followed me, falling into step as we quickly formed a loose circle around the shattered mirror. We couldn't protect it for long, but we could protect long enough for the Snow Queen and the five kings to arrive. I may not trust five mortal kings with the shards any more than I trusted the rabble of men and women in front of me, but I trusted the Snow Queen.

The five mortal kings hurried into the chamber, their clothing rich enough to save entire villages from starvation, and dressed in jewels and rings. A creeping coldness filled the room, hoar frost forming along the walls. The darkness of the shadows receded. The Snow Queen had an ethereal beauty like all the fae; she was tall and slender, pale blonde hair almost silver in the darkness. But the flash of her emerald eyes in the torchlight chilled the blood of more than one man in the room.

Our young mage stepped forward, pale and exhausted. He bowed his head. "There were thirteen souls trapped within the mirror, and they wrested control from me. I don't know if they intended to destroy it—or if the intent was to reflect the curse back from the heavens above. But the mirror shattered. I think we've avoided one tragedy but created another."

Her green eyes flicked to me. "You've confirmed the Dark Mage is dead?"

I nodded, keeping my attention on the mob now encircling Fergal, Fiana, and me.

She turned to the mortal kings. "We've destroyed the Mage, his cursed mirror, and freed the thirteen trapped souls. Take your spoils of war and leave now."

She strode towards the shattered mirror, pushing the young mage aside. He protested noisily, but she ignored him. She crouched to collect four shards from the splinters, shards and fragments of the mirror. The mortal kings rushed forward, jostling each other for the largest pieces.

King Ezmeth glared at the Snow Queen, face red with outrage. "Why should you take four pieces and us expected to take only one?"

"One shard is for myself; the others are for each of my three champions who led this party to vanquish the Dark Mage."

The king quietened, glared accusingly at his fellows as if

expecting them to voice their outrage. They did not. He glowered darkly at them, fingering his knife hilt.

The Snow Queen turned to me, and with subtle nod, Fergal, Fiana, and I stepped aside. A crowd had rapidly grown with the spread of the word that the Dark Mage was dead. Fergal and Fiana followed me to a narrow alcove where we rested. From where I was concealed, I watched the coblynau slip from the great chamber without even glancing at the shards. I still felt an indescribable power turning within them.

The Snow Queen ruled the most powerful fae kingdoms. Our return to Darkthron Castle was greeted with a blizzard of unheralded praise. While Fiana and Fergal spent the nights dancing at dinners, I remained vigilant, unable to shake the foreboding that had followed us home with the four mirror shards our queen had taken. In the depth of the bitterest cold, the Snow Queen called our trio forth to commemorate our victory over the Dark Mage by jewellery she'd crafted especially from the four mirror shards.

Fergal met me in the corridor outside the audience chamber in his finest midnight blue doublet and hose. He pulled at the collar of his shirt as uncomfortable in formal attire as he'd always been.

I grabbed his wrist. "Stop it."

"This is such a pompous waste of time."

"She wishes to honour us. Are you going to question the Snow Queen?"

"No."

"So, we wear whatever she wants us to. Smile, be gentle and accept whatever fineries she's crafted for us."

"Is he still moaning?" Fiana asked, walking up behind us. She wore an dark green dress embroidered with snowflakes, her red hair ornately braided into a circlet of curls.

I nodded. "He is."

"Fergal, I didn't marry you for your fancy clothing. Let me admire you in something fine for once."

Subdued into near-silent muttering, my brother stepped back

allowing me to lead them into the audience chamber.

I swung open the oak doors and strode down the centre aisle, Fergal close behind me, with Fiana walking demurely as the last in our trio. We were met by furious polite clapping, fae lords and ladies that under the dominion of the Snow Queen. Surrounding the audience chamber were mortal servants and a number of the house guard. Fergal, Fiana and I were the only ones to be honoured tonight. I realised that among our mercenary band, I was the only one dressed in ceremonial armour. While we walked to the throne, we received no kind looks from the other fae lords or mortals assembled tonight. Ignoring it all, we proceeded the final steps to the front the room.

The Snow Queen, Holda leaned against her throne as unmoving as if carved from ice. I hesitated, her face unreadable, and her emerald eyes impassive for now. She was dressed in a flowing cape of white fur, and a dark green dress pooling around her feet. But it was the glittering diadem in her pale hair that was skilfully twined in silver to crown her head. I shivered as my pulse quickened in fear.

"Herne, vanquisher of the Dark Mage. You do me great honour."

I stepped onto the ceremonial platform and knelt before the Holda; arms crossed over the breastplate of my armour. I dared a glance up and met her gaze. My smile faded. Dull threads of silver twisted in the iris of her eyes, the darkness still slithered behind her cold smile where once there had been impassiveness. I fought the urge to rise from my knees and flee to the cold might.

She moved to a spindly table at the side of the throne. So captivated by the changes in her, I'd not noticed it until now. She placed hands either side of a massive warrior's helm cast entirely from steel, and smoothed her hands along tall antlers. A single piece of the mirror shard, cut was embedded between the eyes. A cold sweat broke out over my skin and I tried to stand, but one of Holda's own guards pushed me down as she closed the horned helm firmly around my head.

"Herne, keenest of my hunters. May you ride with me and remain forever in my service."

Her words were laced with magic, the curse binding me to

her servitude. I grabbed at the helm, trying to wrench it free, but the steel burned like ice. I grasped at the rack of stag-like antlers adorning the top. The metal numbed my hands, but blood trickled down my forearms from where it'd sliced my palms open. Cursing, I let go.

Where my blood had melded with the steel, Holda's curse came to fruition. My breathing laboured, puffs of icy air before me as I collapsed. Weakened, I screamed but no sound came from my throat. Scrabbling on the platform floor, my blue-tinged fingers confirmed my fears. I'd seen men die of cold. The pain was immense and even if my body fought to live, I'd have eternity trapped by her Holda. I wheezed to Fergal and Fiana to fight, flee, to leave me. But my brother and his wife were loyal. Holda's guards closed in, forcing them to their knees.

I closed my eyes. The frigid agony of drawing air through my lungs had vanished. I was somewhere between life and death, a liminal place beyond pain.

"Fiana, vanquisher of the Dark Mage. You do me great honour."

Holda's command woke me from that painless state and I screamed, lunging forward. Beside me, Fergal fought the arms of Holda's household guard that pinned him. More of the fae guards rushed towards me, holding me still.

Fiana knelt at the foot of the Snow Queen's throne. Holda lifted a fine necklace of silver and pearl, with the centrepiece, another piece of the polished cursed shard.

"May Fate take away all that you have stolen from us," Fiana cursed.

Holda smiled cruelly and touched a bare hand to Fiana's neck as she forced the necklace over her head. Fiana screamed as the pale skin of her neck burned to black with frostbite in the imprint of Holda's hand.

"Fiana, swiftest of my hunters. May you ride with me and remain forever in my service."

Fiana clutched at her chest and the guards let her stumble a few paces forward. She fell to the ground with ragged breaths of icy air from her lungs, lips already turning blue. Helplessly

I watched, unable to do anything for her. Fergal's roar of fury was a battle cry to my soul, but I couldn't help my brother either. Within moments, Fiana stopped moving.

I watched, waiting for her to rise again like I had. Stillness. No breath, no life. Then, the air around Fiana's slender body shimmered as she morphed beneath the power of Holda's transformation curse. Where red-haired Fiana had stood, a chestnut mare stamped her hooves, and tossed her proud head. She neighed shrilly with panic, wild eyes rolling. Woven into the plaited silver chain bridle, the shard glittered from the brow-band between Fiana's eyes.

Fergal's screams were a guttural moaning as men dragged him before Holda. Warriors forced him to his knees as he spat curses and vile insults at the Snow Queen. She remained impassive to his fury. The poison of the cursed shard twisting through her like mercury running through fissures in stone, consuming who she'd been.

"Fergal, vanquisher of the Dark Mage. You do me great honour."

Warriors kept my brother on his knees as a gauntleted fist wrenched his head back by his hair. Holda picked up a long silver shirt pin from the table which had borne our honorary gifts. She took the few steps down from the dais to where Fergal knelt. Carefully holding the pin that glittered with rubies, its top adorned with the polished shard, she pushed it through Fergal's doublet. He winced as the pin pierced his flesh beneath. A drop of blood welled through his shirt collar, smearing Holda's pale fingers.

"Fergal, fiercest of my hunters. May you ride with me and remain forever in my service."

He screamed as the curse took hold, back arching as he refused to relinquish to Holda's will. My brother had never gone down without fighting to the end, and now was no different. Frost-rimed his beard and his lips turned blue as he struggled but no one had ever defeated Holda where she held dominion. He slumped and the warriors slid his body to the flagstones where he convulsed then stilled. I watched in anguish, urging him rise again. This was my brother. If anyone could be stronger than the Snow Queen, it was Fergal.

Faint silvery light moved through the air around Fergal and I recognised the same transformation magic Holda's had performed on Fiana. Fergal's form shrunk beneath the shifting light, limbs contorting as his body changed into a massive grey hunting hound. Weakly he climbed to his long legs and drew his lips back in a snarl showing a fearsome mouth of fangs.

I met Holda's brilliant gaze. "We won't serve you."

"You've no choice. I'll have none but the best in my Hunt."

"What madness is this? Did you forget so quickly the mirror was cursed and every piece of it bears the taint of the original?"

Holda laughed. It was as brittle as a winter's day, and just as unkind. She pushed her will through the three cursed shards we wore, ours linked to the one in her diadem. I landed heavily on bent knee, the weight of the great antlered helm I wore forcing my head into a subservient bow. Fergal growled low, and with a whine, his head dropped onto his paws. To our left, Fiana stamped a hoof and snorted, eyes wild as she lowered her proud head to her chest.

"The three of you should be honoured as leaders of my Hunt, riding beside me into the night. That fat mortal King Ezmeth will understand the wrath of winter and the night. He'll understand why I'm feared."

"Please, Holda," I screamed at her. "Drop you curse against us. The kingdoms don't need another force to fear."

Holda looked pityingly at me. "The curse and truth she desired and can't be un-done, I Ierne."

She raised her hand in a summoning a waiting stablehand. The trembling boy led a white war-horse forward. Still dressed in the white flowing cloak, Holda swung into the saddle, the long green dress split for riding. She gestured to me and Fiana. Fiana didn't walk calmly but ducked and tossed her head.

"If I can save us from this curse, I'll find a way to do it."

Immediately, Fiana stopped circling and stood quietly as I swung into the saddle as I took up her reins. The power of the cursed shards hummed through my veins but I didn't feel the weight of the antlered helm. Holda rode beside me, her white stallion sniping at Fiana as we trotted from the outer chamber. Fergal howled and loped ahead, cleared a path through the gathered Fae lords and ladies and into the castle courtyard.

Outside, I drew Fiana to a reluctant halt. There were only stars above our heads and a chill wind off the snow-capped mountains. Fergal growled in protest, shaking his head at the collar around his neck. A frigid wind blew off the snow-capped mountains and the stars glittered like ice chips in the moonless night sky. Fallen autumn leaves spiralled through the courtyard, then just as quickly, collapsed onto the flagstones. Fiana shifted restless beneath me and Fergal gazed at the drawbridge and the forest beyond.

"Where do we ride, my Queen?" I asked, tilting my horned helm towards the dark branches of the forest.

"We ride the night and the storms."

The wind howled as if with many voices and I understood the terrible and uncanny nature of the Hunt. The witches swept through the branchless forest like wraiths, their voices raised in answer to Holda's summons. These women were beings who shifted between the mortal and uncanny worlds as our trio did. Holda urged her stallion forward into a canter, the steed crossing the drawbridge in moments. Fiana tossed her head and followed and with Fergal's howl echoing through the night, we leapt into a liminal space between life and death. Vast swathes of territory passed below as Holda and I led the Hunt through the starry paths towards our quarry.

Lightning lashed the sky as Holda and I led the witches through the sky towards Trident Keep. King Ezmeth's coastal keep was wild and windswept as Fiana's steel-shod hooves hit the wet stones of the courtyard and she skidded to a halt. The tossed her head, snorting as Holda's stallion pranced closer.

I'd always been an assassin in our mercenary group, but I'd had a choice before. I'd never felt compelled to kill. But now Holda's will drove into the darkest corners of my mind. The pressure of the cursed shard in the horned helm overwhelming. *Kill the king. Kill the king.*

I swung down from the saddle; my steel-heeled boots sharp on stone. In a few strides, I had broadsword from its sheath across my back and kicked the doors to the keep's hall open. Ezmeth's people pleaded and screamed but I didn't hear them. I had focus only for my quarry. King Ezmeth sat slovenly on his throne, protesting noisily at my interruption. Surrounding me, Holda's witches screeched and howled like the winter wind. I strode towards Ezmeth, the steady *click* of my boot heels loud to my ears.

Fergal paced beside me, snarling with lips curled back to reveal unnaturally long fangs. Two strides before I'd reach King Ezmeth's throne and seal his fate. He dashed sideways at the last moment. Fergal leapt, catching Ezmeth's thighs with long claws and tearing the muscle to the bone. I swung the broadsword into Ezmeth's back, splitting spine and exposing viscera.

"Queen Holda wants your soul."

I stepped aside as the darkness of shard overtook Fergal with alarming ferocity and he tore into Ezmeth's chest and throat, silencing the gurgling cries in a bloody spray.

I stalked from the hall, the towering height of my antlered helm dissuading even the bravest of warriors from challenging me. The screams of those remaining in the keep were a din I ignored.

In the courtyard, Fiana bit and kicked at stable hands, hopelessly trying to catch her.

"She's not for taming," I shouted.

The lads turned and paled. Fergal growled until they moved away from the mare. I didn't care whether they watched what Holda demanded of us next or not. I'd fulfilled my role, the king was dead and Holda had his soul for my cursed retinue.

Holda's summons burned through me like the slave brand it was. I swung back into the saddle, spinning Fiana in a tight circle. Holda appeared to my right on her pale stallion and gestured behind us. King Ezmeth rode forward on a black warhorse, his scarred armour reflecting the darkness of the night. On the ground we possessed physical forms, but only when Holda allowed us to ride the land once more. In the sky, we were spectral, cursed souls of a ghostly hunt.

Holda and the witches streamed into the sky and Fiana followed, leaping into the place between sky and land that the hunt rode. We rode like the storm, the corruption of the cursed shard leaching my will and corrupting my mind and soul. *When would I forget what it was to be human and succumb to something other?*

The full moon shone a path of silver across the plains that ran north towards Holda's dominion. A storm grew over the distant snow-capped mountains and thunder rolled through the night, lightning snaking across the clouds. The wind stirred and swung to the north, an icy gale as the Hunt sped onwards.

Holda's pale stallion veered from the sky, plunging towards the ground as I wrenched at Fiana's reins, hauling the unruly mare after Holda. Reluctantly, Fiana heeded my command but Fergal snapped at my boots for being forced from the sky. *Did they not feel the lodestone pulling Holda and I to the plains below?* I spurred Fiana forwards along the moonlit path across the grasslands, racing after Holda's flowing white cape. The witches circled around us in the sky, some riding distaffs, others in owl and bat forms. I felt the potent magic here, almost overwhelming the bonds that forced me into Holda's retinue.

Frustrated, Fiana fought the reins but I let her have her head a moment, the mare galloping past the Holda's stallion, the dark tatters of a once-fine cape flapping behind me.

The crossroads waited ahead, a solemn and ancient symbol in the middle of our path. Beside the churred road, a young lass waited with bundled belongings at her feet. Her blonde hair whipped about her face as we approached, the icy wind no doubt biting her skin but she didn't flinch. I reined Fiana to a sudden halt, clods of earth skidding across the ground as the mare fought me. She loved the freedom of the hunt and endless night skies. Snorting and sidling, she finally obeyed me.

The lass stared up at me, moonlight shining off my antlered helm, but still she didn't move. Behind me, the hunt had halted, horses snorting and harnesses jingling in the night. Holda pushed her way through the middle of the assembled warhorses, her stallion biting any who tarried.

"Child, it's ill luck to meet the Cursed Hunt at a crossroads."

She lifted her chin to meet Holda's gaze. She had ice-blue eyes, the sort I'd seen only in the high blood fae and the royal witch bloodlines but never in a mortal lass. I urged Fiana closer, wondering what trickery this girl might mean for us. Holda studied her intensely, her emerald eyes piercing. I noticed that despite the layers of clothing the girl wore, they didn't hide her reed-thin form, slender arms, and legs and the obvious bruises.

"You're Queen Holda?"

"Who are you to dare summon me and the Hunt to these crossroads?"

"I'm Eimear. I want to ride with you."

Holda laughed but her eyes remained mirthless. "Are you fae or witch, Eimear?"

The lass looked away. "Does it matter? I'm powerful enough to summon you here."

I shifted in my saddle as Fiana side-stepped nervously beneath me. "We're not a resort for lasses running away from home."

"Doesn't the Snow Queen decide who may join the Hunt's retinue?"

Holda stared. "You seem well-versed in Fae lore. Are you one of our orphaned kin?"

Behind us, several knights had grown restless and begun skirmishing among themselves. The witches argued and spun magicks of fate trying to learn Eimear's bloodline before she spoke. But the heavens above reflected the unsettled atmosphere of the Hunt, the constant growls of thunder and lightning zigzagging through the clouds.

"I don't know my heritage, my queen. My life here is cruel and hopeless. I only know that to stay here is to be burned as a witch."

Holda considered the lass, and I prayed some integrity remained in the Snow Queen. To invite Eimear among the hunt but with the freedom granted to the witches and the fae who rode with us, was a fate better than those cursed to serve Holda in my retinue.

"You aren't mortal, Eimear. You'll ride with the Hunt until we are in my domain, and I can decide what to do with you. No descendent of the High blood Fae or Royal witches should be in the mortal world."

Holda held out her gloved hand for Eimear. The stallion tried to bite her, but the lass ignored his ill-temper and moved closer to his shoulder. Holda quickly pulled Eimear up behind her just as the stallion smiled again. The ground white with frost, the stallion prancing in annoyance. The witches circled Holda in a tight spiral, keen to taste the energy of a potential new witch.

"Ride like the winter's fury."

I heeded Holda's summons, leading the Cursed Hunt onwards through the crossroads. Fiana gathered speed as she scented the cold air of the winter skies and the snow-capped mountains. Fergal kept pace beside us, the massive hound baying into the night as he raced Fiana. We reached the sea cliffs and Fiana leapt into the air, front legs reaching between sky and land. We galloped across the sky, the Hunt pursuing Eimear with Holda on my right, and the witches streaming through the sky around us.

I thought about Eimear's knowledge of Fae lore and how she'd summoned the hunt to the crossroads. It was skilful magic, the risk summoning a vengeful Fae to you was not something to be discounted. I wasn't sure she hadn't. The Snow Queen was hardly the most benevolent of the Fae.

I studied Eimear's profile where she rode behind Holda's back. *What is her motive? Why did I feel there is more than a desire to flee the mortal world fuelling her?* She glanced back to me. The ice-blue eyes were assessing and I could discern nothing from their depths.

We arrived at Darkthorn Castle in the fury of a blizzard. Holda reined her stallion and gestured for me to follow to the courtyard below. It had been centuries since I'd been inside Darkthorn Castle. Fiana and Fergal touched the ancient flagstones with an unease that matched my own. I swung down from the saddle, steel-shod boots echoing loudly on the frigid stones.

Holda was already advancing into the hall, hoar-frost lacing the ground in her wake. I gestured to Eimear to follow the Snow Queen and I came last, still uncertain why Holda had drawn the hunt from the skies after so long.

Eimear stepped closer to me as we entered the chamber. "I've read tales about the shattered shards and the cursed mirror; I know a mercenary band was responsible for the downfall of the Dark Mage. You're *the* Herne, Fergal, and Fiana, aren't you?"

I bent the antlered helm, so I was level with Eimear. "Why are you here? Holda is not a fae Queen to be manipulated."

"If you could be free of Holda's servitude, would you?"

"What could force Holda to break her hold on us? We've bought her reputation, titles, land, and wealth through tributes. Besides, Fergal is more hound than man now. Re-transformation isn't an option. The shock on his mind would be terrible and I'd have lost my brother twice-over. The same is true for Fiana. She is more horse than woman, interested only in galloping across the skies."

"Then you'd remain in servitude to Queen Holda?"

"It's not our choice. We've long since lost the ways of men and women. We have no mortal life, only our souls exist in whatever form Holda chooses. We've become as distant from being mortal as the stars."

"I intend to destroy her."

I didn't react, unsure if I'd heard her properly. *This girl intended to kill the Snow Queen? Could Holda even die?* I wasn't certain. I'd never tried to raise a weapon against her again since the first night in when she'd cursed our trio and forced us to join the hunt. Since then, Holda's power had only grown stronger as the shard tainted her magic.

"If you plan to kill Holda, you'll need to be smart about it. I can't promise her magic and the cursed shards won't force me to obey her."

"You never asked why."

"Would it stop you?"

She clenched her jaw. "Holda's right about my lineage but I lied that I didn't know what it was. My bloodlines are high fae and royal witch. I was orphaned in the mortal world after Holda destroyed both lines of my family. I'm the only survivor. I'll have vengeance for my people."

"Do you have a blade?"

Eimear flipped aside her threadbare cloak to reveal a long dagger strapped in a sheathed to one forearm.

"You'll need to get close for that to work."

"That's what I intend."

"I'll be in the audience chamber with Fiana and Fergal. It's going to be a blood frenzy. But during that distraction, go straight for Holda and take your revenge."

Eimear nodded and trotted after Holda, disappearing through the castle's double doors. My bitterness grew and—sensing the murderous rage within me—Fiana trotted over, reins swinging loosely around her neck. I vaulted into the saddle and unsheathed the broadsword from my back. Fergal snarled; hackles raised in response. The Cursed Hunt were near-silent except for the restless shifting of their horses, the music of harnesses and metal weapons sliding from sheaths.

I urged Fiana towards the barred double oak doors. A massive knight rode forward and swung his battle-axe against the doors. They cracked, then swung open. Fiana pushed forward into Queen Holda's audience chamber. The Hunt followed me—the rattle of maces, axes, and swords as we readied weapons for battle. I manoeuvred them as one coherent force, not allowing any cursed soul to rampage and begin hacking at the first mortals they see.

I swung, my sword stabbing one guard in the guts as I turned in the saddle to smash another man's skull in with the pommel of my broadsword. Blood ran down the chamber's steps while the Cursed Hunt sought their vengeance. These were souls who'd found solace on the battlefield—this was the closest thing to freedom they'd experienced for centuries.

The darting blue shape of Eimear dashed along the outer rim of the audience chamber, staying low to the ground and keeping to the shadows. If spotted now, her quest would be for nothing. To keep the guardsmen busy and not notice Eimear, I dismounted from Fiana to fight unrestricted with my broadsword. My boots hit the blood drenched floor, slaughtered nobles and guardsmen surrounding me,.

At the front of the audience chamber a shrill scream echoed above the sound of battle. Near the throne where Holda had been sitting, the queen was now forced to defended herself against Eimear. I glanced to the throne, watching Eimear's deft bladework as she cornered Holda and levelled her blade at her heart. Holda smiled cruelly and I realised Eimear didn't really believe the old tales about how Holda became the Snow Queen. So she might never feel pain again, Holda cut out her heart and buried it somewhere in the snow-covered mountains. A knife or sword to the heart would never kill her. She shouted again and more guardsmen rushed into the chamber.

Hefting my sword again, I charged forward into the new onslaught. The baying of Fergal filled the room, and I turned quickly to see his hackles rise as the war dogs were led into the castle. Focused on the unrelenting sword and axe attacks, I couldn't help Fergal, but I diverted several of the riders from the Hunt to his aid.

A thunderous wave of magic spread through the chamber. Queen Holda staggered and then slumped over her throne. The shine of a dagger hilt buried deep in her chest and a dark trickle of blood from the wound. Eimear was nowhere to be seen but I focused on the guardsman at the base of the dais. They shifted uneasily but moved aside the without challenge.

I looked down at Holda and noticed the dark veins of corruption running below her skin where the power of the shards had tainted her magic. I readied myself, placing my feet a shoulder's width apart. She didn't seem to be aware of me, remaining motionless as though she in sleep. I could see the slight rise of her chest and I knew she still lived. I needed to act quickly. I lifted my sword and brought it down in a single stroke. Holda's severed head hit the dais with two wet *thwacks* before staring accusingly at the fae lords and ladies in the chamber.

I waited for the relief once Holda was dead. But it didn't come. Instead the emptiness remained like an unfulfilled darkness. I turned around, searching for Eimear and where she might be hiding. Where was the girl? My gaze stopped on a track of bloody bootprints leading from behind the throne and down a corridor. Without a second thought, I followed. There were secrets upon secrets with her, and I wasn't certain I'd ever like any of them.

I found her in the outer courtyard that overlooked the gardens. I remembered on a clear day, you could see the plains and rivers to the south that led to the sea. Now the castle was encircled by a blizzard and Eimear was curled with knees to her chest beneath a pear tree. Blood oozed from wounds whose source I couldn't see.

"Eimear? You did it. Holda's dead."

She rolled over slightly. "Are you free? And Fiana and Fergal?"

"We no longer sense Holda's will binding us nor the effects of the shards anymore."

She grimaced in pain."Try to break the curse for me?"

I didn't know if Holda's curses would persist even after her death, or for how long if they did. Remembering the icy burns of the cold steel, I hesitantly reached for the antlered helm, expecting the pain of the curse. The metal was cold, but only from the night and not Holda's cruelty. I wrapped both hands around the antlers and pulled, searched frantically for clasps or some way the helm could be removed—but there was none. Holda had forged the helm without hinges or mechanisms for removal. The realisation was maddening.

"Holda is dead, her throne vacant, Eimear. In the traditions of the time when she cursed my trio, the vanquisher always took the throne. *You* have the bloodlines of witches and fae running through you. I think you know the lore for such situations as this?"

Eimear started to protest but I stopped her with a quick shake of my head.

"Take Holda's throne, command those in your dominion to provide the lifeforce you need. The Fae and witches aren't immortal—as you well know—but power is shared among those in the domain when needed. Call on the witches and fae who owe you allegiance and live, Eimear."

I bent and scooped her up in my arms, her body slight and

bird-like as I carried her back through the passages to the audience chamber. A gathering of fae and witches and had already assembled around Holda's corpse, gesticulating and arguing with passion. They paled at the sight of me, but as they saw Eimear in my arms they grew keen.

"The Snow Queen is in desperate need of healing. If you wish to remain in her favour, I suggest you do not tarry."

The fae hesitated a moment, gaze shrewd as they considered their options and how much they truly owed a new queen. I held Eimear easily in the crook of one arm, and shifted my grip on my sword hilt. The witches immediately muttered apologies and hurried forward to attend their new queen, while the fae lords jostled to be the first to reach her.

Satisfied Eimear would be cared for now, I stood off to the side—guarding her throughout the healing ministrations to be certain no harm came to her. Fergal whined beside me; ears flattened against his head. I stroked his coat, noticing his muzzle was still covered in blood and gore splattered his sides. Fiana whickered at me and swished her tail in frustration. I knew she wanted to return to the sky and I shared her desire for freedom, to escape the world—despite aiding Eimear to defeat Holda, I wanted nothing to do with fae or witch politics.

"What about another ride through the stars, my friends?"

Fergal's ears pricked and Fiana bobbed her head, sidling closer.

"Eimear rules Darkthorn Castle now but has no claim to the Hunt. It's ours to lead."

I strode over to Fiana and swung up into the saddle, already turning her in a circle before I was properly seated. She trotted from the blood slick floors of the chamber with Fergal at her shoulder.

Once we were in the snowy courtyard, I held my hands to the reins. Fiana fought me fiercely before taking the bit between her teeth and ignoring my protestations to slow her speed, she galloped over the drawbridge. We rode—through the small but dense tangle of woods—until the trees thinned and the edge dark cliffs appeared. Without warning, Fiana leapt from the cliffs, hooves landing on a starry sky only she could see, one she'd always followed as it twisting through the night.

I looked below me to the snowy crags and glaciers of the northern mountains. The Hunt still rode behind me, but their role tonight had been purposeful and I was aware of the subtle shifting among the retinue. The witches no longer flew alongside us, their new Queen now resided on land in Darkthorn Castle. Holda and her icy heart had made the Cursed Hunt her personal form of justice, forcing anyone who resisted her will to join us. I hoped those who now followed me shared an interest in removing the unjust, cruel, and evil from this world, and cursing them to ride in my retinue.

Tattermog

Louise Pieper

I took from my childhood a wooden spoon, a goat, and a long, long list of flaws. Someone was always willing to say what was wrong with me. Not my mother, who disappeared when I was six. Not Magi, my twin sister, who loved me as I was. And not often my father, who kept to his tower doing whatever it is that wizards do.

Mostly, it was the village women who came and went like bustling hens. They'd climb the sixty-seven steps to our mountaintop home and cluck and clean and cook and twitch their fingers in ward signs when the shadow of Father's tower touched them. They praised Magi with a catalogue of virtues—she was good and kind and beautiful, and I was… not. They said that, when we were born, I had come bawling and brawling into the world, red-faced with rage, and announced to my horrified mother that the next twin would be more to her liking.

Poxwhallop! I was a precocious child, but not that bad.

It was true that Father preferred Magi. He gave her the clumping name of Magimerismara, like pinning a banner to her dress that said she was a wizard's daughter and not to be trifled with. He gave her a ring of jade and a caged bird to amuse her. He called me Tattermog and shoved a wooden spoon in my mouth when I wailed too loudly while cutting a tooth. Still, I had the best of it. The jade ring shattered and kind-hearted Magi freed the little bird. I kept the spoon, to pin up my hair, and no-one cared if a girl called Tattermog was wild and reckless and made friends with the mountain goats.

When the village women weren't listing my flaws, they would tell us tales of our father's wizardly might. He'd commanded giants to build his castle high in the Tangjat Mountains and smashed the king's army with storms and stones, when they'd ridden to see who dared claim the peaks. The king of Alatay had raged and Father had laughed. Long before, he'd found a way to imprison his death, and since it couldn't find him, he couldn't die. The women said he was the greatest wizard who'd ever lived and that he'd live forever.

He was not so great that he thought to make a place where two little girls might feel at home. The only part of the castle not as grey and bleak as Father's gaze was a walled garden with a spring-fed pool that was the source of the Otysh River. Beside it, three trees hung over a grassy bank. From the pool, a rill ran to the garden wall where a missing stone let the water leap free. It skipped and chuckled down the mountain, merry as a sprite child, joining hands with other streams to flow on to the sea. Tucked in against the rocks and behind the trees, a withy gate opened onto the castle's stone steps.

The village women slipped in through that gate rather than climb another dozen steps and face the dire portal of the wizard's iron-bound castle door. I slipped out through the gate to ride Barleycorn, my favourite goat, over the crags. Magi would sit by the pool, tickling the fish or reading tales. None of us liked that the shadow of Father's tower would sweep across the garden like a bird of prey, spying on us all.

One day in our twelfth summer, when I lay on the grass, exhausted from riding and romping, I said, "Magi, I've been thinking—"

"Oh, we're in trouble." She laughed and plucked a thistle from my tangled hair.

"Remember the songs our mother sang?" I asked.

"Not really." Magi drifted her hand into the water and giggled as a silvery fish rose to nibble her fingertips. "It's been six years. Do you think she'll ever come back?"

"Harkslops! You don't believe that old tale?"

"I don't believe she died of a fever." A frown rippled across my sister's face. "We'd remember that, surely. Maybe a minstrel did come to the village and sing with a voice so lovely he lured her away. Maybe—"

The shadow of the tower covered us and Magi clenched her hand. The fish darted away. Father did not like us to speak of our mother but when we were alone, I kept talking.

"Maybe she wanted to leave this place." I dragged my spoon from my hair and shook it at the tower. "But I don't think she did."

Magi shivered and wrapped her arms around herself.

"Hush, Mog," she cautioned.

"She used to sing about this garden."

"La, la, la, my little…" Magi trailed off, glancing around for any sign of the shadow. "No, I don't remember it."

"Bothersox, you don't! She likened you to this pretty, golden pear and me to this tough old fig, dark and ugly—" I went on over her protest, "—but sweet enough on the inside."

Above us, the branches of the nut tree rustled although the rest of the garden was still.

"She never mentioned a nut tree," I said. We both looked up at the murmuring branches and then down at the tree's dark roots. "I don't think it was here. And in all the years we've played beneath it, has it ever borne a nut?"

"Mog," my sister whispered, "Father says not to trifle with wizards."

"Solspiddle!" I snapped my fingers to show how much I cared for what Father said and sang softly, "Sleep my pretty little fruits: my baby fig, my golden pear. Bless your leaves, your trunks, your roots. Far sweeter crop than trees can bear."

The nut tree shivered and then we froze, Magi and me and the tree, as the light dimmed in the garden again. I gasped a breath of air, cold as spite, and forced out words I knew would scare off our watcher.

"Barleycorn is fighting over the nanny goats on the mountain again, but he's twice as strong as the other billies, and his horns—"

The shadow shuddered and moved on. I stuck out my tongue at its retreat.

"Look," Magi gasped.

A branch of the nut tree dipped towards us with two pale buds at its tip. A sweet scent wrapped around us as it bloomed, the petals fell, and the nuts fattened in a span of moments. Two golden hazelnuts dropped from the branch into our outstretched hands.

"Oh, poor Mama." Magi wept as her fingers closed around the nut.

"Hide it, Mags," I said as I shoved my nut deep into one of my pockets.

For six years we kept the secret, tended the nut tree, and grew as young girls will. Or rather, I grew more wilful and Magi more beautiful. I grew wilder and Magi gentler. I grew more and more restless, chafing against the rule of our distant but always critical, always watchful father. Magi was the only one who could calm me, her cheer and gentle humour like a beacon of lamplight guiding me safely home through the darkness of my savage and stormy tempers.

Then one day, in our eighteenth year, I slipped through the withy gate to find the garden cast in shadow, quivering with my father's shouts and my sister's tears.

"Who?" Father demanded, holding up the little gold nut as if it were a diseased tooth. "Who gave this to you?"

Magi cast me a despairing glance and Father caught her chin, pulling her gaze back to him.

"Answer me, child!"

"My, I mean, a—" She fumbled for words.

"She found it," I said, as Magi burst out with, "A village boy!"

Father glared at me, although my answer was true enough and hers was ridiculous. What villager had gold to give away?

"A boy?" he sneered. In a moment, his rage cooled to icy disdain. "No boy is good enough for you, Magimerismara. Do you think you love him?"

"No!" she cried, truthfully, since he didn't exist.

"And you Tattermog?" His gaze raked over me like the claws of a casually cruel cat. "Have you been trysting with village boys?"

I spread the ragged edges of the three cloaks I wore for warmth and curtseyed to him scornfully.

"I've been riding Barleycorn over the crags," I said. "I'm not interested in boys."

"What boy would be interested in you?" He returned his attention to my sister, holding the gold hazelnut up before her tear-stained face. "But you..."

He flicked the nut into the pool and Magi gasped as one of the silvery fish darted to the surface and gulped it down.

"I see I cannot trust you." Father scowled. "Girls are foolish, weak creatures."

I scowled back, but he paid me no mind.

"I will have to take your soft hearts and keep them safe," he declared.

"T-take our hearts?" Magi stuttered.

"Cobblesnot!" I cried.

"Then you will never fall in love with a man," Father pronounced. In a swirl of shadow, he vanished from the garden to set his plans in motion. Magi ran to me and held me close.

"I don't see how this can end well," I said, and I urged my sister to leave with me at once, to seek our own fortune out in the world for it couldn't be more dangerous than being subject to the whims of an arrogant, headstrong wizard.

"It's not only loving but living for which we need our hearts," Magi sobbed. "Father is angry, but he'll not let us die."

I waved my spoon at the nut tree, but she shook her head, saying, "He will forget that he said such a terrible thing."

I knew our father was too stubborn to do anything of the sort, but we heard nothing more of it until a month later, when a man looked over the withy gate and hailed me away from the side of the pool.

"Hey, lad!" he called and gave me no more than a shrug when I turned. "Is the wizard here?"

The stranger's sharp nose and straggled, grey-speckled beard made him look like a fox with a half-swallowed hen. I returned his shrug and said, "Hey yourself, hogsprat. The wizard's in his tower. Go and knock on his door, if you dare, but he doesn't welcome men here."

"He'll welcome me." The man rested his forearm along the top of the gate. "He wants me to make him a heart-shaped locket for a great working."

I raised my brows at him, though I wanted to curse. "You're a goldsmith?"

Some of the swagger left his face.

"No," he said. "The wizard has a rare and magical shard of fused glass and tin, and I'm the finest whitesmith in Alatay."

"Mog?" Magi called from the other side of the garden. "Where are you?"

"Be off then, dazwaggle," I told the tinker. "Best not keep a wizard waiting."

"Mog?" My sister rounded a screen of pear tree branches and saw the stranger.

"Oh, hello," she said with a small, polite smile.

His face transformed from cocky arrogance to thunderstruck greed.

"Chubblebutt," I muttered, "now he's caught sight of the whole blistering henhouse."

"Tell me your name, Beauty," he said.

Magi's smile dimmed.

"If the wizard finds you know her name, he'll turn you into a snipe," I cautioned.

"You are Beauty." He licked his lips. "The dawning of the sun. The bright gleam of the moon upon still waters…"

Colour rushed into Magi's cheeks as she shook her head.

"Poxpellets, a poet," I cursed as Magi clutched my arm. "Don't trifle with wizards, tinker," I called back to him as we hurried from the garden.

But the damage was done.

Each morning as he climbed the stairs and each evening as he went back to his room in the village, the tinker peered over the withy gate, hoping for a glimpse of Magi. She avoided him, ignored him, told him kindly that she did not wish to further their acquaintance, told him cruelly that she found him old, ugly, and coarse. It was all one to the tinker. At each rebuff he only smiled knowingly and said, "You'll come to love me, my beauty."

"No," Magi answered each time. "I won't."

"Ah." He would wink, or grin, or leer at her. "In time you will."

He ignored me, even when I rapped his fingers with my spoon as he threatened to climb over the gate. He only sucked his knuckles and waggled his eyebrows at my sister. We went inside and bolted the door.

"Why won't he listen?" she cried.

"He doesn't hear what he doesn't like." I scowled. "He thinks he knows best, because he's a man."

"He's a clutbumper," Magi said, which was true enough to make me laugh.

We stayed inside for three days until Father summoned us to his tower. I told Magi we should run away or, better, ride off on Barleycorn. She shook her head.

"He'd find us, Mog. You know he would." She looked down at her pretty dress and soft slippers and added in a whisper, "And then he'd be very angry."

I stuck my spoon in my tangled hair and together, we started up the stairs. The shadows grew denser the higher we climbed.

"Has that tinker gone?" I asked as we came through the door.

Robed and majestic, surrounded by shadows and lit by the glowing coals of his brazier, Father frowned.

"Yes," he said, "although I don't see how that concerns you, Tattermog. His work is done." He unfolded a square of white silk and held out a heart that gleamed like a shimmering star. Father turned, and the tin locket caught the light of the coals, glowing blood red and sullen as a bruise. I shivered.

"Come," Father said, beckoning Magi, but she shook her head.

"Mog was born first," she reminded him.

He sighed but nodded and I stepped forward, with Magi close behind me. I looked around the tower room but I could only see one silk-wrapped heart.

"Hold this," he commanded, passing it to me.

"Will it hurt?" Magi asked, but I had no attention for his reply.

The metal heart was heavy, far heavier than an empty locket made of glass and tin had any right to be, and it filled me with a dark foreboding. I drew back my arm to fling it out of the window so the hateful thing would smash on the rocks of the mountain. I could not bear the thought of its awful weight touching my sister.

Then my father spoke a word of power and plucked out my heart. I froze for a long, empty moment as that single word echoed inside the cavity of my chest.

"Here is a heart to burn within you," Father said, taking a coal from the brazier. "It shall keep you hale and whole, but it shall never love a man."

Father settled the lump of coal into its new home within the cage of my ribs. If I could have moved, I would have shivered from toe to crown as its slow, crackling warmth filled the new silence where my heart had beaten. If I could have spoken, I would have cried out the words that the coal sang into my blood. The creeping, clinging tendrils of the tower's shadows drew back as if my touch offended them, and I grinned. Then my smile fled. Magi stood as still as I had been, her face pinched with pain.

"Broxful addlepate, Father, why did you give her that foul metal?" I demanded.

"Jealous?" he sneered, not sparing me a glance.

"It's cursed, you hootanek!"

"It is ancient and powerful," he said, "as befits a wizard's daughter."

"I'm a wizard's daughter," I shouted. "And now Mags is the cursed child of a pernetticled, durmhangered old fool!"

"Out!" he roared, turning on me. The shadows trembled, but I shook my spoon at him as he raged. "Out you wretched, twisted, little oddsbokken! Back to your rooms, the pair of you. I've wasted enough time on saving you from the folly of your ungrateful, foolish hearts. I have important work—"

Magi shivered and Father shouted. I ignored him and wrapped an arm around my twin to guide her from the tower.

"I'm so cold, Mog," she whispered as we hurried, hand in hand, down the stairs. "Cold and dark, as if I'm filled with shadows. I'm afraid—"

She stumbled on a step and let go of me. Despite the darkness, her eyes flashed like light striking a mirror.

"I hate you," she said, vicious rage strangling her voice and she no longer sounded like my sister. "I'll destroy you. I'll welcome in death and despair to feast on your bones. There's not enough—"

"Hagstabbit," I cried, caught her hand and gasped. How cold she was!

"Mog," she moaned and flung her arms around me. "What has he done?"

I shook my spoon at the shadows that huddled away from me into the corners of the stairwell.

"It looks," I said, "as if Father's made a complete bognobbitted mess of things."

We hurried on, not letting go of each other again. I didn't care about the lump of coal crackling in my chest. I worried over Magi's cursed heart so much that I didn't notice the open withy gate until we were by the pool. Then it was too late.

"Beloved," the tinker cried, flinging himself to his knees before my sister. "I could not leave without you."

"Go away, you nodpot!" I yelled, but he ignored me as usual and grabbed Magi's right hand.

"Come, my love," he said, whiskers twitching as he grinned at her. "Think how happy we'll be, away from these cold mountains." He chaffed her hand between his. "We'll go to Mayminsk and see the king's palace and you'll have a dress as fine as Princess Katiana's and—"

I tugged her left hand. "Back inside, Mags, before—"

She pulled free of us both as the tower's shadow pounced. My sister's eyes flashed white.

"Like a princess?" She drew herself up, lip curling into a sneer that Father would have been proud of. "And you think yourself fit to be my prince?"

Her voice dripped with disdain, every word sharp-edged to cut and wound, but the feckless tinker only grinned.

"Your prince, your hero, your best beloved. I give you my hand, my—"

The shadows drew together with a sound like a thunderclap

and Father appeared in the garden.

"Foolish girl!" he shouted at Magi, ignoring my cries that it was all the tinker's delusion. "I took your heart for a reason and now you throw yourself at this unworthy creature."

"Now there will be a reckoning," my sister snarled in that same broken voice she had used on the stairs. "Now there will be a feast for the crows."

She flung out her hands as if she meant to tear a hole in the world. I lunged, but before I could grab her, Father shouted a word of power and transformed her into a fish. With a flick of his hand, he flipped her into the pool.

"Of all the flat-mangled, bursquatted hampats," I shouted over the tinker's anguished cry.

"I will not be threatened and abused in my castle," Father bellowed. "You're both as faithless and foolish as your mother."

I rounded on him with my spoon raised, fury choking my throat, and Father sneered in contempt.

"I don't need to change you, Tattermog. You are already a heedless, headstrong beast." He swirled the shadows around him and vanished as abruptly as he'd arrived.

"My love!" The tinker dropped to his knees beside the pool.

"Blathercrack!" I thumped him with my spoon. "Nodbuggler!" I hit him again. "This is all your fault. She didn't love you and now she can't and you still—"

Two fish rose to the surface of the pool. Or rather, one pushed another which thrashed and glared. The tinker, with more sense than I thought he had, snatched the angry fish from the water and threw it onto the bank.

"Pestunipent!" I swore, and it transformed, resuming my sister's shape except for her head.

She gave a burbling cry, turned, and ran through the withy gate.

The tinker leapt to his feet.

"Come back, my beautiful glimmering girl," he cried.

I hit him again with my spoon and kicked his shin for good measure, but he only shoved me aside and said, wonderingly, "She called my name."

"We don't even know your name," I said, "and her head—"

"I'll follow her." He clutched at his chest and, for a moment, I felt sorry for him. Surely the curse of the monstrous heart he'd fashioned had poisoned and deluded his own. Then I remembered how he'd leered at my sister before he'd even seen the fused glass and tin that Father had given him to work with. That malevolent shard would have taken root easily in his selfishness.

I slapped him again with my spoon as he cried out, "My Beauty! My love! Though I must search the world, I'll find her again."

"Parsnoodle! Didn't you notice that 'your beauty' now looks like a trout?"

Clearly, he hadn't. Still vowing his devotion, he ran after my sister.

"Good riddance and bad hunting, you bagpusset!" I shouted after him.

How could I restore Magi's head and her heart? I looked around in despair and, from the pool, a fish stared unblinkingly back at me. Was it the same one that had raised my drowning, transformed sister? The same one that had swallowed Magi's golden nut?

I dug through my pockets, finding string and straw, crushed flowers and dry corn cobs, stones and, finally, my mother's gift. I glanced at the nut tree and nodded.

"Brettlespelt," I said, flicking the nut into the air. "Help me, Mother, if you can. The only way Father will give back Magi's head and heart is if I have something he values more."

The fish leapt to catch the nut, then splashed back into the pool. It rose again, opened its mouth and sang, "A box without hinges, key or lid, inside a golden treasure is hid."

"Mama used to sing that to us," I said, frowning to recall the song. "In a stone, a cage, a chest. On a bed though it doesn't rest. Past the mouth that doesn't eat. At the end of the royal street." I grinned at my new piscine friend. "A riddle song and you know the answer, don't you? It must be where he keeps his death."

With a flick of its tail, the little trout leapt from the pool into the rill and slipped like a gleaming arrow through the hole in the garden wall. I tucked my spoon into my tangled hair and whistled for Barleycorn, who met me at the withy gate. Together we clattered down the steps to the village in a headlong, whooping rush to follow a fish, find my sister, and save us both.

Magi was easy to find. Her curse meant she had to stay near water. A deep pool, overhung by spindle-willow, lay a mile beyond the village. My sister had her head in the water when I arrived, but I threw myself off Barleycorn and caught her before she could run off. I held her while she sobbed. There could be no drying her tears, of course. She stared at me with her great, glaucous fishy eyes and shook her head when I asked if she could talk. The light danced and glimmered on her silvery scales. I draped one of my cloaks over her head and told her of my plan.

"Such as it is," I admitted, "but the fish has our golden hazelnuts and perhaps our mother's spirit will help."

Magi gestured to the pool where the silver trout lay in the shallows.

"Then listen," I said, squeezing my sister's hand, "Tiffle and taff, Father may search, and that wretched tinker may hunt, but they won't find we four. We'll follow the river and keep your scales wet, Magi dear. We'll ride Barleycorn and Sweetfish will lead us wherever we must go."

I got to my feet and helped my sister stand.

"Does that cold and deadly heart trouble you, Mags?"

In answer, she clung to my hand while the fish sang a sad ballad about a cursed maiden.

"Gallpins," I said and bound our hands together with a strip torn from one of my cloaks before we scrambled onto Barleycorn's back.

It was as well I did, for that terrible metal locket our father had gifted her was a burden of doom that we hauled on every step of that weary journey. It was worse at night when Magi and I were tired and the curse seemed at its strongest. I would jolt from sleep to Barleycorn's bleating to find Magi asleep and the dark thing that rode in her heart looking out through her silvered fish eyes, making her fingers pluck at the knotted cloth binding our hands. I would take my sister in my arms and let the glowing lump of coal inside me warm us both while Sweetfish sang our mother's lullabies.

So we went from the Tangjat Mountains to the sea, following the Otysh River—tripping and slipping, bounding and pounding, over rocks and through forests, past farms and villages, crossing the broad and fertile plains of Alatay where the roads merged to become the King's Way. At last, we reached the great city of Mayminsk, where the river mouth yawned and gushed its tales of travel into the sea.

A mouth that didn't eat at the end of a royal street… surely, we were close now?

I tugged the cloak close about Magi's head to hide her from the city folk. They stared enough at two young women riding on a shaggy mountain goat.

"Slushputtles!" I shouted at one group of gawkers. "Look any harder and I'll scoop out your eyes with my spoon."

We rode past the docks and the harbour wall, and Barleycorn bounded down a steep set of steps onto a little beach shaped like a shell. High, high above, on a great ridge of black stone, loomed the king's castle. Wide, wide before us stretched the sea, foam-flecked and writhing, and there was Sweetfish, leaping amongst the waves.

"Costering hellican, how do we follow you now?" I called.

Sweetfish raised her head from the water and sang a snatch of song.

"An' it's ho, ho, the wind'll blow, and the master'll tell ye what ye would know."

It echoed a memory of my mother's voice and I joined in singing the verse.

"You must find me an acre of land betwixt the salt water and the sea strand. And plough it up with a devil goat's horn and sow it over with one grain of corn." I grinned at Magi. "We can do that."

I dug a piece of corn out of a pocket and Magi held it while I ground it to dust with my spoon. Then Barleycorn ploughed and Magi sowed and Sweetfish and I sang the song through. Laughter echoed from the harbour wall, but I paid the city folk no mind until a fanfare of trumpets made me turn. Two royal persons, who could only be the prince and princess of Alatay, approached across the sand. I tightened my grip on Magi's hand and Barleycorn's horn, and we stared as boldly as they did.

"We saw you from the castle," the princess said. Her eyes were as blue as the sea and they sparkled with the same humour that twitched her lips.

"And wondered what you did." Her twin brother took her hand, and they mirrored us, except, of course, that I also held a goat.

"Ashputtle, strumpiggle, gallow and glass," I said. "Our work is done. We have ploughed with a devil goat's horn and sown the acre with one grain of corn."

"Ploughed and sown, a job well done," the princess said. I liked the way her voice sounded as sweet as a high meadow lark but with cool depths like a forest pool.

"Only we wondered why?" The prince's smile faded as he looked from my sister's pretty gown to the tattered cloak that concealed her head. "And, er, who you are?"

"We are Katiana and Zhenya," the princess said. "The king of Alatay is our father."

"We are Tattermog and Magimerismara," I replied. "The wizard of the Tangjat Mountains is our father." That widened their eyes, but I went on. "And this is Barleycorn, and that is Sweetfish, and we are here to lift a curse."

I glanced at Magi, and with a shrug, she unbound her head from the cloak.

Matching frowns marred the royal countenances and then the princess stepped forward and took my sister's other hand.

"Cursed?" she said. "Is it painful?" She reached for Magi's cheek and laid her hand against the scales.

"Cursed?" said the prince. "How can we help you?"

I'd not expected their kindness and had to swallow down a sudden surge of heat from the coal inside my chest.

"I think that this—" I nodded at a great wave rushing towards the beach. "—is who we must ask for help."

The crowd on the harbour wall shrieked warnings as the

prince and princess turned. I feared the wave would crush us but, at the last possible moment, it disappeared into itself, and a man stood on the beach. Well, no, not a man but shaped like one with scales and fins. Waves of kelp fell to his shoulders from beneath a coral crown, and his robes were a swirling froth of pearls and sea foam.

"You have sown and now you will reap," he said in a voice like the pounding of surf onto the rocks. "For what purpose have you called forth King Ichthyic?"

"We have sown for—"

He raised a webbed hand to cut me off and said, gazing at Magi, "What vision of loveliness is this?"

"This poor maiden has been cursed," Prince Zhenya said, laying his hand on the hilt of his sword. "She does not deserve your mockery."

"Mockery?" The Fish King's gills flared. "I do not mock."

Princess Katiana rolled her eyes, making me snort with smothered laughter.

"Bosstockets!" I shouted. "The reaping must be reckoned."

The king and the prince bristled, but I went on.

"King Ichthyic, Master of the Sea, the reaping is yours for the doing of a task and the task is no burden to one of your talents. Only follow dear Sweetfish down to the seabed and bring us the chest that lies there."

In less time than it takes to tell, the Fish King returned holding a great iron-bound, barnacle-crusted chest. While I cursed and struggled one-handed to break the hasp with my spoon, he wooed my sister. While I swore and reached within the chest to draw out a copper cage, he promised Magi all the riches of the sea. While I cursed again and unlocked the cage to take out a stone, he asked her to marry him. While I pounded my spoon against it to split the stone to free an egg, Mags shook her head, and King Ichthyic scowled while Prince Zhenya smiled.

"All for an egg?" the princess said, kneeling in the sand beside me.

"It's a box without hinges, key or lid," I said, "and the golden treasure inside…"

I squeezed the egg and, as I'd hoped, a bolt of shadows struck the beach and Father appeared, shaking his fist at me.

"Ungrateful, wretched oddsbokken!" he cried. "Leave my death alone."

"Gladly," I said, "but you must first return our hearts."

"What good will that do you?" He scowled. "Love a man and he will betray you."

"As you betrayed our mother?" I squeezed the egg again and shrugged as he shuddered. "That shard you had the tinker fashion into Magi's heart is cursed," I said. "Take it out and return our hearts, or—" I squeezed a little harder.

"Stop it, you unnatural child. I am your father."

"For all the good that does us," I said, resting the egg on my knee and raising my spoon. I looked him in the eye so he could see that I meant to smash his death to pieces.

"Very well," he cried. He held out his hand, murmured an arcane word, and two red pouches appeared on his palm. "You can have your worthless hearts back but—" He smiled like winter. "—your sister will still have the head of a fish."

Magi gurgled a protest, and I squeezed her hand. King Ichthyic smiled.

"But she must recover if the curse is removed," Princess Katiana protested.

Father shrugged.

"You must give her back her head as well," Prince Zhenya said.

Father sneered.

"I do not have the strength for more than two great workings," he said, "when my death is being squeezed and threatened."

"Yelpwallop," I swore and pointed my spoon at him. "Then here is my bargain. Restore Magi's own head and her heart. I'll get by without mine and I won't break your death. Agreed?"

"You put my death back in the sea, where it's safe," Father said, "and I agree."

I shoved my spoon in my hair and handed the egg to the princess to hold as Magi helped me to my feet, our hands still bound. Father tucked one scarlet pouch into his robe. Then we drew circles of binding on our foreheads with our left thumbs to show the bargain was set.

"Head or heart first?" Father asked, and I said, "That cursed shard of tin."

He spoke the word of power and swapped the evil replica for Magi's true heart.

"Hold this," he said, and passed me the locket. He turned back to Magi and held her fish head as he chanted, his words flowing thickly as if he poured them from a jar of cold honey. Through our bound hands, I felt the magic push against the lingering stain of the curse and Father's folly, seeking her true form.

The mirrored tin heart glinted in my left hand, hot and heavy as a grudge. I looked up into the princess' wide blue eyes. The egg which held Father's death nestled cold and pale in her hands.

"Let me help you," Katiana said. She reached over, her arm brushing mine, and opened the clasp on the side of the locket I nodded my silent agreement, and she tucked the egg inside and snapped it shut.

"Hempsnoggle," I said and the cloth that bound my hand to Magi's unwound.

"Mog!" my sister cried, and Barleycorn bucked and jostled her into the prince's arms.

"What a tragic end to such beauty," the Fish King said and threw himself into the sea.

Father dusted a scattering of scales off his hands and reached for the copper cage.

"Now, Tattermog, my death," he said.

"Goes back in the sea, as promised." I flung the cursed heart as hard as I could but, before it hit the water, Sweetfish leapt up and snatched it.

"No!" Father shrieked. He ran towards the sea and, mid-stride, transformed himself into a sleek, black fish that cut through the next wave and swam after Sweetfish. I could only laugh because by tiffle and taff I had sworn Father could search but he would not find us. Well, bad luck and good riddance to him. It was all he deserved, to chase our mother's spirit and try to reclaim his death.

"Thank you," I said, turning to Princess Katiana.

"I was happy to help," she replied, "and you had your hands full." Her smile flashed as she tipped her head to where our siblings stood, locked in an embrace. "As do they."

"You were so brave," Prince Zhenya murmured.

"You were so kind," Magi replied.

"How could I not love you?" they said together.

The princess rolled her eyes, and I snorted as I tried to smother my laughter. She held out her hand and said, "Will you come up to the palace with me? We must let my father know the good news."

"That the wizard of the Tangjat Mountains is gone chasing his own death?"

She flicked another glance towards Magi and the prince and said, "That also, I suppose."

Katiana was right, of course. The real news was that my sister and Prince Zhenya had found a love that would launch a thousand ballads. The king, though he might have worried that Magi was the daughter of his old enemy and sister to a tattered oddsbokken, looked from his son's smitten grin to his daughter's imperiously raised eyebrows and agreed that they should be married as soon as they wished. Which was as soon as the very next day.

We rode to their wedding side-by-side, the princess and I—Katiana on a dainty little white mare, me on Barleycorn—and though we had talked the whole night through, she was strangely silent. The road was long, but not as long as my list of flaws. I could not stop them from jostling for room in my mind.

"Hogswaggle," I swore at last. "Does it bother you that I ride on a shaggy mountain goat and not a beautiful horse?"

She shook her head. "Barleycorn is your friend," she said. "Why should it bother me?"

We rode a little further, but still she was silent.

"Rumdumpling," I cursed. "Does it bother you that I carry this wooden spoon?"

"Your spoon?" A smile twitched her lips. "You can call it that if you like, but I know a wizard's wand when I see one."

She said no more, and we rode until I could no longer bear the silence.

"Scalderpot," I said. "Does it bother you that I'm not as beautiful as my sister?"

"Who says it is so?" Katiana shook her head. "You are more beautiful to me than anyone I've ever met."

"Then what is wrong?" I cried, even as her words fanned the coal within my chest, a flush rising in my cheeks.

"Your heart is gone," she said, dashing tears from her eyes, "and you'll never feel for me as I feel for you."

"Blastgopple," I swore, and tucked my spoon into my hair so I could reach over and take her hand. "I didn't care about my old heart and Father's spell because I never wanted to love a man. I don't need that soggy heart to fall in love with you…" I grinned at her and warmed through when she smiled back. "I've done that with a lump of coal."

The Withered

Mendel Mire

The sorcerer approached, riding from the woodlands to the west. He seemed to carry with him a darkness that distorted his surrounds, like the blurring of letters on a wet page. Dion sat upon his horse, accompanied by a score of castle guards. He could not be too careful when addressing such matters with a practitioner of the arcane arts.

Dion cleared his throat and spoke up before the lone, cloaked rider. "I must regrettably halt you here, friend, and inform you that the young Duchess has found love for another."

The noon sun bathed the realm in midsummer warmth. The tall spire of the Castle Čelebice stood proudly, overlooking the surrounding plains to the west of the mountains and the fields were peppered with the golden blossoms of the summer dandelions. It was a productive time for the Duchy, the lands teeming with fertility, excitement, and promise of growth and prosperity. But tensions had arisen over matters of the heart. The Sorcerer Mackivel could not have known that when he came to the castle to court the young and beautiful Lorraine Belladoire, her heart had already been won by another—the handsome Dion Boulangère; son of the renowned horse breeders of the Čelebice stables. The menacing confrontation coming to pass cast a blackened shadow over the otherwise magnificent day.

The rider came to a stop before them, his face concealed within the darkness of his hood. A silence lingered for what seemed too long. Dion concealed his anxiety. It was always difficult to deal with such peoples—these owners of unknown capabilities.

A sudden gust of wind startled the horses. It tore many dandelions from their stalks. The yellow flowers tumbled through the party of guards, seemingly fleeing the scene. Dion watched them disappear in the distance with a genuine envy.

"I see," the rider finally said. "It seems a rose once bloomed is no sooner picked."

"My guards here are concerned you may try something rash," Dion said, gesturing to his unflinching support.

The Sorcerer Mackivel lowered his hood. The face revealed was nothing more than the ordinary, hairless face of a man. The face smiled warmly towards Dion and his guards. Dion relaxed a little.

"On the contrary," the visitor said, patting the side of his horse. "The steeds of the Čelebice stables are indeed the best in the land. I would prefer not to part on bad terms."

"Very good," answered Dion. "Under normal circumstances, it is our custom to invite guests into our home to feast and learn from one another. But there remains an unfortunate distrust for your kind among the residents of the Duchy."

"I understand," said Mackivel. He reached a slender hand into his cloak.

A cacophony of unsheathing weapons and drawing of bows erupted all around Dion. He tensed at the sudden escalation. But as the sorcerer revealed two small metallic objects upon his palm, he commanded his company to lower sword and arrow.

"As a parting gift, I offer the Duchess these rings. I intended for them to be ours, but now present them as a token of my support for her union."

Dion eyed the two rings. The bands were silver, each with a matching metallic crystal set upon a butternut clasp. The jewels shimmered in brilliant unison, reflecting the blue skies above. Dion knew of no stones with such properties.

"The stones on the rings. What are they?"

"They are not stones, Dion Boulangère."

Hearing his name from the sorcerer's lips sent a chill down Dion's spine. He swore he had never mentioned it. But he silently reasoned it may have been learned during past stable dealings.

The sorcerer continued. “They belong to a shard of the Mirror of Souls. The shard was split into two pieces, each crafted by the Fei into the jewels you see before you. The shard of mirror contains a human soul, now cleaved in two. These rings must remain close for the soul to be complete.”

The offer surprised Dion. He'd certainly expected worse under the circumstances. The rings shimmered together, beckoning Dion. Enamoured by the tale, he knew Lorraine would be equally smitten by them.

He took the rings. “Thank you for the gift. You are most gracious.”

The Sorcerer bowed and lifted his hood, turning his horse back to the woodlands. Shortly after, Dion and the guards began their return to the castle. As he rode, he examined the rings closely. They seemed to fall closer and closer together in his palm with each step of his horse. Two rings that must remain close to make a soul whole, Mackivel had said. It was romantic, in a way. Lorraine would love them. They would match perfectly with the red dress he'd bought her one day prior.

The visitor had been surprisingly gracious in defeat. He could not wait to show her the spoils. With such a gift, surely their lives were destined to bloom for an age.

But that was a long time ago.

Dion stepped from the stables into the castle courtyard. Glancing upward, his clouded eyes could just make out the twisted silhouette of the castle's dilapidated spire. Previous years had seen it stand tall and proud. But like all things, the years had wilted it to a flaccid droop—now a crude joke among the common folk. It seemed no beautiful thing was safe from the withering of time.

Hobbling to a barrel of water beside the granary, Dion splashed shaky handfuls of it across his weathered face. He then drew it back across his grey, wiry hair, and wiped the drops from the embroidered white rose of the Familie Belladoire upon his leathers. Dion adjusted the ring on his forefinger. The mounted jewel glistened against the morning sun but, like all else, seemed to have faded of late. Some fifty years had passed since he had come into possession of the rings. He often recalled the day he received them.

It was the first day of Spring. The day the Duchess Lorraine Belladoire had chosen so long ago to perform her annual clandestine rite of youth. Today, Fileneros the satyr would shed a tear into the blood of a maiden sacrifice—a preternatural lotion to restore the Duchess' youth and preserve the Duchy. This divine ingredient was crucial for the charm's efficacy. Yet, Dion and Lorraine had swiftly learned how difficult it was to extract a tear from a satyr. Fortunately, they had discovered early that Fileneros held a weakness for the innocent. And so, for their first decade, the couple had slaughtered a puppy before the satyr's eyes; the act proving enough to retrieve a stubborn teardrop. But these last years had been different. Fileneros had learned to bring forth a tear of his own volition and no puppy had been slaughtered since. This annual gift he would presently bring to the satyr was now more a formality—a reward for his contribution.

Dion crossed the courtyard and met with his blind ward, Taryn. The boy stood outside the castle keep. A thin blindfold covered his empty, scarred eye-sockets Lorraine had gifted him. He held a basket in arm, the newly weaned puppy within it, kept secure and comfortable beneath a sheet. Dion took Taryn's other arm, and the boy led him to the stairwell of the keep. They began the laborious task of climbing the stairs to the upper floors of the keep.

Dion guided the pair, Taryn helping his poor old knees support his weight. Somewhere in the decrepit, twisted stairwell, he stumbled a little. The boy saved him from a nasty fall.

"Thank you, dear boy," he said.

Taryn didn't respond. He rarely did anymore. At such a young age, the poor boy's spirit had been shattered by Lorraine's recent spate of cruelty. Truth be told, the fool should have known better than to touch himself while she bathed. An act for which she had her guards scrape clean his eye sockets.

After what seemed an eternity, they reached the hall of the

upper floor of the keep. Crashing and jovial song rang down the corridor from beyond the door ahead, accompanied by the familiar rattling of chains and the click-clack of cloven hooves on stone.

Reaching the solid oak door at the end of the corridor and the boudoir beyond, Dion took the basket from Taryn. It was time to get in there before Fileneros, the damned fool, destroyed the entire castle.

The boudoir was in a state. The bed was indiscernible beneath the mess. The tapestry, a collage of Belladoire white roses, was missing an entire section from its centre. The empty, ornate ceremonial bath sat near the door, splashed throughout with wine. And in the centre of the room, fastened to the wall by the long chain around his ankle as he had been for decades, was the satyr, Fileneros.

The creature swayed. Shreds of tapestry hung from one of his horns. He sprawled his goat-like legs to steady himself and squinted through drunken eyes.

"Dion!" Fileneros blurted. He raced forward, draping a muscular arm around Dion's shoulders. "Come, sing with me—"

> Oh, with love habits of rabbits and the might of a steer,
> Young maidens'll journey from afar to be near,
> This satyr of old, with his pisser hard-as-rock ready.
> And they'll toil to walk straight after taking cock steady!
> For hours upon hours they'll—

Fileneros' yearling pup had remained hidden away in the corner of the room, frightened by the commotion. It howled in time with the satyr's slurred words.

"Quiet you," Fileneros spat.

The pup shrank low with fear. True to his shallow self, Fileneros only cared for the puppies while they remained pups. After a year, and when it had outgrown its smallness and innocence, the satyr lost interest in the pup. And with it, any love he bore for them. So, each year, Dion brought a replacement. This year's offering remained tucked away in Dion's basket throughout the commotion.

As Fileneros roared at the older dog in the room's corner, Dion saw the flash of the many scars across the satyr's back. Scars that stretched from shoulder to waist—the innumerable lashings he had received for soiling so many maidens prior to previous rites. The satyr was certainly gifted at bending a young maiden's will to serve his own. A skill the Duchess had used to her own gain in preparing the annual ritual. But this had occasionally come at a cost all involved; to the Duchess in losing her tribute, to the maiden in losing her virtue, and to Fileneros himself in the form of punishment. It had happened often enough the guards had given the punishment of lashings a name—'being dragged through the rose bush'. Fileneros had indeed paid a visit to the bush many times.

"It's good to see you, old friend," Fileneros said, turning back to Dion.

The satyr lifted flagon to lips and guzzled the contents, a stream of red wine running down his hairy chest and belly, dripping from the plump end of his enormous penis. After upending the flagon, he looked at the basket Dion held. He wiped his goatee dry with the back of his forearm.

He belched. "Is that what I think it is?" He lifted the sheet covering the basket and cried out with joy. "Oh Dion. He's beautiful."

Dropping the empty flagon to the floor, Fileneros lifted the puppy from the basket and brought it close to his face in a tight, infantile hug.

"You've chosen well, Chamberlain. A worthy companion for this coming year."

Completely forgotten in the uproar, Dion now moved Taryn to the far corner of the room and handed him the yearling dog. It was for the best. Without Fileneros' affections, it was certain to succumb to neglect. With a whisper, Dion sent the boy back to the kitchens with the unwanted older dog and returned his attention the satyr, the creature's attention solely focused his new pup. By all accounts, satyrs were believed extinct. But Dion and Lorraine had found one. Fileneros had been young then, growing up in a monastery under the monks' tutelage. When Dion had learned of the power a satyr's tears contained, he'd obtained the beast from the monastery personally. The Duchess had kept Fileneros under lock and key ever since.

Dion moved to the bed. He gathered the soaked and stained sheets together. Lorraine had clearly paid a visit.

Fileneros looked up and grinned. "Our Duchess was particularly vigorous this morning."

"I'm sure she was," Dion replied, unsurprised. Lorraine had been using Fileneros for her own pleasure for some years now.

"You know, she still thinks of you frequently, Dion—well, at least how you used to be."

"Is that so?" he asked.

"Might you consider my offer this year?"

He raised an eyebrow. "Offer?"

"We go over this every year, Dion. You unlock me. I give you one of my tears. I jump from the window into the moat and escape to my freedom. You use my tear to regain your youth and be with your beloved Duchess for the rest of your days."

Dion's finger itched beneath his ring. The band irritated his skin sometimes. But he couldn't take it off anymore if he tried. He twisted the ring back and forth a little, rubbing the skin beneath.

"Oh, yes. I would trade anything for my youth again. To be young with Lorraine. But my answer is still no, Fileneros. I must lead by example, and hope that she will one day put an end to this obsession herself."

Fileneros snorted. "I'll never understand you, Chamberlain. You condemn yourself to love a woman who only sees herself. The twilight of your life is now upon you. And for what?"

Dion gave no response. Truth be told, he considered Fileneros' offer frequently. And usually found the idea humorous. Preposterous even. But today felt different. Fileneros was right. His years were numbered, his end approaching. And Lorraine showed no desire to even resist her compulsion to be forever young.

Fileneros launched himself through the air, crashing onto the bed. "Oh, Dion," he rolled over the sheets. "This is no place to spend eternity."

Dion worked around where Fileneros lay on the bed. He was no stranger to his histrionics.

"You have everything any man could dream of, you fool. Unlimited food, a bottomless flagon of wine, eternal youth, and sex aplenty."

"But only with one woman, Dion! A satyr needs variety. How would you feel if they cooped you up in your kitchens for years with naught but smelly old onions to cook with every day?"

"I'm not sure the Duchess would like being compared to smelly old onions."

"Oh fine. But trade the smelly onions for the finest of caviar and the result is the same after over fifty years. I need to sample more of the delights of the world! All the flavours of the banquet. All the colours of the rainbow," he sighed. "I can't do that in here." Fileneros rolled over towards Dion and rested his horned head upon his hand. "Do you at least remember where she keeps the key to these?" he raised his leg, chain swaying from his ankle. The iron lock hung at Dion's eye level.

"Of course, I remember."

"Well, just think on it. Please?"

Outside the keep, the sudden cries of horses and the rattling of a carriage carried into the boudoir as it approached the gates. The gears of the portcullis groaned into action and Fileneros straightened on the bed.

"Ah, the tribute arrives," he said.

The satyr launched onto his hooves and trotted towards the window. The chain stopped him mere steps from the ledge and view of the lands beyond.

Dion hobbled past Fileneros to the window ledge. The moat was eerily silent. Years ago, children would have swum and played there, and peasants would have fished its waters, but those days had passed and it had fallen into neglect, much like the rest of the castle. Dion's fading eyesight could just make out the carriage now crossing the dark waters above the moat using the lowered drawbridge, over by the western barbican.

"You best meet the young lady," Fileneros said.

On the arrival of the carriage, the satyr's demeanour changed.

The infantile exuberance of earlier transformed into a confident countenance that Dion thought made Fileneros look almost majestic. There was a duality to the satyr. In some ways, he was a gormless fool, yet in others, he was a master of seduction.

She was a lovely young lady. No older than fifteen. Another invisible orphan fed the same pauper-to-princess tale by the Lorraine's scouts. Dion washed her, dressed her, and took her to her room to await her ceremonial bathing that evening.

Dion then made the long walk to Lorraine's boudoir. Closing the solid oak door behind him, he surveyed the enormous canopy bed, positioned where it always had been throughout their marriage, in the corner by the door, blood-red drapery tied back to the posts. The mahogany dresser, surrounded in a crescent of mirrors, midway along the opposing wall. And, as always, the large wooden divider ran the length of the room, partitioning off an excessive wardrobe.

"Lorraine?" Dion called.

"By the window, Dion."

Lorraine wore her full-length coverings, her arms, legs, and face concealed beneath a swathe of dark cloth and a veil. In more recent years, the people had become suspicious of her youthful appearance. Word of witchcraft had spread throughout the surrounding Duchy. Now concealing her appearance was a necessity, her visage only seen by her closest servants and personal guard—all paid handsomely with gold, land, and a promise their own young daughters would be exempt from the annual rite.

She straightened from her practised hunch and moved towards Dion with elegance and grace. As she lifted her veil, even Dion's failing eyesight could not deny the beauty that she was. Only seven years younger than Dion, she appeared in her mid-twenties; hair still black as the night sky, her skin still smooth and youthful.

His heart skipped a beat. "You look wonderful, Lorraine."

The Duchess giggled and ran to Dion. She hugged him tight, swirling him in a circle. A coy smile on her lips, she grabbed his hand, briefly passing a finger over the ring he wore with a knowing a smile. As her own ring brushed past his, the two jewels shimmered in unison, the soul trapped within the jewels intact for a brief moment. She pulled Dion close, and they swayed in slow circles to a silent tune. Finally, Dion brought them to a stop.

He cleared his throat. "I was wondering if—"

"I know what brings you to my chambers," she hushed him, restarting their dance. "You wish to know if this is the year that I come back to you. But my dearest Dion, you know I can't do that."

"But why?"

"Well, who would look after my lands and my people?"

"Somebody. Anybody. You can't keep this up forever. Rumours in the Duchy now tell of an imposter hiding beneath the veil of the Duchess. There's only so long the people of the castle will keep their lips sealed before word reaches the common folk of the dark magic we brought here—"

Lorraine chuckled.

Dion's lips trembled. His heart ached so completely, he feared it would stop beating altogether. He felt his eyes brim with unshed tears. It pained him to straighten his hunched spine to look into hers, but he did so anyway.

"Please Lorraine." His old voice cracked past the lump in his throat. "We were supposed to grow old *together*."

Silence. The gentle swaying ceased. Lorraine pushed away, turning a furious gaze on her husband.

"Are you forgetting Dion? This is your fault. You wanted this. Don't you remember?"

"I do. I remember everything—"

"I just wanted your love," she continued to bear down over him. "But you wanted me to stay young for you. To lose the wrinkles. To have these full lips and these firm breasts. You kidnapped the satyr. You arranged my first bath. You killed the first girl. You were the monster, not me. I did this for you. And then, no sooner do your manly virtues wane, you want me to be old for you now instead?"

Dion had no words. Gazing to the floor, his tears dripped to the faded rug they stood upon. They soaked into the fibres and brought forth a dark colouration—a hint of former vibrance.

The anger drained from Lorraine's face, and she rubbed the skin beneath her own ring before embracing his withered frame. "My dear sweet Dion. Perhaps next year?"

Dion felt the warmth of her embrace. All his joints ached, but he didn't care. He was exactly where he wanted to be. Not just for love, but also remorse. Because it was true—it was all his fault. Lorraine's addiction to eternal youth, the evil things they'd both done to maintain it. And the vile acts she'd visited upon her own subjects since. Perhaps Fileneros was right. If he started all this, he really should finish it while he still had the capacity to do so. Perhaps if he forced Lorraine to return to her true age, her gentle soul would return with it. He looked at the far wall and her large dresser. His gaze drifted lower to the drawer where she kept the key to Fileneros' chains.

Dion bowed his head. "I understand, Lorraine."

She kissed him on the forehead. "You'll always be that handsome young man I fell in love with."

He smiled, though sadness and regret muddied his thoughts. He knew what he must do. His body was failing him more and more each day and if he left it any longer, he may never have the chance to put this right.

He brightened. "I was wondering if you wouldn't mind putting on the dress?"

"Of course, my love," she said with a grin, skipping behind the divider to rummage through her clothes.

Dion didn't have much time. He moved as swiftly as he could to the dresser and carefully opened the drawer.

"You'll be present this evening, yes?" she called out.

"Yes, of course." He stared at the key to the satyr's chains exactly where he expected it to be, then lifted the key quietly from the drawer.

Then he saw them—a pair of eyes staring back at him. They were in a glass jar on the dresser preserved in honey, the whites lined with pale strands of torn muscle. They were young eyes. Taryn's eyes.

"Good," Lorraine continued. "I need you to watch that beast, Fileneros. Make sure he behaves himself around the tribute."

The boy's disembodied eyes stared ceaselessly at Dion, penetrating his soul. His fingers trembled. The key slid from his shaking grip. Dion's stomach dropped with the key until it bounced silently onto the rug at his feet.

Frantically, Dion glanced to the divider. Lorraine was still changing. Moving as fast as his stiff knees would allow, he bent over. Swollen knuckles grasped the key and he pushed the drawer closed behind him, slipping the key under his belt.

"This dress?" Lorraine emerged from behind the divider, as Dion rose to face her. She wore the red dress he'd given her so long ago. "How do I look?" she twirled with slow and perfect grace.

"Beautiful as ever."

But her beauty was no longer the same. Her stunning exterior had once complimented a kind heart. The young Lorraine that Dion had fallen for decades ago would never have taken a boy's sight away; and certainly would never have kept his eyes in a jar. The promise of eternal beauty had changed Lorraine into something else—something terrifying. As if in the absence of ageing flesh, her soul had withered in its place.

Dion gestured towards the jar. "Why are those in here?"

"Your ward enjoyed watching me so much. Now he can watch me forever."

"He's just a boy, Lorraine."

"A boy that couldn't control himself in my presence. He betrayed my trust for a simple, forgettable pleasure. If today he forsakes his duties to please himself, tomorrow he'll divulge our secrets to the ladies of the night. He became a liability. Or have you forgotten?"

"I haven't," he stuttered, trembling with anxiety.

Lorraine pursed her lips. She seemed to sense something was amiss. "You need to promise me, Dion, always remember there is a price for betrayal in Castle Čelebice."

"I won't forget, Lorraine. I promise you. I should prepare the boudoir for tonight." He gestured to the door.

She smiled and kissed him on the lips. "It's funny. Aside from a little cloudiness, those handsome eyes of yours have barely changed. You'll always be my beautiful stableboy. My dashing Dion Boulangère."

In the boudoir, Taryn had prepared for the evening's rite when Dion arrived. Beside the steamy bath the small cherry oak table with a hand mirror. The bath's jewel-encrusted arm and neck rests were open in splendour like gilded flowers, their true sinister purpose concealed for now.

Fileneros was sprawled across the bed, swinging his tail in hand. He gazed wistfully at the window. His new puppy played at his side, chewing on the long locks of his mane.

"Oh, look Taryn, our Chamberlain returns. Happy to pass another year over to the fates, it appears," Fileneros began in mockery.

He stopped, leaning his head back with a frown, and sniffed at the air, like a wolf catching the scent of prey. He pushed the puppy off the bed. It toppled into its basket with a small thud and rolled over in a daze. Fileneros stood up with a dignified and almost regal poise. Dion frowned. This was that other side of the satyr—the side the legends speak of.

Behind Dion, the young maiden had entered the bedchamber. She gasped at the sight of the satyr, her eyes growing wide. Only a handful of people would ever see such a creature. Naturally, her gaze lowered to his enormous and swollen erection.

"My Lady," Fileneros said in a deep, seductive growl.

The girl stood motionless with the familiar doe-eyed look Dion had seen maidens give the satyr so many times before.

Dion stood next to Taryn, arms crossed, observing as Fileneros whispered his sweet nothings into the maiden's virgin ears. 'Fileneros the Philanderer', the monks had called him—the same ascetic monks who raised him and had hated that moniker with passion. They had tried extremely hard to civilise him, but to no avail.

"Come along," Fileneros purred, holding out a hand in a coaxing manner. "Let's get you into the bath and ready to meet the Duchess."

The girl followed his lead to the water.

Silently, Dion ushered Taryn from the boudoir while Fileneros disrobed the trembling maiden.

"You needn't fear me, my love," Fileneros whispered to her. "I am forbidden to give into your desires on this night, lest I receive further lashings."

The girl nodded, entranced by his strange allure even as she sunk into the warm water in the bath.

Slowly, Fileneros ran his large, firm hands over her body, ostensibly rinsing her down. She breathed heavily at his touch. Gently, he guided her arms into the rests on the side of the tub, easing her head back into the brace. Then he bent forward, kissed her on the forehead, and coupled the two halves of the ornate clamp across her neck. After then closing the arm clamps about her forearms, she was completely secure and still oblivious to what had occurred. This was the true power of the satyr's seduction.

Without hesitation, Fileneros thrust the gems of the arm rests along their guides, sliding the concealed blades along the flesh of the maiden's wrists. Blood gushed down the chutes at the end of each restraint, pouring freely into the bath water.

Fileneros placed a hand gently across the girl's mouth and stared mournfully to the window as she thrashed weakly. Her struggling soon ceased and within moments, Fileneros grimly lifted her body from the water, placing it to the side and covering her corpse with a blanket. He rested against the bathtub rim for a moment and met Dion's gaze. A single tear welled in his left eye.

"Such a waste!" Fileneros lamented.

The tear dripped from Fileneros' cheek and into the bloodied bath water. A silver sheen briefly traced the surface. Then the youth ritual was ready for Lorraine.

Dion glanced at the puppy. It slept in its basket, clueless to the fate it had evaded. If partaking in the murder of a young girl was enough to inspire a tear from the satyr these days, perhaps the creature had found a conscience over the years, as surely as the Duchess had lost her own. Dion looked to the window. He felt for the key, still tucked behind his belt. The time was now or never.

"Fileneros, my old friend. I've decided to release you," he pulled the key from his pocket. "Let us see this madness end."

Fileneros' sadness turned to ecstasy. His ears pricked, and he smiled broadly with excitement, his tail flicking. "Really, Dion?"

"This is the last time."

Dion bent down and slid the key into the lock at Fileneros' ankle. Once the satyr was gone, Lorraine would have no choice but to succumb to the ageing process she'd become determined to avoid. Then they would be together again, just as she had promised. They could complete their lives, reminiscing over their love and adventures, and he would forget none of it. He promised her that day he'd never forget—

His finger itched intensely. He racked his brain but could not recall. What was it again? What did he promise her he'd never forget? He felt his old heart sinking. He knew he had made a promise to Lorraine that day. But for the life of him, he could not remember what it was. He rubbed the ring back and forth, trying to ease the discomfort. He had the same thoughts over and over: *What have I forgotten? Was it fundamental to our love?* His mind struggled for clarity, straining to recall the details.

His finger burned. It hadn't been this intense for a long time, he knew that much. The ring had not been so irritating since the day he'd taken Fileneros away from the monastery. That was so long ago now, but the discomfort that day had driven him close to madness. He looked to the bath, brimming with blood-red water. For the first time, he knew with certainty that something *had* faded from his memory. If he was forgetting now, how much had he already forgotten? What did he have left? He thought: *Who am I if I can't remember? What if I forget Lorraine?* Dion panicked. He had to save himself. To hold onto his memories, he would need to take that bath himself. It was the only way to preserve what remained.

Unlocking the chains that bound Fileneros, Dion asked the satyr to help him into the water.

He hurriedly removed his clothes and, with Fileneros' assistance, he climbed into the bath. He splashed the red liquid all over himself as he had seen Lorraine do so many times before. Within moments, he felt the ritual take effect, the de-ageing clawing back the years. He held out his arms, watching his swollen knuckles shrink. He balled his fists and opened them again with ease. The skin on his hands became smooth and supple, the creases and freckles fading.

"Incredible," Dion laughed. "Are you seeing this Fileneros?"

"Indeed. You're looking more like your former self already."

Dion felt the renewed energy surge through his body. The underlying strength and ambition of youth. He felt all his desires renewed and he laughed again at the prospect of opportunity—

But this time the laughter sounded strange, like childish chuckles. He looked up at Fileneros—the satyr's smile had vanished.

"What's wrong?" Dion asked. But instead of a man's voice, it was of higher pitch, youthful, like that of a boy. He again looked at his hands. Now they were small. Delicate. Not those of a man's at all. "No," he stammered. He felt his face. All signs of stubble had vanished, leaving only smooth skin.

"What have you done to me, satyr?" Dion demanded. "The lotion has gone too far! It's turned me into a boy!"

Fileneros sniffed at the air with surprise. "No Dion. Not a boy."

Dion glanced down at his small, lean body soaking in the bloody water. Where once his broad chest had been, there was now a slender frame with round, firm breasts. Where once his manhood had been, now naught but a light bush of hair.

"I didn't know it worked like this. I'm sorry," Fileneros lamented.

Dion snatched the mirror from the table beside him and stared into it. The reflection was familiar, and yet not his. The face looking back at him had all of his features, but transposed upon the framework of a stunning young woman, her face matted with long, blood-soaked locks of dark hair.

"No," Dion shrieked over and over. "No, no, no!"

Fileneros' ears perked at the sound of shuffling armour beyond the door. The guards had heard the screams. "I must take my leave. I'm sorry Dion."

"Don't you dare leave me, satyr!" Dion cried, but the creature had already bounded across the room. He had just reached the window when the door swung open.

Filerenos stood immobile. The warm evening sun shone on his face as he felt it's touch for the first time in an age. But he smiled with pure joy only for a moment. When his gaze lowered to the moat below, all excitement drained from his face.

He moaned softly. "Impossible."

Fileneros looked back at Dion still in the bath, then surveyed the guards edging into the room. Flicking his gaze back to the moat below and across the valley beyond the castle walls, he released an animal hiss of realisation. Fileneros climbed up onto the window's ledge and leapt.

Dion looked at the empty window. He couldn't stay in the castle like this either. Thoughts of what Lorraine would do to him flooded his mind, the terror squeezing tight onto his small, delicate spine. He had to escape too. He pushed himself from the bath, hurrying past the guards to the window. Dion looked down at the moat with his fresh, young eyes, no longer clouded by age.

All hope left him.

Empty. The moat was empty. The dark, muddy waters he thought he'd seen earlier were in fact a muddy mire where waters once flowed. The jump was too high. An impossible task. Far below him, a maimed Fileneros wailed in the mud. He writhed in pain clutching at his leg, most likely broken.

Any chance of escape was lost. The panic overcame him. Dion swayed with a sudden dizziness and fell to the floor at the guards' feet.

"Tell me what happened," Lorraine commanded.

The guard recounted the events as best he could. As the Duchess listened, she kicked the blanket aside, exposing the body of the maiden tribute beneath. She glanced up at the other young girl, now wrapped in a blanket adorned with embroidered white roses and tied at the wrists.

"Two tributes? It can't be." She grabbed the girl by the chin, inspecting her closely.

"I know those eyes." Lorraine hissed.

The Duchess snatched the young lady's hand. She spied the ring upon the small, delicate finger and glanced between Fileneros and the girl. "Dion? What have you done?" she chuckled. "Did you perform the rite yourself? And become a young girl?"

Several of the guards burst into laughter. Another guard handed Lorraine the key to the satyr's chains. She stared at it, seeming to weigh it in her palm.

"Why would you do this, Dion?"

"I needed you to stop. Too many innocent people have been hurt."

Lorraine laughed. "Come now, if you really cared for the innocent, you would have helped that poor girl," she gestured to the corpse. "No, Dion. You did this for yourself."

Lorraine turned her attention back to Fileneros, secured by several guards. Injured from his fall, he leant all his weight on a single leg, now again secured to the chains. He remained silent. She sneered at Fileneros. "And you? Did you think you were the first to try escaping via the moat? It's been empty for a decade. Did you forget we drained the moat, Dion? It was your idea. We laughed for hours about how the satyr approached you each year with his infantile plan of escape. Since when were these beasts ever known for their cunning?"

Lorraine paced around the bath, running her fingertips along the worn roses of the faded tapestry on the wall. "Send for another maiden," she commanded. A guard left the room as Lorraine scrutinised Dion's delicate, feminine frame.

"This is certainly an interesting revelation," the Duchess continued. "Perhaps if you hadn't massacred the monks when you abducted Fileneros so long ago, you would have known this would happen. Or perhaps you would have forgotten about that too. It's amusing, really. I'm not sure what you were hoping for. Without Fileneros, you're useless to me, anyway."

"How can you say that? I've looked after you for decades."

Lorraine smiled. "Tell me, Dion. What do you think brings a tear to our dear satyr's eye?"

Dion's mind swirled with confusion. He looked at the naked body on the floor.

"Surely you don't think it's the maidens? When has he ever shown a single care for a woman's wellbeing? He doesn't even care if the pleasure of his own endowments ravages the insides of a woman. How could he ever see them as anything more than a thing to be tasted? No, Dion. There is a reason I've kept you close all these years. You're the source, my love. The inspiration for his tears."

"What? Fileneros, tell her the truth," Dion cried.

Fileneros hung his head, his will broken. He offered no response.

"Oh, that is the truth. It seems our dear satyr sees no greater tragedy than a man's own wilful enslavement. And you, my dear Dion, have pathetically enslaved yourself for decades. Your ridiculous hope that things between us could ever return to as they once were. It's enough to tease a tear from the hardest of satyrs. I can find anybody to change my bedpan and fuss over my appearance. I've only kept you around to this end alone."

Dion's legs gave way. He collapsed to the tiles with a thud, tears pouring down his face.

"Well, those tears don't do us any good," Lorraine said, leaning closer to Fileneros. "But I'll require another tear from *you* though."

She traced a finger down Fileneros' naked chest and stomach. "But, of course, we know how difficult a task this is for you. Tell me, are you happy with your latest present? You don't seem to be since you were so eager to leave your puppy behind."

Fileneros' eyes widened. His face flushed. He glanced at the basket where his new puppy sat. "No, don't you hurt it!"

Lorraine strode to the basket and lifted the puppy from its basket. She lightly bounced it in her arm like a newborn baby, toying her finger about its mouth. It nibbled playfully as Fileneros struggled uselessly against the guards.

The Duchess leaned in close to Fileneros, scanning his eyes for any sign of tears. Despite the obvious upset to the satyr, no tears came.

"Don't worry. I won't hurt your pet," she said, stroking the puppy. "After all, you are going to need something new to play with." The words rang with malicious intent.

The Duchess pursed her lips.

"We've had so many fun moments together, haven't we, Fileneros? But I need more of your tears," she whispered in his ear.

A guard spoke up. "Shall we drag him through the rose bushes again, my Lady?"

"No," she sighed. "I think not."

Fileneros' ears perked up. His eyes met Lorraine's, with hope renewed.

Lorraine straightened. "Guard!" she commanded, stepping back. "Bring me his cock."

Fileneros' ears wilted. He panicked. Struggling against the guards, he released a shrill cry as his hooves scraped against the stone tiles.

"There's nothing to be found beyond the confines of this room that you don't already have, Fileneros. You need to understand that."

Dion watched helplessly. The guard offered a sympathetic shrug to the struggling satyr, before drawing his blade.

Lorraine sat on the floor beside Dion, ignoring the satyr's screams echoing through the keep. When the guard finished his grisly task, he handed the severed penis to the Duchess.

"I should give you to the guards after what you did," Lorraine said to Dion. "But it seems I too need a new plaything." She tossed the penis aside with a nonchalant look. "I'm curious, what do you think would happen if we used a boy's blood on you next? I know just the boy for the job—your ward Taryn won't see it coming, would he? Or perhaps we could use dog's blood? Or a pig's? I have many satyr tears to collect. This could be fun, Dion." She took his hand in her own and squeezed it. "Don't worry, my love. You'll never lose me. I'm going to keep you close for a very long time."

Dion looked down at his small hand in hers. The jewels on their rings twinkled together, a brilliance that only shone when they were side by side. Together, they were a soul complete—an eternal union, now closer than ever. Now that Dion was destined to partake in Lorraine's cruel experiments for all time, he stared at the rings which had bound them throughout their marriage. For the first time in all their years together he thought perhaps these symbols of their enduring love carried a curse of some kind. Perhaps a curse that somehow drove the events leading to this very moment. He couldn't help but wonder if perhaps the Sorcerer Mackivel had not been so gracious in defeat after all.

The Phantom Queen

K. B. Elijah

In the petrichor scent of the forest, I smelled blood and piss. In the call of a crow from within its shadowy depths, I heard the desperate scream of a man who knows death is close. Instead of swaying branches, I saw the clash of swords, and felt a blade come down on my shoulder, cleaving flesh from bone…

I gasped, coming back to myself. It wasn't the cruel edge of an axe that pressed down on me, but a hand. A gentle touch that belonged to Macha, proprietor of *The One-Eyed Queen,* the last inn on the road before it reached the *foraoise domhain*—the deep forest—and veered westwards along its border before eventually trailing back down the coast to link the harbours to the mountain passes. Yet with the great rivers that carved through the heart of our land, it was easier to transport goods by water than road, making the travellers on this path few, and decidedly odder than ones encountered in the east.

It was why I'd been so grateful to find Macha and her inn, a small but neat two-storey building that didn't care for the politics and struggles that usually graced the fae and mortal kingdoms. Its vine-strewn outer walls and scrubbed wooden tables lent me a sense of peace I hadn't felt in a long time, as did Macha and her chicken stew that had warmed me to the core both last night and this morn.

Darragh would like it here. Maybe… maybe when he returns to me, I shall bring him to this very spot. Call it a holiday, and then convince him to stay with me, where no man can ever find him again…

I pushed the fantasy away and turned to Macha, forcing a

smile onto my face. "You didn't have to see me off."

"Nonsense, sweet *cailín,*" Macha fussed, tucking my hair behind my ears as she had done innumerable times since I found my way to her inn's door last night. Her baby started crying from somewhere in the house behind us, although I'd never laid eyes on the child. "Do you have the bread I put aside for you?"

"I do," I mumbled, feeling awkward about the lengths she had gone to help me. Thanks to her, I had as much food as I could fit in my bag, and a hardier cloak made of spun grey wool to replace the one I'd worn through on my way here. People generally weren't this *nice,* and now that a good night's sleep had cured my exhaustion from the previous day, it was putting me on edge.

Macha sighed. "And there is nothing I can say to dissuade you from this foolish quest?"

"No." *It's for Darragh. And Ma, and Pa, and Cormac and Niamh and-*

And me.

My fingers sought the comfort of my triskele necklace, tracing each of the three swirls, as was my habit. Macha's eyes followed the movements.

"Tell me, *cailín.* Why are *you* here?"

Something about the way she put emphasis on the word made me feel judged. I expected I wasn't as fearsome as the usual warriors and knights that passed this way, but did that make me any less worthy to *try?*

So I just shrugged, hoisting my bag more securely onto my shoulder. "Thank you for your hospitality. I really must get going."

"Yes, I suppose you must," Macha said in a low breath, giving me a final pat on the shoulder as the baby's cries increased in both volume and ferocity. I imagined that as innkeeper here, Macha must have seen more than one traveller enter the *foraoise domhain* to seek the Phantom Queen and not return. The way was treacherous for body, mind and soul, but everyone knew the legend.

Find the Morrigan. Answer her three questions honestly. And

you will have three of your own to which she must respond.

No one in the world of man could—or *would*—tell me where Darragh was.

So, I had to seek my answers in the world of the fae.

I had expected the sights, sounds and smells of battle to continue to haunt me, but the moment I breached the perimeter of the woods, I felt like I'd dropped into the water. Both colour and noise were muted. I had to blink to see through the fog-like glow of the trees and could barely hear even my own footsteps. Whatever magic enveloped this place was strong indeed.

The absence of senses was eerily distracting, and I was focusing so hard on hearing what wasn't there that I almost missed what *was*.

The crack of twigs. The crunch of foliage being dislodged by a huge body. And heavy huffing breaths mere feet behind me.

My own breath paused as I stilled, turning my head slowly so not to attract the attention of whatever was stalking me.

A massive bull, its pelt clearly once white but now a stained grey, whether from its life in the forest or the way my eyes could no longer see in vivid colour. Its ears were stained red, a flicker of dull pigment against the green frondescence.

The creature shook its head, huffing angrily with its dull teeth bared. Its black gaze fixed firmly on my own, its hooves gouging into the dead leaves on the ground as it pawed them in clear threat.

I put my hands out, palms first, and wondered if that meant anything to a bovine or I was just risking pissing it off further. Why was a bull of its size wandering around in the *foraoise domhain*? Why was it so angry with me?

My questions were best saved for *after* I'd escaped a nasty goring. For the horns were longer than any I'd seen on any bulls from Miss O'Brien's farm, curved ivory points that jutted at least a foot in front of its head. *Shit.* If it caught up to me without at least a tree between us, I'd get to see just how well the forest muted the colour of blood.

"Settle," I breathed. "I'm just passing throu-"

The bull dipped its head and charged, and then there was no more time for silly human words. If it had been the plains of Dirn, I'd have had no chance at all, but the dense trees and gnarly underbrush stopped the creature from gathering full momentum, and I had just enough time to dodge behind a thick oak before it was on me, one horn lodging in the bark even as the other scratched down my shoulder. I hadn't been quick enough, and I was paying for it. Red-hot pain flashed from my arm. I clapped my other hand down on the wound with one question answered—blood was the colour of brick here—and scrambled around the base of the tree as the bull thrashed angrily, twisting and pawing at the ground to pull itself free.

I had a small knife in my bag, but that was for skinning rabbits and cutting stray threads from my cloak, not felling beasts as huge as this. Even if I stuck the blade all the way into its flank, I'd be dead before I even got to see whether I'd done more than tickle it. Perhaps it would have more effect if I could get it in the bull's eye?

Yeah, the eye. The part of the animal that's directly guarded by those almost sword-length horns. That's a wonderful *idea.*

I sidled further around the tree as the bull followed, circling further as it tried to catch me, and we played the deadly game for the next few minutes while I fought to catch both my breath and a half-decent idea.

Could I climb the tree? Doubtful. The lowest branches were at least twice my height. Could I make a run for it?

I'd assumed the creature would have continued in its endless widdershins prowl for as long as it remained interested in me, but when I took another step around the tree and came face to face with the huffing thing, I realised that the only dumb animal here was me.

Shit.

I ducked as it tossed its great head in my direction. Letting out a rather unladylike yowl, I stumbled backwards, away from the safety of the oak's trunk. And then I was scrambling to my feet and running, darting in uneven zigzag lines to get as many of the smaller surrounding trees between me and it as possible.

Right, left, right, left, shit, there's a creek—right, right, right-

I felt a whisper of heat on my back. Whether it was the bull's hot breath, the graze of its horns on my skin or just the magic of the forest, I didn't have a clue, but I knew my time had run out. I threw myself to the left, closing my eyes and entrusting myself to the hands of the fates.

I slid down the muddy bank, graceless and cursing: first out loud, and then when I got a mouthful of sludge, limiting it to a mental tirade. The bull bellowed and then its warm flank smacked against my wounded shoulder and then my stomach, driving the remaining breath from my body. Heaving and spitting, we tumbled down towards the creek, the unexpected splash of cold water announcing a halt to our fall.

Swiping a hand from my face to clear the worst of the mud, I drew in a breath and scrambled backwards out of the shallow water, away from the thrashing creature. I was lucky that its body had only brushed me in the descent and hadn't landed on me; this close, I could appreciate how huge it really was. Its muscles quivered as it fought to right itself, its red ears tinged with mud and its eyes wild and hateful.

My shoulder throbbed. My wet clothes sent chills through me, and I was finding it hard to stay upright. If that bull regained its feet before I could get away…

The creature flailed again, and I saw its front right leg had twisted at an unnatural angle, bent in a way that limbs should not bend.

Thank the fates.

I heard the distant cry of a crow, the symbol of the being I sought. I could take this encounter with the bull as the warning it was clearly meant to be. Turn around, leave the forest, forget the Morrigan.

I was here for Darragh, but there was no guarantee that the Phantom Queen would tell me what I needed to know. Or that such knowledge could save him. And what if I wandered for months and never found her?

My dirty fingers found the comforting spirals of my necklace, the one constant in my life. The leather cord that held it had never once snapped. I'd never dropped or misplaced it, and even that terrible day when Ma and Pa had… well. The thief had taken all of our belongings, even the wooden goat Pa had carved for me, but had somehow missed my triskele necklace.

It had stayed with me when my parents were gone, through the hard years that followed, and during the tragic ends of Cormac and Niamh and the Wallaces. A steady, reassuring presence. A lump of metal couldn't judge you. Couldn't hate you. Couldn't *blame* you.

I will leave the forest.

I will continue.

I will leave the forest.

I will continue.

I spoke each decision out loud as my finger rounded another of the spiral loops until I reached the centre. I might have accused myself of orchestrating the outcome, but for the inexplicable fact that every time I sought the guidance of the triskele, it offered a different answer. I knew logically that it must have a static number of whorls, and yet that did not explain why sometimes it gave the even answer, and other times the odd.

Tucking the necklace back into my tunic, I clambered back up the slope and followed the caw of the unseen crows, leaving the frenzied white bull and its broken leg in the mud.

At first, I thought the sight of the wooden lodge was a symptom of my pain-induced delirium. It had been, by my reckoning, sixteen hours since I'd first entered the *foraoise domhain,* yet the light hadn't changed. It was the steady glow of dawn or dusk, a greenish glow where no shadows were ever cast.

No, that wasn't correct. There were plenty of shadows—creeping around the base of the great trees, skulking at my feet and twisting their way up through vines. But the shadows weren't being *cast,* not by anything I could determine. Some fell to the left, others to the right. Some were long, some short, and some had disappeared when I looked back at them a moment later. All this magic was giving me a headache, and the timelessness of the place confounded me.

So, when I saw the lodge, I knew it wasn't real. That it *couldn't* be real—who would live this deep within the Phantom Queen's domain? Yet my weary feet took me in that direction, seeking comfort even as my brain attempted to rationalise the mirage.

I closed the distance in what felt like only two steps, rapping my knuckles to the roughly hewn door only to find it cave open at my touch. The space beyond was larger than the outside of the lodge would have suggested, but it was the crackling fire that drew my attention.

Warmth. Safety.

Dropping to my knees by the edge of the hearth, I held out my freezing hands to the flames, seeking the heat but frustrated when it was barely tepid against my muted senses.

"What in the fates' name are you doing, girl?"

The sharp voice made me flinch, and I looked over my shoulder to find an old white woman nestled in a chair, beady eyes peering at me suspiciously. Her legs were propped up on a little footstool, a knitted blanket tucked in neatly around her lower half.

"I… I'm sorry, I didn't realise you were here," I said, glancing at my muddy footprints on the floor.

She sniffed, curling her mouth downwards as she took me in, head to toe. "And what's that got to do with anything? Do you make a habit of barging into people's houses?"

"Are you *real*?" I asked, because it hardly made sense that this grumpy little lady would live out her retirement in the middle of a cursed forest filled with murderous white bulls.

"Out!" she shrieked, tossing off the blanket and trying to get to her feet, but her spindly wrists on the arms of the chair couldn't support her weight. She mewled like a newborn kitten as she went down on one of her frail legs, and I rushed forward to help her. "Off, off, off! Get your filthy hands *off* me!"

"Sorry," I said again, supporting her weight so she could shuffle back into the chair. The cushion was shaped to her bony bottom, as if she'd been in this seat for a long time. "I was just tired and hoping for the warmth of a fire."

"Ain't no warmth here," she said. "Badb will take a look at that shoulder now."

I blinked. "I… er… *what?*"

"Your shoulder," she hissed, tugging me close.

Had this old woman once been like me? Had she wandered into the forest in search of the Phantom Queen, and become tangled in the forest's impossible infinity, trapped until the years stole the strength from her body and replaced it with wrinkles and rheumy eyes?

She tsked. "Badb will see that sorted, she will. It'll just take the press of a feather and the click of a beak."

She's crazy.

"Badb? Is that your name?" I said, desperate to restore some semblance of sense to the situation.

"Of course, Badb is Badb," she hissed, shoving her pale finger into the crevice the bull had left in my skin. I yelped at the pain and tried to pull away from the psychotic old lady, but she held me in place with a surprisingly firm grip. "What kind of question is that?"

Questions. I have to be much more careful when I find the Morrigan. What if I waste my three questions on something trivial?

"I don't… think you're… helping…" I gasped. "Can you please stop poking me?"

She did, only to jerk me forward and replace her bloodied finger with the slick lap of her tongue. It felt odd, like a round tongue instead of flat, and put me in mind of a wriggling worm trying to burrow into my body through my wound.

"What the fuck?" I howled. I finally pulled myself away.

She just freaking licked me!

"Badb has done all she can for you," she said, and waved a dismissive hand at me. "You may now leave."

"With pleasure," I shot back, wincing as I peeled myself off her floor, the mud that had dried from the fire cracking off my skin. I hightailed it to the door to the sound of her low chuckle, not bothering to close it behind me.

I should have known that only crazy people live in the foraoise domhain. No more visiting people's houses, no matter how enticing they look, okay?

I was so busy fuming about the strange encounter that it took me over an hour to realise my shoulder had stopped hurting. I peeled the fabric away from the wound to find that despite the mass of blood and dirt on my skin, there was no wound. I was once again whole.

I'd met a witch. A real one. A real, talking-in-the-third-person psycho of a witch.

It had been two days. Two days of putting one foot in front of the other, feeling like I hadn't gone anywhere in the unchanging light and the ceaseless foliage. Two days of nibbling beef jerky after Macha's bread had run out. I knew the forest wasn't large enough for me to have walked in a single direction this whole time and not have reached the other edge, yet here I was, still in the depths of the monotonous green glow of the *foraoise domhain*. It was an eternity, and it was both terrifying and *exhausting*.

I knew from maps that the forest wasn't large. A mere cluster of trees, by all accounts, just big enough to house a legend. Certainly not of a size to explain how I hadn't yet reached the other side several times over, considering it only took a couple of hours to travel around, according to the merchants I'd met on the road.

Caw!

I glanced up, startled, to find a huge crow seated on the branch above me. It shook its glossy feathers and opened its beak again, delivering a scathing sound that was more a shriek than a squawk.

Crows are a good sign, right?

"Are you of the Morrigan?" I asked or tried to. My tongue stuck to the roof of my mouth, and my words were the croak of a dehydrated frog. "Please, take me to her!"

The bird tilted its head to one side.

"Please," I begged again, my hand seeking my triskele necklace for comfort. "I must know if my Darragh lives."

Spreading its wings, the crow tensed on the branch for a moment before erupting forwards, trailing a path through the trees.

Yes!

I sprinted to keep up, forcing my weary body into the movement. I didn't dare take my gaze from the avian that led the way, but out of the corner of my eye, I could see other movement, the beating of black wings and the flash of jewelled eyes.

Caw! Caw!

The calls grew into a cacophony, louder than anything I had heard here so far. So loud that it felt like *real* sound again, the shrieks puncturing through the muted haze of the *foraoise domhain*. These crows were something that existed apart from the forest, and that of itself was enough to keep me moving long after I should have otherwise collapsed.

My sore feet pounded tirelessly in front of the other until-

The crow landed on a sweeping horizontal branch near a wide pool of water draped in shadow, the bow dipping under its weight.

"Is this… is this where the Phantom Queen lives?" I asked the bird. I looked around but couldn't see any huts or tombs or whatever else a goddess of death may reside in.

The crow blinked at me and promptly began to preen.

"I don't understand. Is that… a code?"

It continued to work through its plumage.

"Does the tidying of your tail feathers mean *yes*?"

The bird shifted position.

"Oh," I said. "Feet cleaning is *no?*"

"Love," a voice called. "It's just a bird. If you try to see portents and meaning in everything, you'll go mad. Trust me."

I started at the unexpected noise, whipping my head around. It took me three wild glances to notice the girl almost lost in the dark water: black hair cascaded over skin the colour of mahogany, her eyes that of a midnight sky without stars. It was only when she grinned at me, and the perfect white of her teeth gleamed in the darkness, that I realised she was closer than I had first thought.

She beckoned me closer with the curve of a finger, and I obeyed.

"Are you… are you the-"

"Shush," the girl murmured, and a gentle warmth spread around my chest. I was already shoulder deep in the water with no memory of how I'd moved or when I'd entered the pool.

We were submerged in the dark pool, heads and shoulders barely above the surface, when the girl reached up a hand to touch my cheek. Her fingers were warm and dry, despite having lifted from the water only the moment before, and she grazed her knuckles down my jaw with a sudden intake of breath.

"Oh," she said, and her ebony eyes filled with tears. Her gaze seemed to look past mine as if she was watching something *within*.

I let out a low noise, suddenly uncomfortable at the depths of emotion from this stranger.

"Nemain," she said. Her voice was a mellifluous whisper, a promise on a breeze, and I'd never heard anything so beautiful. It was as if every sound in my life to date was discordant in contrast, a crude noise that insulted her with its every thrash and rasp.

I wanted to give her my name in turn, but knew my voice would ruin her perfection, so I just smiled.

Nemain trailed her fingers through my hair, somehow avoiding all the knots and tangles the blonde locks had collected in my excursion through the trees. Her touch came to rest on my shoulder, at the exact place the bull had gored me. But she couldn't have known, for Badb's licking of me—her *magic*, I told myself crossly, whatever odd form it may have manifested in—had healed the wound. Perhaps her fingers felt the uneven stitches I'd made in my clothing to seal the tears.

"What makes your soul so sad?" Nemain asked, blinking those beautiful eyes at me.

I thought of Niamh, her small body lying broken at the base of that wall. I thought of Ma's unseeing stare, the blood that had seeped out of the mouth already infested with flies. I thought of John, his skin splotchy and red, as he choked at my feet.

And then I looked at the girl before me, her perfect, unblemished skin and her beautiful smile, and I despaired.

"Are you the Morrigan?" She winced at my question, turning away from me.

I'd been right: the awful screech of my human voice had hurt her with its discordance. I wasn't fit to stand in her presence, let alone ask of her what I-

And suddenly Nemain was gone, pulled under the water with such grace that for a moment, I wondered if she'd swum away of her own accord. And then I played back the moment, how her eyes had widened fractionally, how her fingers had twitched as she attempted to hold on to me, and I reached out instinctively, seeking to pull her back to the surface. But my hands flapped through the water without result, clawing at the darkness.

The pool was only shoulder height. How could I have missed her? I glanced around with frantic desperation, as if there would be someone on the bank who could help. But the only footprints that marred the soft earth were mine. The *foraoise domhain* remained silent and still but for the crows, which were gathered in the bows of the willows, silently passing judgment.

Fuck.

I dived beneath the black surface of the water, clumsily swishing my hands in front of me in the futile hope that I'd have the luck of the fates to guide my direction.

Memories flashed through my mind, of the bubbles surfacing above Cormac, of our laughs at the prank when he didn't immediately surface, our worry when it continued past the point of humour. The awkward splash as the miller jumped in after him, his face white as he surfaced with Cormac's body in his arms. They said his hair had caught in the mill wheel, words which made no sense. My brother fixed things all the time—he'd unclogged the wheel six times this season alone. How could… how could a lock of his fucking hair take him from us?

Not like this. Don't let the water take her too.

"Nemain!" I shouted as the seconds turned to minutes, too foolish to realise that it would do anything but draw water into my lungs. But to my surprise, the name echoed around me as if I'd yelled it into a barrel, haunting and desperate.

Shock drove my eyes open, the darkness of the pond replaced with a blue-tinged clarity. The surface of the water may have been impenetrable, but underneath it was crystal clear.

Movement to my left caught my eye; only a handful of yards

away, Nemain thrashed in the grip of an enormous monster. An eel, it looked like, thrice the size of any I'd ever even heard of, let alone had the bad fortune to see, and its smooth body already coiled around Nemain's neck.

I swam closer, fighting off the uncanny dizziness that being able to breathe underwater did to one's head. The girl's movements slowed and then ceased entirely.

No.

I grabbed hold of the eel before I could consider the danger, wrenching it out of its deadly embrace. The eel lashed out, and I screamed as it reared for my face, falling backwards as if I was at the precipice of a mountain instead of at the bottom of a lake. I squeezed what was in my grasp as tightly as I could, wincing as slimy flesh pulped between my fingers.

Impossible tears fell from my eyes, only to be caught by the water and swirl around my face, cloudy orbs against the clearness of the pool.

I floated there for what felt like an age, the lifeless body of the eel drifting away from my hands, before a familiar touch landed on my shoulder.

Macha.

But the hand was dark, not pale, and Macha wasn't here.

Nemain peered at me, her other hand massaging her ravaged throat. The bluish light emphasised the marks left behind with ugly black splotches on her perfect skin.

We surfaced together, breaching the patina of the water to greet the stillness of the forest. The crows had disappeared, and the air seemed stuffy after the weightless clarity of underwater.

"Are you alright?" I asked.

Nemain shook her head and pressed a gentle kiss to my forehead. "The question is, are *you,* the one who would face darkness to save a stranger?" Her voice was scratchy, and I almost wept at the loss of the former beauty.

I flushed. "Anyone would have done it to save you."

Just look at you. I almost spoke the words, but common sense held me back from such foolishness. Mere seconds in her presence, and I was smitten. What was wrong with me?

But it felt so right. Her gentle hands, her boundless smile. I could lose myself in her eyes, the eternal promise of a night's sky, and-

Darragh.

I pulled my hands from hers. When had they joined?

"I have to find the Morrigan. I have to know if Darragh, my... betrothed, still lives."

Nemain's lashes fluttered, and her lips pulled downwards into a disappointed curve.

"Then go," she hissed, and when I blinked, she'd disappeared. I looked down at the undisturbed pool, and knew that this time, she hadn't been taken from me. I'd driven her away.

Listen to yourself. Falling head over heels for a strange girl doing fates only knows what this deep in the foraoise domhain? It's the magic of the forest playing more tricks on your mind, that's all.

So instead of staring into the black pool hoping to see a flash of white teeth or dark silky hair, I traipsed out of the water, feeling my mood darken with every step.

Bloody fae.

I didn't care what direction I'd come from, or in which I was now going. I'd long since realised it didn't matter in this accursed place. The Morrigan would find me when she deigned to do so, and in the meantime, the forest would hold me tight in its timeless embrace.

The crows had come and gone several times, appearing in a breath of fluttering wings around me, their beaks cracked open as if tasting the scent of my passing. Whatever it told them, it clearly wasn't enough for their mistress, as they would disappear just as quickly, leaving me alone once more. As the days passed, I'd tried pleading with the murder. Then cajoling, even threatening, but nothing I said or did persuaded them to give me even the slightest indication that I was close to the Morrigan and the end of my quest.

I often thought of Nemain, and whether I should have stayed with her. If I was to be stuck in the forest, at least it would have been with company.

The gentle crunch of a leaf behind me almost made me falter, but I forced myself to keep walking, my eyes still locked forward as if I hadn't heard it.

And when the creature pounced a moment later, I was ready. I ducked, spinning on my left heel and firmly driving the branch I held into its stomach. The wolf grunted as I drove its breath from its body, crumpling to the ground at my feet.

I swung the branch before me. "You think you could catch me unawares again?" I asked the forest, my voice hoarse from underuse. "When there was clearly one more beast to face?"

The Morrigan was of the sacred number. Three answers, three questions. The appearance of the bull had been too random, and after the encounter with the eel, it had become clear. I wouldn't reach the centre of the forest and find the Morrigan until I'd faced her quota of tests.

I'd been waiting for this third beast for days, frustrated when it didn't immediately appear. My nerves were shot after keeping my senses alert step after never-ending step. My food had run out long ago. But if water couldn't drown me, it was clear that the *foraoise domhain* had me in its safekeeping, so I ignored my grumbling stomach and was rewarded when it eventually ceased, fading into a dull ache like the muting of my other senses.

The wolf whimpered in the dirt at my feet, and I hefted the branch higher, ready to bring it down on the creature again if that's what it would take to—

"Cailín."

That voice. That voice, *here,* when…

Oh, you stupid, stupid girl. You thought you were so very clever with the three beasts, but you completely missed the most obvious thing of all.

I dropped the branch and turned, falling to my knees in front of Macha. "Mother Morrigan," I wailed, clutching at her skirts. "Why did you not tell me you were she?"

The innkeeper's face was impassive. "You didn't answer my questions," she said.

"Nor mine," Badb said, as Macha's features turned into those of the old woman, her height shrinking and her skin withering.

"Nor mine," Nemain said, as the deity's skin darkened into ebony, and she stood straight once more.

I hadn't, I realised. Despite my encounters with each of these women, I had not truthfully answered three questions by any of them. I had been too busy seeking my own answers.

"If you were any other soul, you would have been left to walk beneath these trees forever," Nemain chastised, and then morphed back into the kindly face of Macha. "Thrice you squandered what we gave you." She yanked her dress from my grip, then winced and pressed a hand to her ribs as if they pained her.

"I'm sorry," I begged, "I didn't-"

No. She's heard this all before. You know she has. You're just embarrassing yourself.

I took a breath and got to my feet. "You stand here before me once more, so I can only assume you've granted me one final chance to prove my honesty. Ask me what you will."

Macha dipped her head in acknowledgement, and I noticed her neck was swollen and bruised, as Nemain's had been. I wondered if the injuries transferred between the three manifestations of the Phantom Queen, and if that meant Nemain and Macha bore Badb's bad leg.

I had my answer when she stepped closer to me, favouring her left leg, and lifted my chin with one delicate finger.

"What is the worst thing to have ever happened to you, sweet *cailín?*"

My instinct was to shy away from the question. Bite back, change the subject, anything but relive…

For Darragh.

"I would say I have too many," I said, pain dripping from the bitter words. "Death haunts those I care about. My brother, Cormac, drowned in the millpond. Niamh, my sister, fell from a roof. My Ma and Pa were shot by a highwayman with a skittish trigger finger, and my best friends were slain by wild fae. Even…" I gave a cold chuckle, although there was nothing remotely funny about the situation. "Even the boy who gave me my first kiss didn't make it to his fourteenth winter. John was poisoned by the same food we'd eaten together—tell me how that is *fair?"*

I closed my eyes, aware I hadn't yet directly answered the question, and worried I'd already rambled too much. "So, my answer, Mother Morrigan, is to have to stand before you at all. To be so fucking *sure* that my betrothed will die that I had to seek out a legend in the slimmest of hopes that I can prevent it. That so much death has followed me for this to even be a necessity. *That* is the worst thing that has ever happened to me."

I heaved in air, tears trailing down my cheeks. Macha made no move to comfort me, merely cocking her head to the side and becoming Badb in the space between one breath and the next.

"What is the worst thing you have ever done, girl?" The elderly woman peered at me, scrunching her eyes into tight knots of scrutiny even as her fingers tightened around my jaw.

This was an easy question to find the answer to, if hard to actually answer.

"Seeing the pattern and still letting them in," I snarled with my eyes closed, unable to look at Badb and her rancorous sneer. "Of ignoring the voice that told me they would die too, and not caring because I was so *lonely*. Pretending it was a coincidence just to ease my conscience in allowing them to get close, even though it killed them. I let Darragh court and propose to me, knowing what it would cost."

When I opened my eyes, Badb had become Nemain. Her fingers unclenched until she was caressing my chin instead of holding it.

But my body was tense, attempting to brace itself against the third of the deity's questions. How many more of my soul would I have to expose?

The question, when it came, was entirely unexpected.

"Where did you get your necklace, love?" Nemain asked, her voice still affected by the eel's attempted strangulation.

I started. "I… this?" My fingers reached for the triskele around my throat. Worried that my question would ruin my ability to answer, I added, "I was given it as a child."

Nemain was still, seemingly expecting more, so I continued.

"I met a fae in the market. Her eyes were like emeralds. She held out the necklace and told me it would keep me safe." I let out a low laugh. "Even at that age I knew it was bullshit, but I was five years old, dirt poor, and it was very pretty."

I smiled at the memory, tracing a finger around the swirls. "We've seen a lot together, this and me. But if I'd been smart, I'd have given it to Ma and never let her take it off. Maybe then she'd be alive."

"And you'd be dead."

Nemain's abrupt statement made me frown, as did the look of hatred she shot at my chest. I pulled back, affronted.

"That thing," she said, jabbing a finger at the triskele but not quite touching the metal, "is a curse. It keeps you safe, certainly, but at the cost of the lives of those around you."

"That's… that's not," I spluttered, unable to form the right words to object to such a ridiculous statement. "It's not-"

"It's *dark magic,*" Nemain hissed, "and the only reason you survived such tragedies growing up. I'm sorry, but those deaths were meant for you, sweet *cailín,* and when the fates could not take you when your time was owed, it forced their hands elsewhere. Time and time again, they tried to take you for their own, only to be thwarted."

No. No, no, no, that was just-

"I'm… I'm the reason that they're all…" I couldn't finish a sentence, a *thought,* couldn't possibly comprehend the *terror* that swamped me.

"You have three questions," Badb snapped, "and don't dawdle!"

I stared at her, having missed the transition. How could she expect me to think of…?

Darragh. That's why you're here.

"Is Darragh still alive?" I asked, my voice torn as if I'd wept for hours. Perhaps I had.

Badb frowned, tilting her face up to the green canopy above us. She opened her mouth, and a fully formed crow burst forth, its wings trailing an inky shadow in their wake as the bird shot upwards.

The forest was still bathed in that same timeless light, but my body knew it was no longer the same day it had been when it entered the *foraoise domhain,* and it was *tired.*

"Yes," the Morrigan said simply, and the relief I felt at those words was a physical thing, alighting from my shoulders to join the ranks of crows circling above us. And Badb seemed to feel it too, for she shook out her bad right leg as if it no longer ailed her.

"How much time does he have left, before… before I kill him?" My second question.

Badb became Macha, whose fingers swelled until each of the ten digits was a crow, dancing and writhing on her hand in a blurred mass of feathers.

"The necklace only takes those who you grow close to. While he's still deployed in the war, he is safe, at least from your curse. But should he return to you, as is foretold in less than the cycle of two moons, he won't survive the week."

I took that grim news silently, even as the marks around Macha's neck mysteriously disappeared. I'd known that coming here wouldn't give me pleasant answers; one didn't seek the Phantom Queen for good news. But to hear that Darragh would likely survive the war only to die because of me made me want to empty the contents of my stomach.

"My third question," I gasped after I'd done just that. "How do I save him?"

Macha was silent for a long while, and I worried that I'd accidentally already used up all three questions without realising. But she shifted into her Nemain form and gave me a heavy sigh, even as crows burst from tendrils of her black hair, swooping and fluttering around the both of us.

"You cannot take the necklace off without death finding you to recoup the debt you owe," she said, in the angelic voice she'd had before the eel had attacked. "But your betrothed will also live if you keep distance between the two of you. Don't give death another life to steal instead."

"I… I have to give him up?"

The Morrigan inclined her head in a graceful nod, and finally peeled her other hand from her side, straightening to her full height.

The injured leg, the strangulation marks, the broken ribs. All the injuries I'd done to the three beasts of the *foraoise domhain*, now healed with my three questions.

"You cannot see your Darragh again," she confirmed. "Not if you want him to live."

Of course I want him to live!

"But what... what do I do?" I asked, my voice small and lost. "Where do I go?"

Nemain leaned forward and kissed me, her lips soft and full on mine.

"Death cannot touch the Phantom Queen," she breathed. "Stay with *me*."

Lady Marian's Gambit

CLARE RHODEN

Chapter 1

Once upon a time, in an enchanted forest near Hazelmister, a lady of the Fae High Court bore twins. She named them Bramble and Briar for the way they clung together.

Like all other Fae babies, they were tiny and perfect, and the stubs of their immature wings made birthing them a gruelling, painful, and chancy affair. Yet from their earliest months, their mother doted on them. Whenever Nanny—a stout Old One of enslaved dwarf stock, with several centuries of experience and a reputation for discipline—brought her charges to the sheltered garden favoured by the High Court ladies, everyone commended their beauty. Most High Fae women avoided the risky task of pregnancy, relying on potions, charms, and curses—not to mention occasional violence to relevant portions of their male partners' bodies—to fend off the perils of procreation. Infants were rare and much prized, but who wanted the bother of bearing and rearing them, or the ennui of waiting for them to grow up and become interesting? Everyone agreed it was far better for *other* women to tackle such risks.

Generating two healthy babies in a single pregnancy was a triumph. But all achievement comes at a cost, as the twins learned one fateful day.

Chapter 2

In a courtyard where delicate vines screen the sunlight, pillars of blue-veined marble support swags of pale pink, heavily scented roses. Fancifully carved wooden benches rest on a sward of flowering chamomile, with trails of violets leading hither and thither. Dozens of willowy, great-eyed women idle in the summer warmth, chatting lightly in the absence of any new gossip.

One delightful damsel—after holding her tongue, really, for as long as she could—remarks on the agreeable picture the twins make, crawling about their mother's feet, their diligent little fingers pulling petals to shreds.

"Look how pretty they are, the darlings! Such sweet teeny faces!" She catches the matron's glance and smiles. "You mustn't count the cost, my dear. Don't give it a thought! What's the loss of one's looks, or one's figure, or one's desirability? If no courageous woman steps up to sacrifice her beauty and allure, where would we be?"

Hear the moment of shocked silence from the ladies. Their eyes goggle as they look at each other, and then at the stunned mother, with dark circles under her eyes and an air of refined exhaustion, her mouth opened in a dainty 'oh.'

Breaking the tension, another beauty titters, "Oh, I agree, Sylvia! Velia looks so content with her little winged ones by her. I'm with you. I won't hear a word said against her. I'm sure we all think the same. We are ever so grateful to you, Velia! Foregoing your own loveliness to spare the rest of us from, from all that."

The others gush insincere agreement, showering the hapless Velia with assurances that her descent into unsightliness is utterly worthwhile. Velia, with ashen face and eyes full of furious tears, toes both babies in Nanny's direction and flees the garden.

Hurrying up the circular staircase that leads to her bower, Velia runs to the ornate mirror that graces one wall. Of an unusual lightning bolt shape, the antique looking-glass—a family heirloom—has always dominated the chamber. Velia often spends hours before it, admiring herself in the sumptuous costumes she loves, the ones that emphasise her opulent figure. In a society over-full of slender androgynes, her shapeliness is a point of pride. The perfect globes of her breasts, her tiny waist, and the sweet flare of her hips are envied at the court.

Velia observes that her favourite gown of amber silk gapes

over her flat chest, that it drains all colour from her cheeks and bunches around her thickened middle. She throws back her head, screaming as loudly as she ever did in the birthing chamber.

A knock sounds on the door. Velia rips the mirror from the wall and lobs it with deadly accuracy, uncaring of who dares interrupt her frenzy of despair.

The biggest shard of glass slashes Nanny's boulderish head from her wide throat. Her blood spurts in dense gouts over the infants cradled in her arms. She drops lifeless in the doorway.

Poor little Bramble lands unhappily among the debris, one budding wing sliced off in an instant. Briar, falling to the other side of the headless dwarf, severs the other. Velia, still shrieking like a banshee, stomps over to them with a look of horror on her face. Not for the nanny's death or the maiming of the children, but aghast at the life of ugliness ahead. Before anyone else probes the commotion, she seizes a chunk of glass and plunges it into her own neck.

The twins, each now the irate possessor of a useless wing, sit bloodied and screeching among the ruins until the ladies arrive. Fragments of the cursed mirror cover them like a thick scattering of rock salt. A sole fine sliver works its way into Briar's heart; another splinter destroys one of Bramble's eyes.

As their mother bleeds untidily to death beside them, they each select some larger portions of mirror to hold close, like beloved playthings. Curiously, both immediately stop crying.

Chapter 3

Fae babies are resilient, as they must be. So few are born that each inherits a ruthless desire to survive. The twins inherited double the ruthlessness. That is how it is with the twins. The minor matter of their mother's demise does nothing to hinder them. The Fae can easily replace a dwarf nanny from the herds of downtrodden Old Ones. When the new nurse grows too unforgiving of their vicious games, Briar and Bramble know what to do. A simple matter of deploying their beloved mirror shards, kept in their toy box, and awaiting events.

Sometimes, the next minder is more to their taste, and they're allowed to remain for months. Others disappear within days.

Chapter 4

Inevitably, time passes, and the twins become adults, needing nobody else but each other. They are curiosities, High Fae without a full set of wings—although, as the wittier remark, they have one set between them! They have no ties to any adult at court, Velia never divulging the father of her offspring.

With their luxuriant dark hair and brilliant silver eyes, the pair resemble their beautiful mother in her heyday more than any other member of the court. Speculation arises perhaps she created them with a spell—a curse, more like whispers the court—and never bothered to involve a male faery at all. Both twins affect a defiant impetuosity, accentuated by their addiction to everything dark and forbidden. They saved every tiny fragment of mirror, and as each day passes, more and more of the shining slivers decorate their bodies. Briar pierces her perfectly pointed ears with dozens of needle-like fragments and wears several spear-shaped pieces through her one remaining wing like perilous brooches. Bramble, outrageously, uses jagged slivers to pin together the lids of his useless eye. The twins defy the beauty standards of the High Court and delight in terrifying the few younger Fae who follow them into the world. The ladies pity their unhappiness until their antics become too irksome to bear.

Habitually, Bramble and Briar make pests of themselves with lethal practical jokes. They are so constantly out of favour that nobody is much surprised when Queen Titania banishes them in the wake of an especially gory game that decimates the slave caste.

Henceforth, they remove to a neglected tract of land called Thornhallow, soon capturing enough free Old Ones to act as servants. They devote their energies to tormenting mortals, whose sole purpose in life can only be to amuse immortals.

Eventually the twins adopt their Shards of Oakendoire plan, when Briar and Bramble pit a royal against an outlaw, with unexpected results.

Chapter 5

"And you're certain that this is going to work?" asks the prince. Again.

Briar compresses her lips. Mortals are so stupid. Honestly, they can't hold a single thought for more than two minutes at a time. Fortunately, they only live a few short decades. They'd never manage with the centuries of memories the Fae carry.

Bramble looks up with a feral grin, his sole silver eye flashing in delight. He stands beside the prince, watching the goblin blacksmith labour over the new weapon. The goblin smith, bowed like an ancient tree, her scant grey hair erupting from her scaly pink scalp in clumps, stands over the sparking forge fire—hence the thick lumpy scars that cover her. She lifts the hammer repeatedly, scrawny arms corded with ropey muscles as she bashes the red-hot iron against the anvil. She could snap the royal in two with a single flick of her long, bony fingers.

The prince. Briar considers him. He is of middling height for a mortal, which is disgustingly short by Fae standards. Bramble is clad in his customary black, a cloak of plaited deer-and-bear-hide flung back from his shoulders. The forge fire glints off the wicked glass shards that seal his blind eye shut. Briar admits that Bramble is terrifyingly beautiful, by the standards of any race. Clever too, curse him. In this latest bout of their long rivalry, she had the first choice of player: a royal prince or a scruffy, no-account outlaw living like a bear in the woods? She chose the high-caste mortal.

The scion of a royal house, Prince John, is full of guile, loaded with evil intentions, a right beast around women. All of that argued a certain rat cunning, perfect for the ongoing tussle between herself and Bramble. Sadly, John is also rather stupid, his avaricious nature regularly clouding his judgement.

Briar doubts that he has a single rational thought in his head. John's the kind of man who jumps at anything shiny, too acquisitive to consider that there might be other costs. He denies himself no pleasure and rarely thinks of the consequences. Fool. Divert those tax monies from his brother Richard's war chest? Easy, until the king demanded repayment and took three castles from him as forfeit. Jump on that plump damsel and pin her to the ground with one hand over her mouth and the other up her skirts? Delicious, until her husband demanded that he pay for the upkeep of the resulting royal bastard.

Briar narrows her eyes to study her chosen pawn. Prince John is not exactly ugly for a human, being merely average. Briar deems him absolutely hideous. But he is her choice, and she's damned if she was going to let Bramble win again. John might be pathetic, but she is his patron, and she is mighty. She steps towards the fire.

"This will certainly work," she tells him, her voice rich as her favourite fermented mead. "The magic shard within the sword will seek your enemy. See that glow?" As the smith finesses along one narrow edge, the whole clearing flushes red, radiance springing from the sword's tip. For a moment, it resembles a burning brand more than a weapon.

Bramble whoops. Briar's blood sings in answer to the glare of the blade. Her heart beats in time with the smith's last strokes. "What do you say, my lord? Speak your desire to the shard of power." She smiles, taking care not to show her teeth, filed to sharp points. Mortals spooked at the sight.

John stares, mouth open. Briar claps her hands, recalling him.

"I, yes, I," he stammers, then pulls himself together. "I, John, prince and heir of this realm, regent in my brother's stead and ruler of all its peoples, desire the heart's blood of Robin Greenhood, so-called master of the forest, by the power invested in this sword."

Eye-stabbing light bursts through the clearing. They throw their arms up at the stupendous glare as the sword erupts vividly and then subsides. By the time Briar looks again, the weapon is on the anvil, slowly dulling as it cools. The goblin throws water on it, and it steams furiously. By the third dousing, only a dull ticking sounds from the blade. The smith picks it up, beginning to polish it.

"Your wish is heard," Briar says. "The blade is complete. Come within reach of your enemy, and the shard of power will blaze."

"Ha! And I'll finally defeat Robin Greenhood! He won't tell any more tales to my brother!" Prince John beams at her. "How can I ever repay you, my lady?"

Briar inclines her head regally, while Bramble scoffs.

"Carry the blade into the mortal realm, and your debt is more than repaid."

The twins signal a gaggle of their Old Ones—the lesser Fae, hobgoblins, sylphs, and dryads—to escort the royal fool back to mortal lands. Briar's mood shifts, as always, when she gives over a fragment of the mirror. She wonders if there is any point to the centuries-long rivalry that she and Bramble adore. The cyclic nature of their life in exile angers her. The stakes are flimsy—some or many human lives—and the satisfaction of all those bloody deaths brief. There's always another bout, another wager, another contest.

Frowning malevolently, she accompanies Bramble deeper into the forest to the meeting place with Robin Greenhood. Bramble mocks the prince's pernickety ways and Briar growls at him, baring her teeth. Not since they were very small, have they exchanged kind word.

Not since their mother marooned them in a sea of cursed shards.

Chapter 6

Robin Greenhood is not at the appointed place.

Briar sniggers. Bramble puts hands on hips and glares at the bloated gnome in charge of this clearing, where Thornhallow meets Oakendoire. The portly Old One scurries away in terror. Two standing stones half-buried by time mark the narrow path between the realms, radiant with sunlight from the mortal world.

"At least my sorry pawn showed up!"

"He'll be here," answers Bramble. "Time runs differently across the veil."

Briar guffaws. "Indeed, it does! Let us walk about a little. The shade of these oaks is rather pleasant, don't you agree?"

Her twin sneers. They wander along the path that leads from the clearing to another neglected standing stone. They pause there a moment, Briar wondering aloud what the strange sigils carved into the north face of the stone might mean. This was an idle and transient query which teased them intermittently during the years since they'd made themselves at home in Thornhallow, a narrow swathe of land butting up against Oakendoire. Similar ancient sentinels guard each of the twelve border crossings, all carved with a script that not even the Old Ones could read. Inconceivable that a civilisation existed before their time. Bramble shrugs indifferently. They retrace their steps.

This time the outlaw awaits them, fidgeting. Robin is striking more for his litheness than his face. Like his enemy Prince John, he is only average human height. But in contrast to the royal, Robin's proportions are splendid, and his eyes have a bright, intelligent glint that most humans lack. Briar peers at him sidewise, peeved that he kept the appointment. She'd heard about Robin Greenhood, and she was astounded that he'd fallen into Bramble's hands. The fellow looked capable of bettering his royal rival without magical aid.

How much more amusing if Robin failed to turn up at all. "I wish," she says to Bramble, "that we never had to use humans at all."

"Wishing is all very well," Bramble replies. "I wish we'd never come to this place."

Briar scoffed. "Ha! It was you who got us banished at the end!"

"Pfft! Those idiotic Old Ones were no use, anyway. They would have died sooner or later. Titania overreacted."

"Whatever." Arguing with Bramble was second nature to Briar, but their arguments led nowhere. Anything that could be said had been said, and more than once, over the years. Briar wished their life hadn't become so dull. If not for meddling with mortals, they'd have nothing to do.

"My lord, my lady," Robin hails them. "Well met in Oakendoire."

"We are not precisely *in* Oakendoire," says Bramble, dripping disapproval. "And you, fine sir, are late for our appointment."

"I am," agrees Robin, ducking his head irreverently. "My apologies."

"Hmm."

Briar puts a hand over her lips to quell the hilarity that bubbles up at this ridiculous human's impertinence. She wants to applaud his glibness but jumps when Robin looks at her.

Scowling, she steps back to let Bramble deal with the fellow.

Her twin is more than happy to do so. "One would think that you did not want our help. We offer our aid to so few humans. One would expect it to be prized."

The outlaw smiles. "One would." He pares his voice to the exact, crisp tones of the High Fae. Then he drops into his ordinary accent. "But—tell me if I have this wrong—it was you who offered me your help. I am no beggar at your table."

Bramble bridles, drawing himself up to his full height. His dark aspect is menacing and his shard-threaded eyelashes glitter. "I had not thought you so unworthy," he declares. "You may leave."

"Fair doings," says the outlaw. "Marian warned me you were tricksy."

Briar scoffs. "What would she know? A foolhardy mortal scrabbling about with the Old Ones and their pathetic little magics. Imps are tricksy, my fine sir. *We* are deadly."

"I do not care for your tone," replies Robin, inclining his head as though speaking to royalty. "Or your company, come to that," he adds with an irreverent grin. On the words, he flings them a half-salute and turns back to the standing stones.

"Wait!" yells Bramble, with all the clout of his centuries of bullying and a decent dollop of magic.

The single word reverberates off the stone sentinels and the trees, making the hair stand up on Briar's arms. As for the human, he springs to face them, sword drawn. She's glad to see his face turned ashen, though his hand is steady. A worthy pawn, this Robin. Again, she curses Bramble for saving the stronger human for himself. But only if the wretched man is made to accept the shard-tipped arrow that Bramble has bespoken.

Robin takes a breath and puts up his sword. "It's only polite to listen to your proposal," he says. "I won't promise to do your bidding but say what you want." He crosses his arms, feet spread wide on the uneven ground, a picture of confidence. Despite herself, Briar finds much to approve in the jut of his chin and the light in his eyes. He would taste delicious.

Bramble sees it differently. "Your impudence does not reassure me," he thunders. "I need someone who can put aside useless emotions, someone with the will and the strength to carry out a dangerous, difficult mission. Probably beyond your powers, outlaw."

Robin, bless his pitiful human heart, tries to shrug this off, but they see his instinctive response. Robin Greenhood rates himself highly, and won't swallow being called too cowardly, emotional, or incompetent to dare anything. "I'm listening."

Bramble chuckles. "I should think so. You're not a fool, by what I hear. I'm offering you a chance to rid the country of a milksop regent, a second-rate prince who doesn't deserve his place."

"Go on."

Briar is amazed at the human's discourteous tone. Directed at anyone but her twin, it would seriously anger her.

Bramble glares down into Robin's face. Briar holds her breath, waiting for the outcome. Perhaps the meeting itself will turn bloody.

"I have at my disposal an arrow such as you have never seen," says Bramble. "An arrow that cannot possibly miss its target, no matter how unskilled the bowman."

Robin stares up at the beautiful Fae. "Then you are speaking to the wrong man."

Bramble gapes for a shocked moment, but his recovery is swift and brutal. He thrusts out an arm and throws the outlaw onto his back. With one knee on Robin's neck, he jeers. "Then I shall offer it to your enemy, the Hazelminster Sheriff. It makes no odds to me what stupid games you mortals play. I have no objection if you die."

"The Sheriff would never deal with the likes of you." Robin's voice grates against the pressure on his throat.

Bramble chortles. "Fool! Every mortal wants Fae magic."

Robin shakes off the offending knee and scrambles to his feet. "Not him. He's the worst kind of new religious. Stupid enough to think the old ways belong in the past. He doesn't believe in the powers of the land and the creatures that dwell on it. More interested in a so-called church that cares for the rich and spits on the poor. Nah, the Sheriff won't help you get whatever it is you want."

Robin brushed off his hose, *tsking,* and pointed a finger at Bramble. "And I'm thinking it's a bad idea to get involved with you at all. I like my partners more on the friendly side. If you don't mind me saying so."

Before Bramble can roar his anger at the reckless mortal, Briar intervenes. "Our offer stands. Take it or leave it but be aware that the gateway back to your beloved Oakendoire could close on you."

"Indeed, it could!" agrees Bramble, catching on. "A pity should you find yourself on this side of the veil with no magical weapon to wield."

The outlaw narrows his eyes at them before glancing over his shoulder. Briar and Bramble each flurry with one dark, tattered, shard-pierced wing. The passageway grows dim, as though night reigns on the other side of the veil. Robin Greenhood turns back to them.

"No point in leaving such a weapon unused." He shrugs his shoulders. "You may as well let me have it."

"Tut tut," says Briar. Bramble snarls.

"My lord, my lady," amends the outlaw, obviously fearing to be trapped this side of the doorway. "I beg you, please allow me to use the charmed weapon."

"Make your vow." Bramble pulls forth the shard-tipped arrow.

Robin directs a look of annoyance at Bramble. "I swear to use this weapon against my greatest enemy, to make his downfall as public and humiliating as possible. I'll always do everything in my power to protect the forest and all who dwell within."

The arrowhead flashes crimson. Lightning bursts over the clearing, turning the shadows black as death. When the dazzle fades, Bramble recovers first. "Go now, human, and use this weapon with all your puny might. The Hazelminster Fair is in two days' time. We expect results."

The hue of Robin Greenhood's face suits his name. He's clearly shaken, try as he might to hide it. He rolls the shaft of the arrow in his palm and raises a mocking grin. "Results you shall have. By your leave!"

With unexpected swiftness, he turns about and sprints through the spinney. Bramble calls after him. "Cowardly human! Don't dare cross us!"

There's no answer. The veil closes and Briar takes her brother's arm. "Let's go home. There's nothing more to do until the game is played."

Bramble grunts. Stepping into the shadows of Thornhallow, they are lost to sight.

Chapter 7

"Robin, give it to me."

Lady Marian of Westhaven pouts at her lover. Ever since they hatched this plan to thwart Prince John's devious ways, Robin has doubted that the High Fae would want to give him a bespelled arrow. For pity's sake, everyone with ears knows that he's the most accurate marksman in the country. Nobody has less need for magic. Even King Richard himself praised Robin, back in the days when he was naught but a long bowman in the motley army fighting the Wreadae hordes. Bestowed with the manor of Garretsey after one especially amazing act of courage, Robin came home as a hero and a landowner.

Until John decided that Garretsey manor and its lands were better used to support the King's court in his absence. Thrown out of his demesne, Robin joined the masterless men of the forest, vowing to protect the poor from the most rapacious of the regent's decrees. Marian, meeting him as a newly made noble, recognised him for something special. As well as being an adept and inventive lover, Robin afforded the perfect cover for her spying at the court. John might rail against Robin Garretsey all he liked, little knowing that it was Marian who sent Richard all those reports. Robin was nothing more than a diversion from her crucial errand.

Make that *errands,* she thinks. She needs Richard safe on the throne to protect her and those like her, according to the deal she and her sister witches struck, to save the natural magics of the land. Spying on his brother and reporting back was simply a side-game in her larger plan.

Marian's going to bring down everyone who scorns Creiland wise women and penalises their power, High Fae, and royalty alike. The witches and the Old Ones have a plan that's close to fruition. She can hardly contain her excitement at the thought that the Old Ways will soon return. First, though, to bring this sadly expendable, though delightful, man to heel. "Robin, darling, remember what we said?"

The outlaw looks up from the arrow. His eyes are dark, the pupils enormously dilated. "What?" he asks. The influence of any cursed shard on ordinary humans is strong, and even though Robin is several steps above average in ordinary human terms, he's flummoxed. Marian steps closer and puts a hand on his shoulder. Such a broad, delectable shoulder.

"My darling, this is dangerous. Let me have it." She kneads the nape of his neck, whispering a word or two of charm-laced comfort at the same time. "There! Nasty thing." Taking it in her gloved hand, she thrusts it into the pocket concealed in a fold of her riding habit. Robin blinks, frowning at her.

"What?" he asks again.

"You're the most wonderful man," she assures him, standing on her toes to reach her lips to his. "Thank you. That was so dangerous, alone in the deep of Thornhallow with those rogue High Fae. You are so brave."

Robin, his face regaining some of its colour, pulls her into his arms. "It was nothing. I'd do anything for you, my love. Anything so that we can be together."

Marian sighs and settles her head against his broad chest. "Everything will be better, after the Fair. You'll see."

She smiles to herself. Everything indeed.

Chapter 8

"Do we have it? The shard-cursed arrow?"

Marian puts her hand on Mother Shipton's shoulder. "Yes. Robin fetched it for me. Rest easy."

"And he agrees to the terms? His life's blood against the Dark Fae?"

"Robin will do as I ask."

"Humph." The hag pulls herself out from under Marian's hand to return to the pot simmering over her hearth fire. "There's a lot could still go awry, missy. Not least if that cowardly regent loses his nerve."

"I know. I'll do what I can to give him an obvious opportunity."

"Humph. Just make sure—ah, you know what to do, girl."

"I do. But if you don't mind my asking, Mother, are you sure this is the only way?"

"Worrying about your lover, are you?" The old woman barks a laugh. "Well, he's pretty enough. I'll give you that."

Marian bites her lip. "If there's any other way... No, I know there isn't. Don't mind me, Mother. We'll all play our parts." She looks through Mother Shipton's doorway to where her sisters wait. The time to act is upon them.

Chapter 9

The Hazelminster Fair dawns fine and clear—no great matter for Marian to arrange with a dozen weather witches on hand.

Marian takes her place beside the Sheriff on the raised dais, smiling sweetly at his acidic comments. Amusing in his own sour way, the Sheriff is an old noble who suffers from gout. He's the King's man from the top of his velveteen cap to the elongated toes of his suede boots, but he's not the cleverest of officials. He always appreciates her suggestions about handling John's contemptible demands, and never notices her influence over all decisions made at Hazelminster Castle.

"Is he here yet, the mincing ninny?" The Sheriff does not try to hide his disgust at the King's little brother.

"Oh, Sheriff, you are wicked! I believe we will soon see his grace. Hark! Is that not a hunting horn I hear?"

"Huh."

A flourish of trumpets announces the regent Prince John. Guards clear a way through the crowds so that the Prince's outriders can proceed to the dais, while the Regent's litter is carried to the very steps. The people of Hazelminster ooh and aah as the royal visitor emerges.

John makes quite an impression. He's clad in a cloth of gold and his cloak of red velvet is trimmed with ermine. A gem-set crown rests upon his head. The Sheriff stands to greet the noble visitor, and Lady Marian drops into a deep curtsey. She slides her eyes sideways as the prince mounts the steps. Good, he's definitely carrying the enchanted sword at his hip. Dipping her veiled head even lower as he takes the chair prepared for him beside the Sheriff, Marian ensures she captures the regent's interest.

"My lord," she breathes, casting a glance at him under fluttering lashes. "Welcome to Hazelminster Fair."

"Hmm." John reaches out a finger to lift her chin. She smiles shyly, lids lowered. "Sheriff," says the regent. "Let this noble lady sit by me. Here, my dear, where I can look at you."

"Oh, my lord!" In a pretty show of confusion—half trembling at the royal attention and half unworthy of the royal offer—Marian contrives to have her chair moved to the prince's right, where she keeps a close eye on the sword. With the Sheriff on the Prince's other side, she manages events exactly as planned. Only half a mind is needed to titter sweet responses to the regent's heavy-handed compliments. Marian awaits her moment.

Chapter 10

The Fae twins are not enjoying the fair. "I detest this," complains Bramble as he and his sister trudge through the gates of Hazelminster Castle to join the throng. "It makes me feel—"

"Dirty is the word you're looking for," murmurs Briar. "But we need to see this play out in person."

Bramble grunts. The glamour masking their true appearance is oppressive, like a heavy cloak held over the face. "As ever. The outlaw will skewer the prince, several guards and bandits will kill each other in the aftermath, we'll recover the weapons, and you can pay me the forfeit."

"Huh! When the prince slays the outlaw you can pay *me* the forfeit!"

Bramble laughs. "Well, let's just see what happens." Neither of them admits the forfeit is meaningless, being simply the first choice of pawn in the next round. What excites them both is the bloody combat that their interference instigates among the abject humans.

The day wears on in a succession of woeful contests in several trivial skills, totally unnecessary to the meanest of immortals.

Looking about in boredom at these human antics, Briar notices more than a score of the Old Ones among the crowd. Glamoured to look like human children, they toddle behind this or that middle-aged woman. Usually, these gnomes, sprites, dryads, and hobgoblins avoid crowded places. Perhaps they are perfecting their babyish concealments. Briar sneers. No concern of hers.

It's a dowdy gathering. Briar wishes that the Fair attracted more handsome young men and dainty damsels. Grabbing a couple of tasty youngsters to carry across the veil is one of the juicier outcomes of provoking bloody fights among a mortal crowd. The sweet human playthings don't last very long, but that's the nature of mortals. There are always more to be had. Except here... Ugh. The eligible youth are vastly outnumbered by ancient wrinkled women, dozens of masquerading Old Ones, and a pack of soldiers past their prime. The dreary throng makes the prince look attractive, his female companion—a noblewoman on the wrong side of thirty, Lady Marian something-or-other—quite fair. What a waste of time. Perhaps when Robin arrives... Briar sighs, earning a dark look from her twin. Their cover requires total silence.

The Fair drags on, with none of the usual drunken exuberance the Fae expected. The matrons chat and sort through fabrics and hanks of rough-spun wool; the Old Ones chase each other in flawless simulation of mortal children. The mob of veteran soldiers vies with one another for frivolous prizes.

Finally, the announcement of the longbow contest.

Briar and Bramble worm their way through the crowd, closer to the dais. The prince scans the faces below, a deep frown between his thin eyebrows. Briar is just as peeved. None of the contestants look anything like Robin. There's a giant of a man, almost Fae height, somewhat like Robin's second in command,

'Little' John—but this fellow's too old. A relative, perhaps. Bramble touches her shoulder and points out another competitor in an undyed homespun, with a ragged red kerchief knotted about his brow. Will Scarlet? But Briar shakes her head, searching the line of long bowmen. Too old. All of them were too old for the life of masterless men in Oakendoire.

John rises, disappointment on his face. Robin has not come.

"Waste of our time," breathes Bramble. "I'm going to kill them both."

The prince draws the enchanted sword, raising it over his head to signal the start of the competition. Even the twins gasp as the weapon erupts in blinding light, flying from the prince's hand to slam unerringly through the chest of one contestant, a fellow so ordinary that Briar hadn't even noticed him.

"Is that Robin?" she cries, forgetting to be quiet. "I win! I win!"

"Hush!" Bramble grabs her arm in a painful grip, pulling her towards the gate. "Do you want to get caught in this?"

'This' is the mayhem that follows the launch of the flaring sword. The crowd rushes forward to see. The pretend children dart about, the matrons scream, the soldiers bellow. There's no getting away. The surge pushes Briar and Bramble closer to the dais and the bloody scene below. Lady Marian's down among the peasants, kneeling over the prostrate body. Briar catches a glimpse through a gap in the crowd, and hisses. The battered old soldier is no more: Robin Greenhood lies in Marian's arms, smiling up at her while his heart's blood spurts out. He hands her his longbow, eyes closing, but his smile remains.

Marian bends over him, pulling something from among the folds of her dress. Briar gasps as the crowd suddenly parts to reveal the noblewoman. Notching the shard-tipped arrow, Marian yanks back the bow string and lets it fly in their direction.

Briar feels Bramble tugging at her arm, but it's too late. Drenched in the heart's blood of the hero, guided by the venomous shard, the magicked arrow plunges through Briar's chest and all the way into Bramble behind her.

An enormous flash of lightning blasts from the skewered bodies. For long moments, the afterglow blinds the crowd. When at last they can see again, a shimmering miasma roils about the fallen as their cloaking glamour recedes into the ether. For an instant or two, the twins' shard-pierced wings flutter brokenly.

Marian, standing tall with eyes narrowed, calls out to the amazed assembly.

"Stand back! Stand clear!"

The two tumbled bodies of the Fae explode into flame.

After years of tormenting others and drowning in their own misery, the twins are at last free of the cursed mirror's baleful influence.

Chapter 11

Soon the busy Old Ones throw soiled hay and lumps of wood onto the pyre made by the bodies. How merry they are, like children set free from chores to enjoy the sunny afternoon.

Lady Marian of Steelholde steps back from the outlaw's body, ceding her place to a bevy of women. They surround Robin, screening him from sight. Marian lifts her skirts and returns to the dais, where the Sheriff and several of his soldiers form a protective wall about the prince, shielding him from the chaos in the courtyard.

"My lady," says the Sheriff, somewhat discomposed by events. "Are you safe? You shouldn't have gone down there!"

"I know, Sheriff," Marian answers demurely. "I was quite safe, I assure you." She turns to the prince. "My lord," she says to John, "here is your sword. I can't understand how it flew from your hand."

John grabs eagerly at the weapon, stained crimson with Robin's blood. Marian presses her lips together as the stupid man lifts the blade to his face, as if the smell of the gore pleases him. She clasps her hands near her bodice, fingers tapping an unusual rhythm. John makes a sound of distress.

"What's amiss, my lord?" asks the Sheriff.

"This sword!" cries the prince. "It's ruined!" And indeed, the weapon splits into two long shards as they watch, the bloodstained blade dropping away from the hilt. Oddly, the metal smashes as it hits the cobbled courtyard, shattering more like glass than iron.

Marian murmurs something under her breath. A troop of busy children sweep up the shards and hurl them into the fire, sparking a fine display of green and blue flames that pleases the crowd enormously.

Meanwhile, masked by the thronging folk of Hazelminster, a certain tall bowman and his sure-footed mate whisk Robin away to the forest. The witches have done what they could to repair his heart. Now he needs the rest and quiet that only Oakendoire can provide, surrounded by folk who love him.

Calm and joy descend upon the gathering. The ghastly pyre burns to nothing but ash, its putrid stink soon replaced by the delicious scents of roasting meats and sizzling pancakes. The witches quietly congratulate themselves on their success, and melt away with the joyful Old Ones, all of them impatient to reclaim Thornhallow from the pollution of the twins.

Marian takes a deep breath and squares her shoulders. One lot of cursed shards destroyed. A small tract of ancient Creiland wildwood reclaimed from the all-conquering dark Fae. This county safe with its share of wise women. But so much still to be done!

At least her sweet playfellow is still breathing, she reflects, away in Oakendoire with his fellows. Already planning her next visit to her courageous paramour, Marian holds out her arm to the Sheriff. Together, they watch the unhappy Prince gather his retinue and depart.

The Strength of Bones

McKenzie Richardson

The dark-haired man gazed into the casket. Its occupant appeared at odds with the memory of the one always quick to laugh and ready with a joke.

Clearing his throat, Lorenz opened his mouth, but the words didn't come. There was an emptiness within him, as though he'd been hollowed out. Nothing tied him to this man who'd raised him, who'd loved and cared for him. He may as well have been a stranger. Guilt was all Lorenz felt as he stared death in the face.

His shirt collar scratched at his neck, and he was uncomfortably aware of the sweat soaking his black suit. He shifted self-consciously as the funeral director approached, a surveying shadow materialising right on time.

"Ready to continue?" the director asked. He looked at the man in the casket, rather than Lorenz, as though asking the dead's permission.

Lorenz closed his eyes as slowly as the world turned. "Yes."

Shutting the casket, the director wheeled it from the room.

"I'll bring the ashes by tomorrow," he declared.

With that, the director left Lorenz alone in the room that felt too large.

Walking the few blocks to the toy store, Lorenz found the windows dark. The lights hadn't been on all week.

He paused before unlocking the door. The store would be so empty now its occupant was… gone.

Growing up, the toy store had been a place of wonder, a warm, magical spot nestled within the drudgery of the outside world. With intricate music boxes and clocks that chimed the hour, animals and puppets that moved when you pulled the strings, it was a place packed with sound, movement, and magic.

Without the toymaker to bring them to life, the toys were just things, the store a building rather than a wonderland.

Lorenz did not want to walk across the threshold. Doing so would make it all real. Yet, as is the case with growing up, he pushed himself to do the unpleasant yet necessary thing, despite how unbearable it felt.

When he pushed open the door, a wave of stale air greeted him. He gazed at the beautifully carved toys and trinkets. They looked so lonely on their shelves.

The events of the day weighed heavy on his shoulders. The funeral had been a popular affair. Yet even in the crowded room, Lorenz may as well have been alone, the sole inhabitant on a distant planet witnessing the emptiness of stars.

Climbing the stairs to the little apartment above the store, Lorenz settled onto the thin mattress, trying not to think of its previous occupant's final sleep.

Then he dropped his head in his hands and waited for morning.

The sun rose on signs propped in the shop windows. *Everything must go! Building for sale!*

Strangers recounted tales of the wonders the toymaker had crafted over the years. Some had been coveting items in the shop since childhood. Each time a customer expressed their condolences, the hollow in Lorenz's chest grew.

Closing the shop meant a little piece of magic died in that small town, but Lorenz worked in the city. He couldn't run the store. That's what he told himself, at least.

Besides, he wasn't a woodcarver, a toymaker. He dealt in ceramics. He'd never been able to pull the same life from wood the toymaker had. Closing the shop was the sensible choice. Though perhaps a part of Lorenz hoped doing so would make the empty feeling in his chest subside.

That evening, a heavy knock came at the door. Lorenz knew who it was before he opened it. That dreary sound could only have announced one person.

The funeral director stood in the doorway like a rain cloud incarnate, here to wash away any chance of the peace Lorenz had hoped for. He pressed a jar into Lorenz's grasp and met his eyes. The two shared a look that needed no further explanation, one uncomfortable with death, the other with the living. Then the director departed.

The weight of a human body surprised Lorenz. He set the jar of ashes on the counter, the lid clinking loosely like a final closing.

Anger bubbled inside him. Why hadn't the toymaker told him he was sick? Lorenz hadn't visited as often as he used to, but the toymaker could have written, could have sent word, done something. Not just stayed here alone and suffering.

Betrayal grated at his skin, the secret kept, the anger of those last moments robbed from him.

He would have come if he'd known. He would have. Wouldn't he?

With a burst of rage, Lorenz pushed the jar away, unable to stand the sight of it. It hit a snag in the wood, a patch where a younger Lorenz had attempted carving his initials but only managed a jagged scar. "Sometimes what is broken can be repaired," the woodcutter used to say. But this was not one of those times.

The flimsy jar toppled, and the lid popped off. Its contents spilled out like a billow of dusky snow.

"Damn jar," he muttered, examining the cheap ceramic. He'd have made a better one, one that would not crack or break.

In the city, Lorenz was renowned for his bone-china pieces, their strength and whiteness. His critics said his work was mechanical, that it lacked soul. They said he was an exceptional ceramist, but that he'd never be a craftsman, an artist, until he could feel with an artist's heart. Lorenz waved it away as jealousy, but only partly because he didn't understand what they meant by an artist's heart.

Still grumbling, he scooped up the ashes. There were little specks of white bone poking out of the grey dust.

The whiteness of bone had always fascinated Lorenz. Rolling the fragments between his fingers, an idea took root, gnarled branches brought back to life.

That night, Lorenz entered the workshop for the first time in years. It had always been a sacred place, an essential aspect of the man who'd owned it. It was hard to differentiate the two, to determine where the toymaker ended and the workshop began.

Stepping through the doorway was like overcoming a physical boundary. Lorenz hadn't anticipated how his chest shook as he gazed at its contents. The hammers and chisels, the boxes of wooden gears, the intrusive smell of cut wood, the shavings that littered the floor.

Unwanted memories crept like spiders, guilt slinking along with them. He should've come more often, taken a break from work. He didn't have to be so busy. With a shake of his head, Lorenz pushed away the regrets. He had work to do. He found what he was looking for on the top shelf at the back of the room.

The cavity of the mould held the shape of a cat sitting on its haunches, its tail looped. The toymaker had carved the creature out of wood the day Lorenz had arrived in the world. When Lorenz first showed an interest in ceramics, the woodcutter had created a plaster mould of the figurine.

As he mixed the kaolin with water, Lorenz remembered his childish excitement at the magic of turning powder to liquid to solid creation. As the memories swirled like the smooth paste he'd formed, he sprinkled in the ashes.

Mould filled, he set it to flame in the tiny kiln. The firing process would take the longest. Lorenz dreaded the waiting. To escape his thoughts, he tidied the room.

He couldn't bear to pack away the tools. Not yet. He'd sell them eventually, but for now, they were content where they were.

Lorenz didn't know when he'd fallen asleep. One moment he'd been collecting wood shavings, the next he woke up. His ears rang with the memory of a distant cat's cry.

Shrugging away the dream, he retrieved the mould. When it had cooled, he cracked it open. Inside lay a perfect casting of the cat, so lifelike one would've thought it were moulded from a living creature, not merely a scrap of wood.

Lorenz carried the bone china figurine upstairs and placed it on the bedside table. Then he crawled beneath the blankets and slept deeply for what felt like the first time in years.

Dreams spun their webs inside Lorenz's mind. He was trying to exit the workshop, but a cat the colour of moonlight wound around his legs. Each time he attempted to bypass the creature, it twisted back into his path. Tripping over the smooth feline's body, Lorenz landed hard. The cat leapt onto his chest, weighing him down, squeezing the breath from him.

Lorenz woke with that heavy feeling still on his chest. When he made to sit, the edges of the real world and the dream world seeped together.

"Well, hello there," Lorenz said groggily to the cat perched on his chest. He glanced over to see if the window was open. It wasn't. "How'd you get in here?"

"I've always been here," the animal said in a purring voice. "Don't you recognise me?"

Lorenz gaped. Was he still asleep?

The cat blinked at him slowly, the way only cats can do. As the creature stood and stretched, needle-like claws dug into Lorenz's skin. The pain was proof enough that he was indeed awake.

With a start, Lorenz shot out of bed, upsetting the cat onto the floor. The feline landed gracefully on four delicate paws.

Lorenz gawked at the snow-white creature. "Did you just talk?"

The cat gave a small sneeze that sounded almost like a laugh. "Of course."

"Where'd you come from?"

"You made me."

Lorenz shifted his gaze toward the bedside table. Only the extinguished lantern remained.

"Are you the china-cat then?"

The cat's tail twitched with a slight clinking noise, like pieces of ceramic rustling together. "A bone-china-cat," the snowy creature corrected.

"Bone china," Lorenz repeated in a whisper. His eyes widened as he stared at the animal's unbelievably white coat. "Made with his bones."

The cat nodded its silky head.

"Are… are you him, then?"

Deep golden eyes fixed on Lorenz. "Of course not. I've just told you. I'm a bone-china-cat."

Now that he listened, there was something distinctly feminine in the cat's purring voice.

"But," she continued, "he is a part of me. You used his ashes to make me. I feel him here, his memory."

"His memory?"

"Of this shop, of woodcarving. Many of you. He loved you very much."

Lorenz focused on a spot on the wall.

"He had something he wanted to tell you, something he didn't have a chance to explain. A warning."

The man gazed back at the cat. "What kind of warning?"

"I think it's best I show you."

With a magnificent leap, she pounced on him. Her sharp teeth pierced the flesh of his hand.

Lorenz pulled away at the flash of pain, looking down at the twin puncture wounds. Scarlet blood beaded on the skin, catching the early morning light.

He was about to demand an explanation when the world around him blurred. His vision swayed toward the crimson droplets, and everything else spun away.

Shaking his head, Lorenz looked down at the workshop from the ceiling as though he'd stuck his head through the floorboards. White specks dotted his vision as the cat appeared beside him.

Below was a man with jet-black hair, a work apron around

his waist. Perched at the workbench, he methodically carved a piece of wood. It was impossible not to notice the air of sadness around him, like a cloud hovering over a cheery day. His face was not all that old, but there was a heaviness to it.

Despite the smooth skin and clear eyes, Lorenz recognised the man.

"How is this possible?" he breathed, never taking his gaze from the figure. He wanted to call out to him, the man he knew was dead, but the cat nudged him with her paw.

"We're in a memory. His memory. There's something you need to know about how you came into this world."

A knock at the door stopped Lorenz from further protest. When the figure below answered it, Lorenz had to squint through the resulting brightness. At first, he thought the sun was ablaze, but the light did not reach the small windows. Instead, it streamed through the doorway where a figure stood in radiating brilliance.

"Hello," a sweet voice chimed. It belonged to a girl no more than ten years old. Her hair glowed brightly with azure light, turquoise hues tangled in the stands. Each time Lorenz tried to make out her other features, his gaze returned to the blueness of her hair.

"I have something for you," she cooed. From the folds of her gown, she revealed a small log.

"With this, you can create life," she said cryptically. "I can show you how."

The toymaker's brow worked itself in concentration, the hints of the folds that would come with age already visible.

"Within this wood lies the seed of life from which you may carve a son. Give him what features you deem fitting and he will always be yours."

The toymaker's eyes lit at the prospect of a son, cutting through the surrounding darkness.

"But magic is not so easily gained. If you wish him to live a true life, to be a real child, there's another ingredient you'll need."

With a wave of her hand, a rippling image lit up the shop.

Brighter than any sun, the light emanated from a tiny flower as white as newly fallen snow. It shone as though angels has crafted it from pure illumination, glittering like diamond dust.

"This is a fragment of the Maledetto MirrorThe mirror's properties were too great for any one soul to control. It shattered, but there's power in each of its remaining shards. This one will grant what you seek. To obtain it is difficult and will require persistence. Will you take on this quest?"

The man nodded.

The scene shifted like a kaleidoscope of mingled colours. There were flashes of emerald leaves and blue sands swirling. The voice of the girl with the turquoise hair drifted along with the wind.

"There is a place of blue sand where the Frost Giants took their last stand against the Green long ago. Their remains returned to the earth, but the ice in their bones took longer. Over millennia, it broke down into a desert of blue sand. At the centre of this desert, you'll find a cave."

The scene shifted. At first, Lorenz thought all the colour had drained from the world, but when his eyes adjusted, the mouth of a dark cave loomed.

"You'll meet those who will try to stop you." The scene sped by in rapid succession. Lorenz only made out bits and pieces, a flash of ruby scales, a snaggle-toothed grin, and a bottomless darkness. "But you must persist. Let nothing stand in the way of what you desire."

The intricate lily of pure light crafted from the Cursed Mirror shone like an underground sun. The vision swirled again to reveal the toymaker back in the shop. His body was visibly tired but still tense with hope as he carved a humanoid body from the log the girl had given him.

Lorenz knew the story from there, how the wood had come to life, how he'd been born. The vision faded, the toymaker's memory overpowered by his own.

When Lorenz opened his eyes, he was back in the attic room, the bone-china-cat beside him.

"I never knew all that," he whispered. "He never told me."

"He loved you very much. He'd have moved the world to save you."

"It doesn't matter now. He's… gone."

"Yes, but you are still here. That is what matters."

Lorenz stared at the cat.

"Dense human." She rolled her eyes like a pair of dancing moons. "It's the mirror. The mirror in your heart. It gave you life, but it's tainted. It's what keeps you from feeling whole. The dust inside you keeps everyone at bay, locks your feelings up tight. That mirror keeps you trapped."

A creeping sensation slithered along Lorenz's skin like a silky snake.

"What do I do?" he asked, shaking away the invisible serpent.

The cat's eyes glowed so bright, a mischievous twinkle edging into their light. "The mirror taints you. You must remove the mirror."

A cold bolt of dread pierced Lorenz's gut and lodged there, the impossibility of the cat's declaration like a knife striking to his core.

Lorenz chuckled to hide his fear.

"And just how would I do that? I can't very well rip out my heart."

The dancing moons of the cat's eyes rested steadily on his. "That's exactly what you must do."

The cat perched on the windowsill, tail ticking like a pendulum. Her large golden eyes watched Lorenz prepare for the journey he still suspected was merely a dream.

"You should eat before we go," she advised, crossing the room with clinking strides.

Despite his doubts, Lorenz followed.

"Do you want anything?" he asked as he settled at the table.

The cat's tail flicked. "Don't be silly. I'm made of china. I don't need food."

Under her attentive gaze, Lorenz ate his breakfast, packed a bag, and double-knotted his bootlaces. Then he stood at the door as though unsure how far to take the delusion.

The cat nudged the back of his calf. "Go on," she urged, purring like the lid closing on an earthenware jar. "You've already come this far."

Lorenz emerged into the fresh morning air.

The feline toddled along beside him, each step clicking against the cobblestones. The noise was soothing, something for Lorenz to concentrate on, to take his mind off the madness of whatever was happening. A dream, a delusion, a guilt-soaked hallucination. He did not quite know what it was. But he'd go along with it. For now.

They spent the night at the edge of the blue-sand desert. The snow-white pads of the china-cat's feet showed none of the wear Lorenz's did.

In the morning, Lorenz woke to a weight on his chest that was becoming familiar.

"What's all this about?" he groaned to the cat on his sternum.

"It's dirty here. I don't like dirt."

If he'd had any lingering suspicions, this creature was the toymaker reincarnate, they ended here. The toymaker had been no stranger to clutter. When Lorenz would complain about the disarray in the shop, the old man countered, saying it helped with creativity. Lorenz had always thought it was an excuse to get out of cleaning, but perhaps there was some truth to the logic. The toymaker had created such wonders.

A pang of jealousy crept into his heart at having never captured that same magic. Just as quickly, Lorenz pushed the feeling away. Was this the mirror taking hold? The envy subsided to guilt for selfish thoughts.

"We should be going," his companion interrupted. "Best to reach the cave before nightfall. There's no telling how treacherous the desert will be in the dark."

Lorenz followed the cat from the lushly padded grasses toward the blue sands. Browns and greens gave way to azure. The wind picked up so quickly it caught Lorenz by surprise.

Pulling on the extra layers he'd brought, Lorenz stepped into the skin-slicing rapids of wind. They cut into whatever they came into contact with, boring holes in his leather coverings. The sand ripped at his exposed palms, slicing thin lines of blood into his flesh as he pulled the bone-china-cat beneath his coat.

Guilt took his mind off the pain. He'd never known how the toymaker had struggled to bring him into existence.

By the time the cave materialised like a gaping mouth ready to swallow him whole, Lorenz didn't think he could go any further. He ducked out of the roaring winds. The only sound within the cave was the cat's purr, tumbling over each stone.

"How do we know when we find the right cavern?" he asked the darkness.

"I expect we'll know it when we get there. That's often the way of magic." The cat trotted ahead, so vividly white, she glowed slightly.

As Lorenz followed, a new sound emerged, a rumble deeper than the cat's purr. A streak of white shot toward him. Only when he felt the cat's smooth coat against his leg did he realise she'd retreated to join him, startled by the noise.

The tunnel widened to form a hollow in the rock. It was surprisingly warm for a cave in the middle of Frost Giant sands. Lorenz packed away his extra layers for the return journey. *If I make it that far*, he added to himself.

There was a faint light in the centre of the cavern, like a candle in a bottomless pit.

Remembering the lily's shine, the pair headed toward the light. By the time either realised their mistake, it was already too late.

A massive head rose, weaving through the shadow. The tiny flame intensified, illuminating the huge nostril from which it blazed. A second head joined the first, followed by another and another, until a swarm of scaled faces towered over them on long, spindly necks that tapered together into a single body.

Seven heads observed the adventurers. "Who dares disturb my slumber?" the mouths demanded as one, subtle flames bursting from each snout.

Wide-eyed and mouth gaping, Lorenz was too stunned to answer.

"We apologise for the disturbance," the cat cut in, her clinking voice smooth and silvery. "We're merely two weary travellers."

The seven-headed dragon snorted. "Your apologies mean nothing to me. I'm still awake when I'd rather be asleep." One head slunk forward like a massive branch swaying in the wind. With a great whiff, it breathed in their scent, then scowled at the cat. "Not much use for you. But this one could make a nice treat. Might as well enjoy a meal while I'm awake." A few of the heads chuckled, while the others opened immense jaws.

"Wait!" Lorenz exclaimed. The dragon stopped, fourteen eyes settling upon the man. "What if we provide something other than sustenance? I'm only a bitty morsel for such a great and powerful beast. Not worth the trouble."

The dragon squinted, considering. "There is an oddness to your scent. Perhaps you're right. Best not to risk it."

Ignoring the insult, Lorenz breathed a sigh of relief.

"But what else could such puny creatures offer?"

Lorenz's mind raced. "Entertainment. We could entertain you."

A rumble echoed through the tunnel. At first, Lorenz feared it was the dragon's stomach, but the beast was merely pondering the offer. The great monster's expression lit up. "Riddles," he exclaimed. "I do love a good riddle."

Lorenz's stomach churned. He'd never been much good at wordplay.

"Answer my riddle and you can leave. Fail and…" The dragon smiled, showing far too many teeth. "Well, best hope you can answer."

Lorenz faced the massive creature with as much courage as he could muster. "I accept."

"Very well," the dragon beamed.

> *"A stubborn youth, most uncouth,*
> *looks upon the body of a man,*
> *observes his death mask, given the task*
> *to name him if he can.*
> *The youth dances, as he answers,*
> *speaking cryptically,*

'An only child begets an only child
without the help of a mother.
To my own, that man shares a father
though my father has no brother.'
Who can the dead man be?"

Lorenz's head spun with the rhymes, unable to concentrate under the weight of the bargain. He turned to the cat for help, but her golden eyes stared back like blank porcelain.

"Tick tock," the dragon said, its heads swaying as though keeping time. "Better get guessing if you'd like to stay uneaten."

Lorenz's vision blurred around the edges, casting monstrous shadows to the world.

A sudden pain at his ankle set his vision alight, clearing away the darkness. The cat perched at his feet, eyes fixed on an opening behind a nearby rock. If they were quick, perhaps they could reach it.

As the dragon continued taunting, the seven heads distracted by their waving dance, the pair leapt toward the dark pit. They did not know where it led, but it was almost certainly better than the bottom of a dragon's stomach. Holding the bone-china-cat tightly, Lorenz jumped into the hole.

A blaze of fire erupted behind them, then the deep rumble of laughter. "Run, run, run while you can, little boy," the dragon bellowed. "You'll have to answer sometime."

The echo of the dragon's words followed as they tumbled down the slope.

The body of the bone-china-cat was cool against Lorenz's skin as they slid further into the unknown, bumping and slamming against the uneven terrain.

The slope deposited them into a hollow with a series of less than graceful grunts and unpleasant yowls.

Flat on his back, Lorenz blinked up at the dim ceiling. A patch of scraggly hair disrupted his view.

From beneath the hair emerged a row of craggy teeth, as though stalactites and stalagmites erupted from tarnished gums.

A pair of coal-black eyes appeared above the teeth, gazing upon the new arrivals.

Lorenz scurried back as the cat leapt toward the grinning ghoul.

Clenching his eyes tight to await his fate, Lorenz's ears prickled with every sound. Something reverberated, ominous yet familiar, like the rumble before a storm. He opened his eyes to see the owner of the gruesome grin stroking the bone-china-cat's back. The cat was purring as though nothing were out of the ordinary.

"Mornin'," the old crone croaked.

"Is it?" was all Lorenz could think to say.

"I know why ya here." The snow-white feline rubbed against her hand as the woman spoke. "Come on then, if ya must. I haven't all day ta wait on ya."

The woman turned and went on her way, the cat padding along behind.

"Who are you?" Lorenz asked, getting up and loping after them.

The woman cocked a whiskery eyebrow. "Names're a funny thing. Make people rec'nisable." Her milky eyes intensified as though seeing into Lorenz's soul. "Lost mine long ago. Maybe it was taken. Wherever it was, it ain't here now. They called me a striga before I ended up here. Good a name as any, I s'ppose."

"Where are we going?"

"You're here to put things right, ain't ya?"

Lorenz was silent.

"Ya here ta put the mirror back. I smell it on ya skin. Only two reasons things wind up here. Ta take the mirror or ta put it back. Ya here to purge ya soul."

A knot worked itself into Lorenz's stomach as Striga resumed her trek, expertly dodging the cat that weaved between her ankles, as though they'd been at this intricate dance for years. Taken by her confidence in his purpose, Lorenz followed Striga deeper into the cavern.

The trickle of water echoed through the space. As they neared its source, Lorenz's chest grew heavy. An invisible hand seemed to squeeze his heart, fingers digging into the organ. His breath caught in his throat as another wave of pain rippled through him.

"That's the mirror alright," Striga said, a bit of a cackle in her tone. "Gets ya, donnit?" A toothy grin spread across her face as she led him onward.

Lorenz felt the place before he saw it. The hand on his heart became a vise grip, crushing the life from him. He pictured the organ rupturing, his chest cavity filling with blood, his whole life ending here in a damp cave with a witch and a bone-china-cat.

A touch at his shoulder pulled him from his thoughts. Striga's dark eyes gazed upon him.

"Ain't much, but it'll help with the pain."

Lorenz's head felt heavy as Striga pulled his shirt collar from his neck. When her teeth punctured the skin, the pain set every nerve of his being aflame. He wanted to scream, to pull away, to pound his fits and run. But just as quickly, the sensation gave way to a wave of soothing relief. The whole world felt like the colour blue, his limbs light as air.

"Do what ya must, boy," Striga said.

When the witch released him, Lorenz was sure he'd float off the puddle-strewn ground, but he didn't. The cat strode up and pressed a paw to the back of his leg. That was all the encouragement he needed. He stepped forward.

Some of the feeling had returned to his body now, enough to follow the pull in his chest. The dripping water grew louder. *Plink. Plop. Plink, plink. Plop.* The droplets gathered in puddles, seeping into the holes in his boots. Their echoes lingered in the hollow spaces of the cave like melancholy afterthoughts.

The dripping condensation had carved an indentation into the rocks below, creating a flat space within the stones. It resembled a low shelf or a throne. When Lorenz's eyes fell on the structure, the pull in his heart weakened his legs and his knees crashed into hard stone. He opened his mouth to cry out, but even that felt useless against the mightiness of this place.

The ache in his chest guided him forward, stone snagging his skin as he shuffled along on his knees. His mind floated along, as though outside himself, looking down on the scene from above. His shaky fingers approached the stone.

The jolt shot through his body like a lightning strike. The ghost of a mirror loomed before him, composed of vapours and air. It glowed white-hot before shattering, shards flying in all directions. One headed straight for Lorenz. Along its trajectory, it warped and twisted, distorting itself into the unbelievably delicate form of a lily.

Ghostly hands took hold of the bloom. Lorenz recognised them by their watchful care, the nicks and slivers in the skin, the calloses on the palms and pads of each finger from hours of working with wood.

The memory of the toymaker ground the sparkling lily into a fine dust. When a wooden puppet came into view, Lorenz wanted to look away from his younger self, the version of him that came before, the lifeless lump of wood that would somehow become what he was today.

With the care of handling a newborn, the phantom fingers dusted the powdered lily into the hollow of the puppet's chest. This was where his life began, his unconventional birth. *An only child begets an only child, without the help of a mother.*

The ache in his chest was unbearable now, like a fire had ignited there. He clenched his eyes shut as the world exploded with shades of blue. Stands of azure hair snaked toward him.

"Lorenz," called a voice like nothing he'd heard before. It spoke with the voice of hundreds, maybe thousands. High and low, deep and piercing, the multitude twined together with each word. "How good to see you again."

Before him hovered a girl, the one he'd seen in the shop. The one with the turquoise hair. Her eyes glowed with an unearthly blaze as white as bone-china. Her hair writhed in clumps, reaching for Lorenz, threatening to snag him in their tangled grip.

"Go back," she said in that voice of all voices. "You're nothing without me."

Lorenz fumbled, unsure what to do. The tendrils of blue hair wrapped around his wrist.

As the hair touched his skin, his neck pulsed where Striga had bitten him. Screeching in pain, the girl flinching backward, her hair relinquishing its hold.

"I see you've been talking to my mother," she said, voice hot with anger. "Gave you her protection, did she? What lies has she been telling?"

"I'm here to put the mirror back," Lorenz panted against the pain. The air hurt his skin as though made of fire. It slipped down his throat and into his lungs, burning him from the inside out.

"You can't," the girl bellowed. "I'm what gives you life."

Lorenz's limbs shook as he tried to hold himself up. Everything felt heavy, everything hurt.

A shot of white leapt across his vision and the cat appeared between them.

"Ha! You think a little kitten can stand up to me."

The feline hissed. "I know what happened to you, the promises made. The Dark Mage lied when he lured you to his side, used you as a sacrifice to create his mirror. He tricked you, took advantage of your desires. Now you do the same to those who venture here."

"He did *not* betray me!" the blue-haired girl snarled, saliva flying in her rage. "He gave me everything. Look at me. I'm pure power. I'm unstoppable. He gave me eternal life while all others weaken and die."

"You're just like him, greedy and corrupted, darkness incarnate. You call this a life? Holed up in a cave?"

The girl glared. "I wouldn't be here if it wasn't for Mother. She locked me away, tried to keep me from those I could influence. You saw her, how she's withered and aged, all to convince them to let me be. But I have my ways. I see their desires. I know their hearts are as dark as mine."

The girl's eyes blazed as she turned back to Lorenz. "You know you want the power that beats in your chest. I've helped you all these years. Gave you life, gave you talent. You'd be nowhere if it wasn't for me."

The cat was at Lorenz's side, pushing her smooth head against his skin. "Don't listen. She doesn't care about you. She wants to take over. Don't give in, Lorenz. Fight!"

Lorenz's head throbbed with the heat. Raking his fingers

through his hair, he scratched at his skull as if to dig out the fire burning within.

"Fight it, Lorenz. Fight it," the cat whispered.

"You're weak without me," the girl chuckled. "You'll crumble away. Talentless, soulless. You'll perish like that father of yours, alone and with nothing."

The mention of the toymaker sent a ripple through Lorenz's body. The cat's words echoed in his mind. He couldn't give in. He had to fight.

He struggled to his feet and took a shaking step forward. The girl laughed. Her hair shot out, but a flash of white intercepted. Lorenz made to untangle the cat as she wrestled with the strands, but she batted him away.

"Go!" she demanded. "Get to the throne. You must give up the shard."

One step after another, Lorenz forced himself forward. The fire in his chest was so strong now he could barely breathe. As he approached the throne, the girl swept in front of him. Her eyes flashed like a thousand suns.

"Don't do it. You won't survive."

Despite her words, Lorenz caught the hint of fear in her tone as he lifted his hand toward the stone.

In a last desperate act, the girl made to block him, then howled in pain. Red-black blood dotted the air as she kicked at the cat latched onto her leg.

With a final flail, she freed herself, sending her attacker across the cavern. The cat collided with the rocky wall, shattering into tiny white fragments. They rained down like powdery snow as Lorenz's hand touched the throne.

For a moment, the world went dark.

Then the throne burst into light and the blue girl screamed, pain cutting through her multitude of voices, sending them bouncing off stalactites as though fleeing the scene.

Lorenz's chest burst open, ribs splayed. From the ragged skin, tiny specks of diamond-like stone emerged with bursts of ruby blood. Sweat poured from Lorenz's brow. The fire within had lessened, but he was not sure this fresh pain was any better.

In mid-air, the hovering shards solidified. A stem emerged from the lump, petals unfurled. The lily took shape, blossoming into a sparkling field of light, a darkness hidden within its core. All at once, the pain receded from Lorenz's body, as though an infected organ had been removed.

He breathed in what felt like the first full breath of his life and gazed at the twinkling light. The faint echo of the blue girl's screams barely reached him. All he saw with the lily, the enchantingly immaculate lily, hovering a few inches from his face.

Lorenz reached toward its light. Just before his fingers touched the glass-like stone, something brushed against his leg. He looked down to find the bone-china-cat, transparent like mist blanketing the morning.

The ghostly creature looked up with those golden eyes and her purring voice resounded inside Lorenz's head. *Don't fall prey to the mistakes of your father. You've purged yourself of his unintended darkness, the toxicity he never meant to pass on. Let yourself be whole. Don't give in to temptation. You've already come this far.*

Like vapour on the wind, the cat dematerialised, and Lorenz's hands dropped to his side. He turned away from the lily, a light in the dark that was not quite what it seemed. He raced to the cavern wall where a patch of bone-white china dusted the ground. Tears prickled his eyes, rolling down his checks and mixing with the powder.

The slightest pressure touched his shoulder like a butterfly alighting. Striga's shrivelled face was brighter, as though the burden of a hundred years had lifted from her shoulders.

"Shame," the witch said, scooping the powder into her palm. "Wassa good cat."

"And a good friend." Lorenz tore his sleeve to fashion a pouch. Then he collected the powder inside. "Sometimes what is broken can be repaired."

The old woman nodded as though understanding a universal truth. Then she smiled. "I'm glad ya made it, boy," she said, tonguing the gaps between her teeth.

"There was a girl. A girl with turquoise hair."

The woman's smile broadened. "My Liliana. Ya saw her then? I thought ya might. I lost her long ago. We can't always prevent those we love from comin' to harm. At some point, we have ta stop blamin' ourselves."

"Is that why you stay?"

Striga nodded. "Nice ta be close ta her. I know it ain't the same, but it's all I've got. Livin' in this cave. It's fine by me. I try an' warn those who come seekin' the shard. Tried ta warn ya Pa. But he was determined. My Lily had tempted him with a son. She was always good at that, figurin' out what a person needed."

Lorenz remembered how close he'd come to succumbing to her temptation.

"Do you ever get lonely here?" he asked as he stood.

"A' times. But there are always those who seek the lily, the promises they hope it'll keep. There's always someone comin' this way. Met many ov'r the years. Some give in ta the darkness, some let it consume 'em. The lily returns ta its place once it's eaten away what's left of 'em. You're the first ta willin'ly put it back, though. Seems the world still has some surprises."

Striga pulled him into a hug and Lorenz's heart beat hard as he fell into the embrace. Warmth radiated in his chest, as though glowing from within, not painful like fire, but soothing in its heat.

He pulled back, unsure.

"Ya can feel now, my boy. Joy an' hope an' love. Use this gift wisely. Now you're whole."

Lorenz headed back toward the mouth of the cave. He travelled through blue sand and thick forest until he found his way back home.

Despite the ache in his limbs and the tingle in his skin, Lorenz roused himself early the next morning. In the workshop, he found a scrap of wood and began carving, using the long, careful strokes the toymaker had shown him long ago. He cast the carving in plaster, then mixed the broken bone-china with a fresh batch of clay.

The next morning, he pulled a bone-china-cat from the kiln.

Though similar to the first, this one was not so much a cat, but the essence of a cat, capturing the regal posture, the confident gaze, the feeling that everything about it was right. Never had he created something with such a soul to it before. Perhaps he'd found his artist's heart.

He placed the figurine in the window where its body shone like starlight.

When people stopped in to inquire, to ask if it were the late woodcutter's doing, Lorenz simply replied, "No, it's mine. The woodcutter's son."

They tried to buy it, but he refused whatever the amount. Instead, he promised them another, any animal they wished. He cast bears and dragons, unicorns and birds, but never another cat. There was only the one keeping watch of the little shop.

He hadn't planned on staying. The shop had felt too empty. But as it slowly filled with new wonders, the prospect didn't seem so daunting.

He'd resurrected the magic of the store he'd thought was dead and buried. It was a new sort of magic, one entirely his own.

Before Lorenz went to sleep that night, he thought of the seven-headed dragon's riddle. *To my own, that man shares a father, though my father has no brother.*

Deep in his heart, he'd known the answer. It'd just been too painful to admit.

"My father," he answered. "My father."

That night Lorenz dreamt of witches and mirrors, of bone-china-cats and adventure.

In the morning, he created new fantastical things. Because a heart unburdened is one capable of magic. And magic is all you need to create wonders.

Once Upon an Automaton

Nikky Lee

It was Lysanias' fault. If my brother hadn't boasted about how I'd built an automaton to rival the smithing god himself, I wouldn't be here.

If not for Lysanias, I wouldn't be on my knees in the Queen's throne room with a blade pressed to my throat, waiting for her Highness to pass judgement. And gods be, there is a *lot* of judgment in those eyes right now.

A guard steps forward. "The smithy had this on her person." He holds out a gold locket to Queen Calliade. She takes it, pries it open and lifts out a shard of glass. Obsidian black, it glitters like the oasis waters on a moon-filled night. Its reflection scatters dark mirrors on the floor, pulsing and twisting with the shard's energy.

"What powers it?" she asks.

"Life," I murmur.

"How did you come to possess it?"

I stare into the swirling reflections, hypnotised by their dancing, just as I had been all those months ago when Lysanias had run into my workshop, breathless…

"Savvina! Look at this!" Lysanias exclaimed, waving a small string purse at me.

I rose from the rat trap I'd been setting under a loose floorboard. At the sight of Lysanias' empty rucksack, I scowled.

"Where are my parts?"

I'd given him a list and coin enough for what I needed. Even made him repeat my instructions back to make sure they'd sunk in. My brother waved my question aside and pressed the purse into my hands.

"Just open it," he said, hopping in excitement.

I took the bag. It was light. Felt empty too, except for a lump at its bottom. I opened it. *If he's gone and squandered my coin on some worthless—*

My fingertips brushed something sharp, and a static jolt ran through my hand. I gasped, jerked my hand away, revealing a hair-thin cut to my thumb. Just deep enough to draw blood. Scowling, I upended the purse on my workbench, and with a *plink-plink* a sliver of glass half the length of my little finger fell out. Hot anger licked up my neck and across my cheeks.

"You spent our—*my*—money on a piece of *broken glass*?"

I'd hoped my anger might cow my idiot brother, but it did the exact opposite. He folded his arms and jutted his chin, all haughty-like.

"Not just any piece of broken glass. It's *magicked*."

"Sands and sprites, spare me. I need *parts*, Lysanias. I have orders waiting!" I gestured to my workshop and the two half-finished automatons on my table: the first a mechanical sand cat—all oscillating tail and padding paws—the second a bronze cage with four metal canaries set inside. Both half-finished and now behind schedule. Lysanias held up his hands.

"Hear me out." He motioned for the shard. With a roll of my eyes, I dropped it into his hand, and he picked up the fifth and final canary on my workbench. "Just watch." He placed the shard in the bird's chest, behind its metal-worked wishing bone, right where its spring would have gone.

A heartbeat passed, and a sigh built in my throat.

Then the canary's head lifted; it flapped its wings and sprang to its feet.

My jaw dropped. "Gods above."

Lysanias grinned at me as I dipped my ear to it, listening to the faint whirr and click of its gears and cogs turning.

"What powers it?" I whispered, frightened I might scare the miracle away.

"Magick," Lysanias said.

I shot him an exasperated look. The dessert was home to hundreds of small magickal gifts. As Kralian citizens, we'd been tested for Water Divining—the most coveted gift of our desert kingdom. Suffice to say, neither Lysanias nor I had shown any aptitude for it. I met my brother's gaze. "What *kind* of magick?"

Lysanias swallowed, suddenly unsure. "The old lady mentioned something about lifeforce."

My grip tightened around my workbench. "What old lady?"

"The Fae merchant selling the shard. She bought it off a fisherman from the coast who found it tangled in his nets. 'Didn't know what he had', she said."

True, it sounded dodgy as all hell, but there was no denying the shard's wonder. I mulled a moment, lips pursed. "Did she have more?"

"Just the one," Lysanias reported. His grin returned, "But I thought you could use it for… you know." He nodded to the abandoned humanoid of bronze and wire lying in the corner of my workshop. Twice as tall as a man and same again across, the automaton was my career's work.

And it was in pieces.

Pulled apart one afternoon during a lull in work orders to figure out why the blasted thing wouldn't run. Not that it ever had. Long ago, I'd learned springs were not enough to power something so big. I'd been working on installing a steam contraption, but then summer solstice arrived, and orders flooded in for solstice gifts. I'd not returned to it in months.

Before I could protest, Lysanias pulled the shard from the canary, marched over, and thrust the shard inside the automaton's chest, depositing it inside the miniature boiler I'd installed to run a steam test. With a click, he shut the hatch and scampered away. We held our breath.

Nothing happened.

Lysanias frowned, waited another moment. "Perhaps it's too big."

A snap of a rat trap sounded under the floorboards along with a high-pitched squeal.

"Least something's working," I muttered, crouching to the floorboard and pulling it up. The trap lay underneath, a rat crunched under its hammer, neck at an awkward angle. I was about to release the trap when the dead rat *moved*. Not *moved*, but something in the rat shifted, slipped loose with a faint squeak. Something, not quite a breath, whispered across my fingers and I spun, spotting the shimmer as it slipped into my automaton—right into the boiler.

Lysanias' grip crushed around my arm. "Savvina! Did you see—?"

"I saw."

The automaton hummed. Actually *hummed*. Low, on the edge of my hearing, its static filled the air and pressed against my skin. With a creak of hinges and a wobble, it rose to its feet.

"It's working!" Lysanias circled the machine and tentatively prodded its side. It didn't topple as I half expected it might.

"Working might be an overstatement," I said, circling with him. Magick gave my creation life. Perhaps it could make it move too—the only question was how. "Did the merchant give you instructions? A phrase to say maybe?"

Lysanias shrugged. "She said the magick was malleable. Adaptable. It would respond to whatever use we could imagine for it."

How very vague. Trust Lysanias to be pulled in by the promise and not think to clarify the details. Though his find had my blood thrumming too. *Whatever use we could imagine for it.* Nothing for it but to try. "Can you hear me, automaton?"

A faint squeak emitted from the boiler in its chest.

My brother shot me a look, mouth drawn into a perfect circle. "I'll take that as a yes." He licked his lips. "Step forward, automaton."

The automaton didn't move.

Lysanias scowled. "I am your master, automaton, you answer to me. Step forward."

Not even a tremble. The automaton remained motionless, the glow of its eyes a steady blue.

My brother is not one for patience. He stamped his foot,

champed his teeth. "By the magick that binds you, obey, or I will pull that shard right out of you! Step forward."

I sighed. Better to intervene before my brother took his temper out on my creation and broke it. "Perhaps it can't move. Maybe you need to be more specific, like 'two steps forward, automaton'."

The automaton stepped forward. Twice. Excitement blossomed in Lysanias' face again. He spun back to the machine, eyes turning distant, no doubt imagining some future use for it that I could only guess at. That was his way. Forever running before he could walk. "One step forward, automaton," he commanded.

No movement.

I titled my head, considering. "One step forward, automaton," I echoed.

It stepped again. *Curious.*

"Why only you?" Lysanias pouted.

I stared into my palms, just as mystified as he. Then noticed the cut on my thumb from the shard. What that it? My understanding of magick was minute, but a suspicion formed in my mind. *Blood magic.* I could—*should*—have left it alone, but the part of me that had always envied the power of Kralia's Magi wanted to know if my guess was right.

"Put a drop of blood on the shard," I said.

Lysanias did as I suggested, digging into the automaton's chest and popping open the boiler. Carefully, he pricked his finger on the edge of the shard inside and blood welled, glistening in the lamplight of my workshop. Then it was sucked *into* the shard. Lysanias jerked his hand away.

"Try now," I told my brother.

Lysanias cleared his throat. "Step forward, automaton." It did, and my brother clapped his hands together and danced up to my side, grinning from ear to ear. "This is going to change everything!"

If only I'd thought to wonder what he meant by that.

"You'll have people lining up to order from you," Lysanias said as we set up my stall at the Lower Side markets. "Just think, we could finally get out from Landlord Turik… You could find a bigger workshop."

I'd not cared much about our accommodations or that they were on the wrong side of town, but the thought of a bigger workshop, what I could *do* with enough parts and space, won me over.

Sure enough, people did gather. Their number swelled as they watched my automaton trudge back and forth from the cart and stall carrying smaller automatons and various metal workings—tools, knives, buckles, tack. I busied myself organising my display and pretended not to notice. Until the Magi.

She parted the crowd like the prow of ship; short, stocky, her uniform impeccable with not a mote of Kralia street dust on her. Her cuirass bore an embossed seal of the Queen's guard over her heart. Sharp green eyes drank in my automaton in a heartbeat, tracking its progress as it trudged between cart and stall.

"Can you make another?" she asked.

Lysanias swept in like a vulture, eyes gleaming at the hint of a first sale. "Magi Meteli! We've been expecting you."

Lysanias was always the better barterer, so I let him do the talking.

"As many as you need," he said.

"As many as we have *parts for*," I corrected, shooting my brother a look as the Magi inspected the automaton. While I might have enough parts to create another, there was only one shard, and we barely knew how it worked.

Her gaze swivelled to mine, calculating. "How many?"

I hesitated. If we could replicate the magic, I could make as many as they wanted, provided they supplied a big enough down payment so I could purchase the materials. Lysanias' whisperings of new accommodations and workshop rose in my thoughts again. Damn him, he'd always known how to weasel his way into my head. But the problem was still the magic. If I failed to deliver, my reputation would be ruined. In a city like Kralia, which relied so heavily on trade to survive, reputation was everything.

I opened my mouth, already hating the words I was about to

say. Something along the lines of 'irreplaceable', when Lysanias, in his infinite wisdom, chimed in,

"Why don't we start with a delivery of ten and take it from there?"

"Lysanias!" I grabbed his sleeve and hauled him away with a "Just one second" apology to our Magi customer.

Behind our stall, I shoved him against our unpacked crates. "Are you trying to ruin me? It took me a year to design that automaton! It'll take me *years* to make that many and the magick—"

My brother winced and straightened from the crates, waving off my anger with a hand. "As I recall, it took you a year to *design* it. Putting it together took less than a week once you had it all decided."

"Each one would still take a week, *minimum*! Even if I didn't have to fabricate half the parts for it."

"Then don't," Lysanias said simply, and frowned at me as if *I* was the one being unreasonable. Like *I* was the idiot making outrageous promises while drunk on dreams of a better life. "We'll hire some help with the deposit."

I chewed my lip. Evidently, he *had* put some thought into this. But there was still one gaping hole in his plan. "What about… "—I leaned closer—"*the magick*?"

My brother winked at me, actually winked, and my stomach knotted. "Leave that to me. We're good for this, Savvina. I promise."

I thought of everything we'd worked for. The reputation I'd carved out from the dust of the slums. The years Lysanias had pulled double shifts at the tannery so I could apprentice to Master Skopas and buy the parts for my first automatons to sell at the markets. He'd seen something in those metal workings that I hadn't. Something bigger. A way out. Perhaps this was the same. With a pang, I wondered when I had lost faith in him. I heaved a sigh and rubbed the dust from my eyes.

"All right. You win. I'm trusting you with this. I'll do the automatons. You find a way to do the magic."

Lysanias beamed. "Agreed." He swung back to Magi Meteli. "You have yourself a deal, Master Magi."

I expected Magi Meteli to laugh when Lysanias named the price for our automatons. Instead, Meteli had paused, considering Lysanias, me and the automaton, lingering on the last with a kind of fierce want I'd only seen in gambling dens. With a curt nod and a shake of hands, we sealed the deal.

With the down payment, we relocated to Upper Side. Our house was modest by Upper Side standards, but the barn accompanying it had sold me. Twice the size of my old workshop, we soon had the hay scraped and a forge installed, at which point Lysanias left me to get on with the work of fabricating more automatons.

My original automaton—Talos, I'd called it—was a saving grace. No need to hire an extra hand when I could set it to a task and it would work day and night without tiring. Granted, the tasks had to be menial, but once I had the moulds prepared, it could bang out a full casing in under a week, cogs, pistons, plating all. That left me the task of "stringing it together" as Lysanias had phrased it late one evening after he'd stumbled home from the tavern.

"Have you found a solution to the magick?" I asked, steering him out of my workshop before he broke something.

"All sorted. Jus' you wait," he slurred, patting my head like he'd done when we were children. With a sigh, I put him to bed, certain that his assurance was a lie. He'd done nothing but get drunk and gamble since we'd moved here.

But to my brother's credit, his promise was true. Two days later, I opened my workshop door to a brown-robed Magi on the stoop. We blinked at each other, my gaze darting to his ruffled hair and rumbled robe while his attention fell on my oil-stained tunic and callused hands before he offered a quick bow of introduction.

"Magi Iseas at your service."

I blinked again. No one had ever bowed to me before. Where we came from, that just didn't happen. At my stunned silence, Iseas hesitated, then cleared his throat. "Your, uh, business partner sent for me. Something about sharing a magical power source."

"My brother," I corrected automatically, then remembered my manners and held open the door. "Best come in."

He was thin and bookish, like most Magi were. Young too, scarcely more than twenty. Where had Lysanias dug this one up from? As if on cue, my brother burst into the workshop, still in last night's clothes.

"Iseas, you made it! Come this way, this way." He ushered the Magi into the workshop, directing him to where Talos worked in one corner pounding out a breastplate for a third lifeless automaton lined up against the workshop wall.

"Incredible," Iseas said, circling my bronze creations. "This is very fine work, Master Savinna." He gave me a brief, almost bashful smile in my direction. "I see why the Queen's Magi commissioned you."

Surprised at the compliment, I opened my mouth to stammer a thanks, but Lysanias got in first:

"So, can you do it?" He indicated the three motionless automatons. "Can you spell them to share power from the original?"

The Magi's brow furrowed, considering Talos, and his eyes narrowed to slits as if peering into sun. "Aura's stable," he muttered. "No sign of magical decay." He strode around the automaton again, then titled his head. "Curious magic. Where did you—"

Lysanias cleared his throat. Loudly.

Iseas stiffened. "Right, yes, extra coin if no questions asked." He gave a nod. "A simple enough matter," he concluded, "provided your power source is great enough."

Lysanias whooped. "You hear that Savinna?"

I held up a hand. "What do you mean 'provided the power sourced is great enough'?"

Iseas scratched his chin, gaze roving the workshop as he considered. "Think of it like a river," he said. "You can syphon water off to create a new stream without affecting the flow of the old river. But if the original river is only a stream, syphoning some of it away may stop it flowing altogether. Run it dry."

"I see." I glanced at my brother. He shrugged in response.

That meant the decision was mine. I blew out through my cheeks. "All right, let's do it."

The Magi flashed me a grin and motioned to Talos. "I'll design a set of sigils for you. I'll emboss the alpha sigil on this plate here." He tapped the breastplate on Talos' chest. "When you put the beta sigils on the other automatons, the alpha will syphon power to them."

"See, Savinna? Easy!" Lysanias said, clapping a hand to my shoulder.

I didn't share his optimism. But the Magi drew up the sigils, applied the alpha to Talos' breastplate and instructed us on how to apply the betas—demonstrating as he drew a beta mark on the first of the new automatons. As soon as he was done, the sigil flared white and the beta automaton creaked, lifted itself from the wall, ready for instructions.

"Salute, automaton," Lysanias instructed.

A faint whirr, a click-click of gears and the automaton's arm rose and gestured. I gripped Lysanias' arm and grinned. "Well done, brother!"

Iseas gave a small cough. "About my payment?"

"You shall have it," Lysanias said, sweeping forward to guide Iseas to the door. He pulled a purse of coin from his pocket and dropped it into the Magi's palm. "Enough to clear your debt with the House of Zinon."

My ears pricked, recognising the name of Kralia's second biggest gambling den. So *that's* what he'd been up to. Guilt twinged in my stomach. I'd thought Lysanias had been blowing the last of our down payment on drink and dice. Instead, he'd been blowing the last of our down payment on drink and dice and *finding us a Magi*—one so in debt they'd take any job *and* look the other way...

I should have pried more into the shard's magick. Pressed Lysanias for more details. But I hadn't... Not when we added the beta sigils on the next two automatons saw the glow of Talos' alpha sigil sputter and fade. Not when we frantically searched our new lodgings for more vermin to power the shard. Not when we'd taken to the streets soon after, desperate for a street dog, desert lizard, *anything*…

"It's no good," Lysanias huffed after we'd chased a sand cat up a rise and lost the creature underneath a brothel. "They're too quick."

Together, we flopped onto the roadside, staring out at the oasis' black waters beyond the flat-roofs of Upper Side.

"There… must be something," I gasped.

"Set more traps?" Lysanias suggested.

"No time. Meteli is visiting tomorrow to inspect our progress," I said. In my old workshop, it wouldn't have been a problem: the trap would've filled in an hour. But our new lodgings were frustratingly pest free. I scratched my eyes and searched the street for inspiration. Nothing but sand, dust and a couple of stubborn weeds growing through the cracks of mud-brick wall. How they found enough water to survive, Pantheon only knew. I blinked, the words tumbling in my head. *Water*. My gaze shot up to the oasis, taking in its expanse stretching across to the slums of Lower Side. *Water. Lifeforce.*

I pushed myself up. "Give me the shard."

Lysanias frowned but placed the cloth-wrapped shard in my palm. I beelined for the water. Lysanias trailed behind me in silence, knowing better than to question—he'd learned long ago to trust my ideas.

We found our way to the bank, red sand sticking to our boots, reeds scratching our legs, listening to the croak of frogs calling in the night. I crouched at the waterline and unwrapped the shard, exposing one glistening edge. Holding my breath, I dipped it into the shallows.

"Oh, I *see*," Lysanias whispered.

If only I'd given it more thought. But I was desperate.

The shard hummed in my hand, the force of it resonating through my fingers and up my arm. A heartbeat of nothing, then *whump*. Spray stung my eyes, burned my cheeks. The frogs fell silent. Behind, Lysanias released a strangled cry. I opened my eyes.

The oasis was *gone*. Drained. Bone dry.

Lysanias pulled at my sleeve. "Savvina, what did you *do*?"

Dazed, I didn't answer. Instead, I pressed my fingers into the dirt that had been the oasis' shallows, hoping to see water well up through the sand. Nothing.

"I didn't think it would take it *all*." It had been a long shot, a gamble. How much could one little shard hold?

Down the bank, shouts sounded. Too far away to make out words, but their tone was alarmed, urgent. Three agonising beats later, a bell tolled.

Lysanias pulled at me. "We have to go!" He hauled me to my feet and back into the street. Doors were opening, people blinking out into the night.

"What's going on?" One man asked from his threshold as we passed. "Another raid?"

Lysanias shook his head, feigning bewilderment. "The oasis has gone."

"What?" Frowning, the man pushed past us and down the street. We didn't stick around to see his reaction. I don't remember how we got home, only that it was dark and bumbling as Lysanias half carried, half dragged me there and thumped me down in my workshop.

"What will we drink?" I asked him.

"It'll be fine." Lysanias pried the shard out of my hand and returned it to Talos' boiler. The automaton hummed back to life, a faint sloshing echoing from inside it. A breath later, the first beta winked on… then the second beta straightened, and the third.

"You saved us," Lysanias said.

"But the water…"

"Will come back," he assured. "The oasis has never dried up, not once. Not even in the worst drought. It'll be full again come morning, you'll see."

Morning came and went and the oasis did not return. But Magi Meteli did.

"I had my doubts," she said, striding around the four automatons and nodding appreciatively. "You have done well. I will take these four now. Raiders grow bolder by the day and our caravans need protection." Her gaze slid in the direction of the dry oasis. "Especially in these times."

"P-protection?" I stammered. I'd thought the Magi had wanted the automatons for labour. In the same way Talos had saved me hours of gruelling work, I'd assumed the Queen's Magi had seen a use for them in her own work. "They're not trained to fight."

Meteli grinned at me and something in it set my hairs on end and made my gut cinch tight. "Not yet," she said. "Now, show me how you control them."

The blood drained out of my limbs. Controlling them required her blood on the shard, and a little voice in the back of my head warned that letting Meteli in on that little secret was a bad idea. The silence lengthened.

"Well?" Meteli pressed.

Lysanias cleared his throat and moved in.

"It's simple, really," he said. He turned to Talos and the betas. "Automatons, I command you to obey Magi Meteli's instructions." He bowed to Meteli. "Give them an order."

The Magi licked her lips, considered a moment. "You," she singled out one of the betas. "Kneel."

I gaped as the automaton dropped to one knee.

Meteli turned to us with a nod. "Very good," she said. "I'll increase my order to one hundred."

My stomach seized. "One hundred?" I echoed. Had I heard correctly?

"I'll adjust the down payment, of course," Meteli added. She produced a curled parchment from her robe and held it out to me. "I trust this sum is sufficient?"

With shaking hands, I took the parchment, unfurled it, made out mine and Lysanias'names printed on the page along with the words '*Queen's Treasury*' and a sum so large I had to read it three times before it sank in. It was more money than I had a name for. Lysanias peered over my shoulder and I caught his sharp intake.

"Present this to the treasury and they'll see to your payment," Meteli said. "I expect ten automatons each month until the order is complete." She turned to go. "Come automatons." At once, the four machines fell into file behind her.

"Not this one," I said quickly, pressing a hand against Talos' bronze chest to prevent it from following the others. "It's the original and I've trained it to help me fabricate parts. I'll need it to complete your quotas in time."

Meteli paused, considering. Then nodded. "Keep it."

With that, she left and Lysanias and I sagged against my workbench.

"Let me see that parchment again." Lysanias unpicked my fingers from the parchment. He let out a whistle.

"How did you know you could transfer command of the automatons like that?"

"I didn't," he admitted. "It was a guess. But I figured we didn't want to let Meteli in on the shard. A Magi like her might try to take it." He tapped Talos' bronze chest. "Good thinking with your excuse to keep the original. Better to keep it close."

Talos set the final bronze panel on the eightieth beta and I screwed the edge into place.

"Two more months," I said under my breath. It had become my mantra in the last few weeks. Two more months of this day and day out grind. Twenty more automatons and Lysanias and I would have enough coin to never need to work again. I could choose my commissions, take only the work that captured my interest. A true artisan.

Panel in place, I straightened, rubbed the throb of dehydration behind my temples. True to Lysanias' word, the water had come back, but it was more puddle than oasis. The Queen had sent whole conveys of water diviners into the desert to draw whatever they could from the earth and bring it back. When that hadn't worked, the Queen had commissioned water caravans from Trader's Bay. Even with automatons, not all of them made it.

I scored the beta mark on the new automaton's chest and waited for the glow to spread into the sigil.

It remained dead. Inert.

I checked it again, wondering if I had made an error. No, it was exactly the same as the other seventy-eight automatons I'd marked. Cold dread settled in my gut. "Please, not now."

At the back of my workshop, I pulled the sheet covering the other nine automatons of Meteli's monthly quota. Breathed a sigh of relief. Their beta sigils held, but the one on Number Seventy-Nine had faded, like a flame of a candle shrunk to the end of its wick. "Shit."

"What's shit?" I jumped as Lysanias' voice sounded behind me. He leaned on the workshop's door, looking distinctly out of place in his embroidered velvet tunic and dress boots. Off to a dinner with his Upper Side society friends. Jealousy twanged in my chest and I shoved it down. Lysanias had got us Meteli's commission. He deserved to enjoy his share of the profit.

Even if you're doing ninety percent of the work? whispered the voice at the back of my mind. I ignored it. "The shard's power is fading," I said.

Lysanias straightened. "What?"

I gestured to Number Eighty. "Its sigil won't work." When Lysanias opened his mouth, obvious question on his lips, I said, "I've checked it twice. It's not the sigil."

My brother's attention fell inward as he considered. "Show me the shard." I obliged, opening Talos' chest and boiler. Lysanias plucked the shard from it, wrapped it in a kerchief, and tucked it inside his tunic. "Leave it with me."

"But—"

"Trust me."

With a wave, he set out into the night, whistling as he went.

"You better bring it back in three days," I called after him. "Meteli's quota is due."

"You worry too much, sister," he called back.

The shard was back the following morning—I arrived to Talos hammering out the casing for Number Eighty-One, the alpha sigil glowing on its chest. Across the workshop, Number Seventy-Nine and Eighty's sigils were also bright.

"You did it," I said to Lysanias when he emerged from our accommodations late that morning. He blinked at me once, twice, before a slow smile crept across his face.

"I did," he echoed.

I gripped his shoulder. "You really came through." I hesitated, chewed my lip, about to ask what manner of critter he'd sacrificed—*did I even want to know?*—when my gaze fell on a gold locket strung around his neck, and my thoughts scattered. Such trinkets were popular among lovers in Upper Side. I'd seen well-to-do merchants from the nearby merchant port town selling them in the markets. A grin pulled at my lips, and I gave the trinket a pointed look.

"You going to introduce me?"

He didn't blush as I expected, instead he tucked the locket under his tunic, muttering, "Another time."

I frowned but let it go. "My thanks again for the help. Meteli will be pleased."

And Meteli was pleased. She sent a wagon for the latest load of automatons—these on their way to bolster the city guard—and a pageboy who handed me a note from the Magi.

Take special care with your next batch. They are destined for the Queen's throne room.

—Meteli

I gawped at it the note for several seconds, the heady realisation of it slowly sinking in. My automatons in the Queen's throne room! On display for visiting dignitaries, merchant lords and, on rare occasions, Fae from as far as Darkthorn Castle.

With that promise dangled, I threw myself into my work. Knocking out another two automatons within the week. As soon as their beta sigils were scored on, they were up and helping with the fabrication tasks, speeding the work along even more. It was all going well—too well in hindsight—until I scored the rune onto Number Eighty-Four. Just like Number Eighty, the sigil remained inert and a glance to Number Eight-Three saw the beta markings on its chest piece sputter. I swore under my breath and went to find Lysanias.

"Failing already?" My brother stared at me. "Are you sure?"

"As sure as the sun will rise on the morrow."

It was Lysanias' turn to swear. "Must have been too old," he muttered. He rose from our table, pushing his half-finished luncheon away. "Leave it with me," he promised again.

Relieved, I returned to my workshop and put my mind to the month's quota. The next morning, Number Eighty-Four's beta sigil glowed a steady white. Lysanias had come through once more. With a brief twist in my gut, I again wondered what life Lysanias had found. Sand cat, scorpion, desert fox?

Put it from your mind, a cold, pragmatic part of my brain whispered. *They are serving the greater good now.*

The shard's power failed again on Number Eight-Seven.

"Perhaps it's the strain of all the automatons," I pondered as Lysanias gave an exasperated curse and thumped Eighty-Seven's chest plate with his fist. I hesitated, then spoke what I'd been wondering since Number Eighty's failure. "We could be at the end of the shard's limit."

"No," Lysanias growled. His hand curled around the locket at his neck. "I'll deal with it."

I cast him a doubtful look but left him to it. A day later, Eighty-Seven glowed like the all others. It lasted another two automatons.

"It's the strain," I insisted as he circled Eighty-Nine. "There are too many automatons drawing on it."

"Eleven more," Lysanias muttered. "We'll make it stretch." With a nod, he pulled on his coat and went out into the night.

I didn't ask where he was going.

At the month's end we delivered Eighty-One through to Ninety. Yet when we came to score the beta marks on Number Ninety-One, Ninety-Two and Ninety-Three, each one failed in turn. Each time Lysanias took to the streets in search of fresh life-force. With the oasis dry, he must have had slim pickings, few animals were still around, even in the city, and each day the hollows under Lysanias' eyes grew.

"This isn't good for you," I said, when Number Ninety-Four's sigil wouldn't spark. "Let me go this time."

My brother stayed my hand as I reached for my coat.

"I take care of the magick. You build the automatons," he said, reciting our agreement from all those months ago. With a sigh, I let him go.

It was the same routine with Number Ninety-Five, but Number Ninety-Six took *two* of Lysanias' outings to make its sigil glow. Every bit of power we gave it, the less it seemed to last. *The more the shard demanded.* The thought, when it came, often in the dead of night, chilled me to the bone and left me shivering until morning.

Then the knock came at my workshop door. An old woman in a modest shawl, her skirts dusty from the streets.

"Begging your forgiveness, Master metalsmith." She curtseyed low. "But I'm hoping you might have seen my son, Iseas?"

"Who?" I asked, dumbly.

"Iseas, he worked for you."

It took a long second to remember, but then… *Ah, the Magi Lysanias hired to spell our first sigils.* I cleared my throat. "Apologies, but I haven't seen him in months. Many months."

She blinked up at me. "My Iseas was last seen with your brother two nights ago in Lower Side. I hoped he might know…" she trailed off, shoulders curling over as she shrank into herself. A Lower Side mannerism—I'd seen it often enough—but for the first time I realised how wretched it made a person seem. I straightened.

"I will ask him when he returns." I made to close my door.

"Master, wait!" she wheedled. "One more question, please."

As tempting as it was to slam the door, I huffed, "What?"

"You have ties to Upper Side society and the palace, perhaps you've heard…" she glanced at me then away again, fear turning her body stiff, "… if there's been another murder?"

It was the first I'd heard of it. "There have been murders?"

"Ten of them now. In Lower Side. The killer doesn't take their coin or any valuables. Just leaves the body in an alley." Her chin wobbled, her eyes on the edge of tears. "I told Iseas not to go out, that it was too dangerous…" She shuffled forward on my step. "Might you implore one of the Queen's guard to search? You're one of us, I thought we could—"

At her words, I stiffened. *You're one of us.* A whisper rose in the back of my head, sharp and cold: *How dare she.* I'd worked my heart out to get where I was. Long days, sleepless nights, all so I could be here. And here she was trying to swoop in and use my hard-earned status to search for a son who was probably in a loan shark's prison.

She will bleed you dry. Pull you down to the dregs again, the whisper said. *Get rid of her.* I listened.

"Get off my step."

"But Master Savinna—"

I shoved my door shut, pressed my back to it and waited until her pleas ran silent and her boots shuffled off into the street.

Ten murders. Eleven if Iseas was among them. The same number of times Lysanias had gone out 'hunting'. Too much of a coincidence. My hands shook as I paced the workshop. But to fuel the shard, Lysanias would have needed it with him, and it had been inside Talos the whole time.

I watched the automaton quietly tightening the bolts of Number Ninety-Seven's leg plates. Removing the sigil would have put it out of action until Lysanias returned it, unless...

My gut turned cold.

I strode over to Talos. "Stand up." It did so, and I leaned in to examine the alpha sigil. It wasn't glowing. Someone had traced white paint into the sigil's grooves so that, at a glance, it would appear to be working. My mouth turned dry. *Gods, say it isn't so.* I pulled off Talos' breastplate, popped open its boiler.

Empty.

But how?

Then I saw it. Inscribed on the inside of Talos' breastplate. A beta sigil. My fingers curled around the metal, anger filling my belly. I knew where the alpha sigil was.

I stormed into Lysanias' rooms, startling him from slumber. Never mind it was nearly noon.

"Savvina! Wha—" he began, stumbling upright as I tore the sheets off.

"Give it to me!"

He blinked, his night clothes hanging off him. He'd lost weight—some part of my mind noted. A lot of weight. "I don't—"

Anger blinded me. I swept in, snagged the locket around his neck, and pulled. It came free with a *'plink'* of breaking links. Cheap metal. *Of course it was.* I turned the locket over in my palm, tracing the filigree with a finger. There, disguised among the curling gold wires: an alpha sigil. Just like the one on Talos' chest.

And it *glowed*.

I clawed the locket open, already knowing what I'd find. The shard lay tucked inside, nestled around a scrap of oil-stained cloth. Like that, my anger left and I deflated onto the bed.

"Why?" I asked, staring at the locket in my palm. "You could have used sand cats, mules, even a camel."

Lysanias sank down beside me. "People guard their beasts better than they do themselves." He stared at the shard in my hands. "The first time… I went to Lower Side to find a rat. But I found old Phaon unconscious outside a tavern, drunk to oblivion as usual, and I thought, 'why *not* him?'"

The chill in my gut spread into my chest as the name jogged a memory of an old homeless man, usually passed out somewhere on the east end of Lower Side. No family anyone knew of.

"The next was…" Lysanias began, and I clenched my fingers around the locket and covered my ears.

"I don't want to know."

There, with the locket next to my ear, I heard it: Isaes' voice, as sure as if he were next to me. "… Mercy… have mercy…"

I threw the locket across the room. It hit the wall and bounced to the floor. "*Why?*"

My brother's eyes lingered on the locket. "I thought giving it a soul with magic might make the power go further."

I glared at him, ready to curse him again, to ask why *people,* of all things, when the whisper rose in my head. *Why not people?* The thought sunk in like a burr, and try as I might, I couldn't shake it. In the end, I sagged against the bed and said, "You took the shard from Talos and hid it. Why?"

Lysanias gave a shrug. "I said I'd take care of it. I didn't want you to worry."

Didn't want you to worry, his words circled in my head. Infuriating. For a man who could smooth talk just about anyone, he was frustratingly poor at explaining himself. Lysanias' gaze returned to his knees, knobbly as a grandfather's under his night clothes. "You finished Number Ninety-Seven," he said. "I saw it when I came home last night." A pause. "Did it…?"

My hands curled into fists. "It won't activate." We'd been so close. Three more automatons. Add Talos into the count and we were still two short. Would Meteli accept that?... *Could I?* The thought rose inside me, insidious and grating; twisted around my mind like a piece of crooked wire. My next thought was cold and sharp: *What's two more?*

Lysanias came to his feet and began to dress.

"What are you doing?"

"Ninety-Seven won't activate, you said it yourself." He pulled on a tunic from the floor. Not his usual well-made garment. This one was old, sweat stained around the collar, and scuffed at the hem.

"You're going back to Lower Side."

Wordlessly, he picked up the locket from the floor.

I could have said something then. Argued with him. Locked him in. But as he pushed past me to the door, I stepped aside. *Two more souls,* the thought whispered in my head. *Two more...*

I paced the workshop, anxious for Lysanias' return. Against the far wall, the last two automatons waited, beta sigils dormant. Today was the deadline. Meteli had collected Ninety-One through to Ninety-Seven along with Talos, and I had begged a few days extra to complete the last two.

"Materials are getting difficult to source," I lied to her. "Nearly all caravans are focused on bringing water."

With a grudging nod, Meteli had granted me an extension. "Two days. No later—the caravans are in dire need. I'll pick them up from your workshop."

I checked the street again—no sign—and kept pacing. *Where was he?* It was nearing mid-morning. Meteli would be here any minute. Then, at last:

"...Savvina..." He stumbled across my threshold, clutching a hand to his ribs. His face was black and blue, but behind his swelling jaw, his eyes were dull and cheeks sunken. The broken gold chain dangled from his free hand.

"Gods be, Lysanias, what happened?" I rushed to him, pulling the locket from his fingers as he fell to his knees.

"Lower Siders... found me," he wheezed.

My gut went cold. "Did you get the last two?"

A shake of his head. He winced as it set off something in his side. I peeled the blood-spattered tunic away and saw the bruises extending across his ribs and stomach. A new, unsettling thought sank into my stomach.

"Were you followed here?" I gripped his tunic. "Lysanias!"

"Going to… rest…"

I swore and spun back to the automatons, locket tight in my grip. Both were still; sigils inactive.

"Shit!" I wiped a hand through my hair. *Think, think!*

Need more.

"… Savvina…" Lysanias croaked from the floor.

"Hang on, for gods sake! Let me think." But my brain floundered. *More,* was the only thought I could summon. The locket's filigree wires dug into my skin. *Need more.*

We'd been so close. *I'd* been so close.

A faint moan. Lysanias. "… Forgive me…"

I turned, caught the rasp of air as it sighed from his lungs. I waited for him to suck in another breath. Only he didn't. Instead, his skin shrivelled, receded, and turned to dust. With a sigh, his bones slumped in and a shimmer slipped free and into the locket.

Somewhere deep inside, I registered my own strangled scream.

Against the wall, Number Ninety-Nine hummed to life. I stared at it, then at my brother's bones lying on my workshop floor, adding to its dust. The locket pulsed, throbbing through my hand.

More.

A half sob, half giggle broke from my chest. I held the locket to my ear and listened to the last words of its latest victim.

"… Savvina…"

A bang on the door and daylight flared across the workshop. I looked up to Magi Meteli framed in the open doorway, her face cold as steel.

"What have you done, Master metalsmith?"

The Queen smiles from her throne; judge, jury and executioner. Such is the way of Kralia. We don't have the Fae's courts or Alatay's laws. Here, the Queen's word is absolute.

"I am to die," I say. For the first time in what feels like months, my thoughts are quiet. My own. A veil lifted from my mind as I finished my story. Lysanias is dead. Because of me. For me.

It was my fault.

"Yes," the Queen says.

My heart doesn't sink. It doesn't do anything. It listens numb, feeling the cool of the throne room floor hard on my knees.

"And no," the Queen amends.

I stare, uncomprehending.

She lifts her hand, inspecting the gold filigree locket in her fingertips, and I feel its faint whisper. *More.*

No. Oh gods, please no.

The Queen's lips curl. "There's still one more automaton to power."

The Wraith of Murkdres

Stephen Herczeg

Sparks flew as the swords clashed in the dying light of the day. Beads of sweat ran down Tantalus' brow, stinging his eyes and blurring his vision. With weary arms, he raised his sword, blocking the last thief's downswing. The shudder that ran through his body from such a puny blow told him everything he needed to know.

Gods, I'm tired.

Strength waning under the timid onslaught of his aggressor, Tantalus regretted leaving Mythfe Ennore so soon after the Fomorian incursion. He had answered the call when the sea demons erupted from the waters to the West of the Elven lands and forged even more legends surrounding his name with their defeat. *The Face of Arcadia,* for that was what they called him, would live long in the minds and tales of the elves.

In his own mind, Tantalus was a simple man, with simple tastes, one of which was battle. As drained as he was, Tantalus would not let some country bumpkin with a desire for easy gold be the one to bring him asunder.

Turning beneath the thief's blade, Tantalus swung his sword around in a full arc, straightened it, and slammed the point into the man's back. The blood drenched tip appeared through his stomach, ending the skirmish.

"Idiot. I have plenty to share. If you'd asked nicely, I might have given you coin," Tantalus growled in the dying man's ears as he slid from the blade and bloodied the dirt beneath him.

Staggering several steps, Tantalus dropped to his knees, sucking up breath and gagging on the dry dust kicked up by the fight.

That was much harder than it should have been.

Reflecting on the attitude of the bandits that attempted to rob him, Tantalus presumed his identity was unknown to them. Well known throughout the southern lands, even before his foray into the Elven-Fomorian war, Tantalus came from the fair-haired race of men that dwelt in the cold climes of the North. In the city of Arcadia, where his beauty held him in higher esteem than his physical presence and abilities, the title, *the Face of Arcadia*, had travelled with him for many years.

Looking up at the three cooling bodies before him, he forgave the brutes their ignorance, but had no regrets about their deaths. Attacking and robbing any traveller was something he simply couldn't countenance and had come to the aid of many in his situation before.

A *whinny* and *snort* floated across to his ears. Looking up, he saw Mythana, his large black stallion. The horse had stood its ground during the battle, turning and kicking at one bandit that sent him flying into Tantalus' blade.

There's more bravery in you than in most men.

Struggling to his feet, Tantalus whistled to the horse, who trotted over, ready to be gone from the area. Sheathing his sword to free his hands, Tantalus patted the big stallion before climbing up into the saddle.

Looking through the closing gloom, Tantalus saw a faint glow over the horizon to the East. "If I remember correctly, Mythana, the little town of Alverton, is just over that rise. They have the best beer in the area. I think a mug of ale, plus a soft bed for me, and a dry stable for you, is just what we need."

The horse *whinnied* as Tantalus flicked the reins and trotted off towards the glow.

Alverton was a tiny farming village nestled in the middle of a vast, open plain. To its east, the river Calliffe, fed by Lake Murkdres, ran down to the join Whitrane River which serviced both Mythfe Ennore to the west, and Cursed Cliffs off in the far south-east.

Tantalus had been heading towards Trader's Bay in the south, hoping to catch a boat sailing north towards Crowfell Harbour or even Riverborough. His months of service under the Elven King had been rewarding, but hard work. He wished to return to Arcadia for a long rest, and to attend to his lands, preparing for his eventual retirement.

It had been quite a while since he last set foot in the little town, almost under the same circumstances.

Several years ago, he had narrowly escaped from a major battle in the north-east with only his sword and armour intact. Bleeding from numerous wounds, he had collapsed on the banks of Deadlinet River and resigned himself to death, when fortune struck as a passing merchant boat spied his prostrate form and dragged him aboard. The Captain, Terrogar, rather than ferry the warrior all the way to Mythfe Ennore, instead turned south and traversed the River Calliffe, depositing Tantalus in Alverton at the Old Goat inn.

Vanessa, the barmaid, had tended to him over the next few weeks, returning him to full health, which they tested often and intensely as Tantalus' strength returned.

Eventually, a patrol of soldiers stopped at the inn. One man recognised Tantalus. Arrested and dragged back to stand trial for desertion, Tantalus stated his case to an older officer. Well revered among the others, he stood in defence, and stated his witness to Tantalus' bravery in the face of overwhelming forces, and to seeing the many wounds ravaging his body as the young warrior fled for his life. Originally listed as missing, presumed among the dead and disfigured, Tantalus' charges were dropped after much deliberation and instead he was awarded one of the highest honours. The officials deduced Tantalus had accounted for at least thirty enemy soldiers, a number that washed away any taint of desertion.

Sitting on the small hill overlooking the town, Tantalus realised it hadn't changed at all in the intervening years. He was sure that the people must have changed, though. Surely Vanessa was swept off her feet by some local farm hand with broad shoulders and arms. Spurring his horse onwards, he aimed to find out.

The door of the Old Goat opened onto a scene from his memory. A thick pall of pipe-weed smoke hung in the air, as if made of thick cobwebs draped from the ceiling. A mix of familiar and new faces turned towards the adventurer as his muscle-bound body filled the doorway.

Tantalus was only interested in one set of eyes, and as the owner slowly turned away from her conversation and focused on him, he smiled widely. Vanessa was still as comely as he remembered. She needed no makeup to look striking, and had an arresting figure that still stirred memories deep within him. But her expression didn't brighten with a smile, instead becoming dark as recognition grew within her.

Two yokels sitting at a table near the entrance turned to each other. "Ain't that Tantalus?" said one.

"Yeah, the Face of Arcadia, init?" said the other, "He was here only a little while ago. I still remember it."

"Yeah, like yesterday it was," said the first.

"You fools need to find lives," said Vanessa as she brushed past their table. "It was four long years ago." Looking at the tall, handsome warrior, a slight sneer crossed her lips as she said, "You look almost as dead as the last time you were here."

"And you still look as beautiful," Tantalus said. "You've been well?"

"Peachy," Vanessa almost spat, "For the first two, I watched that door every day, hoping and praying you'd come through. Then I dreaded every time it opened in case it was you. And now, you've returned. What do you want?"

"I can only apologise for my absence. There are many tales I could tell to explain it, but I feel that would be in vain. For now, all I wish is for a good meal and a bed for the night."

"Fine." With a wave of her hand towards an empty bench near the back of the room, Vanessa left, returning to her duties behind the bar, casting only sneering glances at Tantalus as he pushed through the throngs of customers and sat down.

Almost immediately, the grimy visage of a local farmer spun around and stared directly into Tantalus' eyes. "'ere, ain't you that Face of Arcadia bloke? Lobbed in 'ere 'bout four years ago?"

Nodding his weary head, Tantalus answered, "Yes. I was injured in the great battle of the marshes, North of here. A kind citizen brought me to this place to be healed. I owe my life to the owner of this establishment and his wonderful daughter."

A finger extended and waved towards the warrior. "That's right. You had a fling with young Vanessa, dint you? And then up and left. Nairy a word. She don't half go on about it."

A feeling of regret filled his mind as he held his tongue and slowly answered. "I was arrested and taken from here, yes. I could not get word out for over a year while I underwent a trial to determine my innocence. Then I was sent to Arcadia. I have only recently returned to this land. I hope to have words with Vanessa, but she does not seem acceptable to that."

The yokel sat for a moment, digesting Tantalus' words. Just as he opened his mouth to speak, a rasping voice cut him off. "Varmind, leave the poor man alone. I'll not have my guests beset upon by thoughtless questions." The warrior and farmer looked into the ruddy, but kindly face of Ciaran, the landlord of the Old Goat. As the farmer turned away with one final sneer at Tantalus, Ciaran spoke again. "I do apologise. Mr. Tantalus, Vanessa's in a right state, has been for some time. You two had quite a thing when you were last here. She's not got over it."

"I can only apologise to her. It has taken almost every minute of my time simply to return to this place. If you agree, I will stay for a night or two. Maybe I can find a moment to speak with her."

"That would be good. Now, I understand you need a room?" A nod from Tantalus confirmed the fact. "And some food?"

"Yes, Ciaran, thank you. If I could have a pint of your best ale. I still remember how wonderful it tasted."

Ciaran's face flushed red. Several faces turned towards the pair at the mention of beer. "We... we," the landlord stammered, "We don't have any, Sir. There's not been enough water to brew for weeks."

Confused, Tantalus' brow creased. "What? The mighty River Calliffe is mere yards from this place. The winter rains have washed these lands, leaving the fields as green as ever I've seen. Surely, the river isn't befouled or something?"

Before Ciaran could respond, another man from a nearby table spoke up. “No. It’s worse than befoulment. It’s bewitchment.”

“What do you mean?” asked Tantalus, glancing around and noticing that all conversation had ceased, with all eyes directed at him.

“There’s a spirit,” came a voice from behind him, followed by a barrage of voices.

“Evil spirit,” said another.

“She kills, and poisons the water,” said another.

“No, she doesn’t,” contradicted the first voice. “She’s blocked off the stream from the lake. It won’t flow no more.”

“Aye, that’s what it is. The stream’s been dammed, and we’ve all been damned.”

“It’s evil.”

“We’ll all die.”

Holding up his hands to call for calm, Tantalus, “Woh, please one at a time. Can someone just tell me what’s going on, calmly?” He stared at Ciaran, hoping the landlord would relate the tale.

Obliging, he started. “Several months ago, we noticed the river’s waters drop to a trickle and then stop altogether.”

“Not a drought?”

“No, as you’ve said, we had plenty of rain. The well is full, but we’ve only enough for drinking water. A month after it started, a group went upriver to see what had happened. We thought there must be a blockage, trees down or something. Only one man returned.”

“Mad he was,” said someone near the back. “Went crazy.”

“Yes, he could only talk about a ghost or a monster. Another group went upriver. They wanted to reach Lake Murkdres. That’s where the river starts. They rode more carefully, and returned quickly, with the same tales as the madman.”

“A ghost?”

Nodding, with a murmur of agreement behind him, Ciaran continued, “Yes, they say that the stream is blocked by rocks, and when they approached the lake, it was all quiet and still, until night set. Then they saw her. A shimmering spirit. It was a woman, all dressed in a wedding gown or something similar.

Floating over the still lake, leaving a trail of light on the water."

"Sounds like a wraith," said a quiet, lone voice behind Tantalus.

He turned and spied a hooded figure sitting quietly in the corner of the room, away from all prying eyes. If he didn't know better, Tantalus would have dismissed the figure as a mere shadow, but he had seen his like before. "Madragore?" he said. "I'm surprised to see you in such a well-populated area."

Sitting forward and flicking his hood back to reveal a long mane of raven black hair, with a sharply defined aquiline face, Madragore smiled at Tantalus and replied, "Even mages need to eat."

By way of introducing the spellcaster, Tantalus said, "People of Alverton, let me introduce Madragore of Sefardican. We recently fought the Fomorian sea demons on the shores of the Elven Sea, many leagues from here. A more formidable magician I have never seen. What do you know of these wraiths, then?"

"Nasty. Not easy to kill. Full of vengeance, as they are the spirits of one killed for some petty reason. Pride, jealousy, envy." Madragore sipped from the cup of wine before him, thinking. "If this one has blocked off the river, then it seeks vengeance against someone in this village, or further downstream."

All eyes looked around the room, each man casting suspicious glares at their neighbour.

"How does one stop it?"

"Silver sword would be best. Need to find what binds it to this plane first. May also be some sort of talisman that has caused the wraith's formation. They are very rare, and very dangerous."

"Danger does not frighten me," said Tantalus, "But where will I find such a weapon?"

A deep voice piped up from the other end of the room. "I can probably help you there." Tantalus searched for the owner and spied a dwarf swigging from a bottle of whisky. From the bulging muscles in the arm gripping the bottle, Tantalus realised he had all the hallmarks of a blacksmith. Staring straight back into Tantalus' eyes and ignoring the surrounding mob, he said, "I'm Colm, by the way. The local smithy, but you look like you've figured that out already."

"You have enough silver in stock?" said Tantalus, stepping around from his table and moving towards Colm.

"Nay, but if this lot want that wraith gone, then you, armed with one of my swords," he said, striking his chest with his fist, "Are their best bet."

Thrusting a hand into the satchel slung around his shoulder before slamming it down on the table in front of the dwarf, Tantalus revealed several shiny coins, a necklace and torc made from solid silver. "There, I'm not a man who doesn't put his own money where his mouth is." Turning to face the crowd, he added, "What of the rest of you? I will rid this town of that wraith. I deem it payment for the kind of treatment I received four years ago. Colm here needs silver to forge a weapon capable of dispatching the spectre. How badly do you want it gone?"

A murmur rose amongst the crowd. Many of their heads hung low, the owners avoiding all eye contact with Tantalus.

When no-one moved for several moments, Tantalus shook his head and reached for his donation. "That disappoints me more than anything," he said, grasping the coins and jewellery, dragging it across the table to make his point.

As he raises his fist, ready to place the silver back into his satchel, a female voice broke the silence. "Stop," said Vanessa, pushing her way through the crowd and stopping before Tantalus. Staring the warrior in the eyes, she said, "You'd do this? For us? For no reward?"

Nodding, he said, "The only reward would be to taste the first barrel of beer brewed from those waters."

"Then have done of it," Vanessa said, slamming a fistful of silver jewellery, and the other holding three silver goblets onto the table. "These are mine," she added, turning towards her father. "I'm sure there are other trinkets in this place, to add to the pile."

"Oh, right you are," came Ciaran's reply, as he scooped up several items from behind the bar and trotted on over. As his collection clattered down, the crowd seemed to disappear, clearing out and leaving the room empty of all but those who had donated to the pile of silver items.

"Is that enough?" asked Tantalus.

Colm picked up several pieces and examined them, cocking his head slightly to catch what light he could. "Not quite. I'll lose a lot from separating out the silver and other alloys."

"Damn," said Tantalus, just as the door burst open once more and the motley crew of farmers and tradesmen entered, striding up to the table and dumping their loads of family treasures and knick-knacks onto the growing pile.

Once finished, a slight smile grew on Colm's face. "Now we should have enough."

"How long to finish it?"

Downing the dregs of his wine, before wrapping his huge arms around a collection of the choicer pieces, the smith said, "A few days. I'll get started right away. I've always preferred beer, anyway." Nodding at the remaining pile of metal items, he added, "Get one of these louts to bring the rest of that over to me shop."

"Anall nathrach oothvas bethud doe-chiele dienvay."

"That's right, then your arm must be higher, your hand facing away before you throw your palm down. Try it again. You're almost there."

Tantalus had been working with Madragore for three days to perfect the *Charm of Corporation*. His mind was as fatigued as his body. Sweat beaded on his skin; his brain ached from the tedious repetition of the spell.

Standing still, he took a deep breath, closed his eyes, and calmed his mind. Repeating the incantation, he spun, reached up high, then cast his hand down, opening it at the last moment as if throwing the conjuring across the ground like a handful of dirt.

A tingling sensation erupted from his fingertips. He opened his eyes and almost yelled in delight as a bright purple circle formed, the almost invisible walls shimmering before him.

"Well done. I'll make a mage of you yet," said Madragore.

Stepping through the barrier with ease, Tantalus joined Madragore to study the magical trap he'd created. It glistened in the harsh sunlight, harmless to humans, but a disorienting experience for spirits, forcing them to take form and therefore able to be attacked.

"How long does it last?"

"Depends on the strength of the mage. For you, I'd say thirty seconds." As Madragore finished his sentence, the glittering spectral confine disappeared from view. "It gives you time to attack the wraith, but obviously, you must be quick. Stay inside until the ghost joins you, then exit and give yourself room. You should be able to attack from outside, but be quick. It will recover quickly once it can phase out again."

"You'll be needing more than just a pretty cage then," said a gravelly voice behind them. Tantalus turned to see Colm stride up, holding a weapon sheathed in a new leather scabbard. He handed the weapon to the warrior. "This should help."

Tantalus drew the sword. The blade caught the sunlight and cast a bright shine around the area. The silver had been polished to a gleaming brilliance. "That's magnificent," said Tantalus.

The dwarf stood with his arms crossed across his massive chest and a smile on his face. "Yes, it is, even if I do say so myself. That blade is as keen as any other I've ever forged. I have to say I'm very proud of it. I just hope you can use it to send this wraith thingy off to wherever it should be."

"With this," said Tantalus, holding the sword high, "and Madragore's spell, it should be a simple matter."

The mage didn't look convinced. "I wouldn't get overly cocky if I were you. Not many have faced one and lived to tell the tale."

Early the next morning as Tantalus prepared Mythana for the day long trek to the lake, a lone figure stepped into the stables. A slight grin came to the warrior's face as he recognised Vanessa. Over the last couple of days, he had found time to talk with her. At first, she had been reluctant to even speak with him, but with successive attempts had finally warmed and allowed him to explain.

"Just wanted to wish you good fortune. This is a generous thing you're doing. Any other warrior would just skip out and leave us to our misery," she said.

Tightening the straps holding his breastplate and pauldrons in place, he smiled and said, "This town was kind to me when it didn't need to be. And you were more than kind. If I hadn't been dragged away in chains, I might never have left. When I vanquish this wraith, you never know I may not leave here, or if I do, it may not be alone." The sly grin on his face, giving his countenance an ethereal beauty for which he was well known, and over which he never wore a helmet.

Vanessa, failing to stop a coy grin breaking out on her face, said, "Then we may need to talk when you get back." Turning, she added, "Away with you. The sooner you leave, the sooner you return."

The journey up the deep and normally wide River Calliffe proved quicker and easier than Tantalus has estimated. As the river was little more than a trickle, Tantalus urged Mythana to follow the riverbed, skirting any remaining ponds or puddles along the way. From studying the only map in the town, his best guess was that Murkdres was around ten leagues from Alverton.

The sun was still well above the western horizon when he finally reached the source of the river. The wide headwater, blocked by piles of rocks and tree logs, looked as if a storm had ravaged the lake and pushed them across the path of the stream.

Riding Mythana up the left-hand bank, he hitched him to a sturdy tree and moved to examine the makeshift dam. Water dribbled through the rock pile, telling Tantalus that the pressure was building, and he realised it would be a simple matter of mechanics to loose the torrent once more.

Pulling a slender, but tough looking tree bough from the pile, Tantalus jammed it into a small hole leaking a significant amount. Pulling it towards himself, he strained with all his might before he felt the rock above shift. Smiling, he pulled harder, his arms and chest striving and near to bursting with the effort. Suddenly thrown back against the loose rock wall. The stone gave way and tumbled down into the dry bed below, heralding the return of the mighty river.

With one stone freed, the rest of the wall succumbed to the pressure and flow cascading through the gap in the dam. Wood and rocks toppled from the dam wall, washed away downstream.

Climbing the small rise to the edge of the lake, Tantalus stared at the calm waters of Murkdres, gently lapping at the rock and sand lined shore. Beyond, the mountain range climbed up to the wide barren plateau marking the realm of Kralia, bordered the southern edge, with the late sunlight shimmering off the myriad streams that fed Murkdres with the purest of waters.

On the eastern shore, Tantalus spied two small buildings, possibly fishermen's huts, used by nearby farmers on trips to supplement their marketable crops. Legends told of the teeming fish life in Lake Murkdres.

A gentle breeze blew Tantalus' long golden hair, his nose immediately recoiling in disgust at the smell it brought. The stench of rot suddenly enveloped him in its folds. Burying his nose into the crook of his arm, Tantalus studied the corpses. They lay where they'd died. Their eyes were wide in terror. Their faces and chests split wide with multiple long and deep wounds. From their dress, he realised these were the men sent from Alverton.

These are not knife or sword wounds.

Tantalus studied the long lacerations criss-crossing the nearest corpse's chest.

Almost like beast claws.

Glancing around, he sought any evidence of paw marks, but the boggy ground belied all suggestion. The only prints were those of the men.

The wraith then.

Looking once more at the unfortunate townsfolk, Tantalus committed to a proper burial when time permitted. He turned and led Mythana towards the fishing shack. Night was coming. He needed shelter and a safe haven.

Finding a small, grassed area behind the shack, Tantalus took the saddle from his horse's back and let him graze in peace. Stepping onto the porch, he placed the saddle and bags down before trying the door. It opened easily, allowing him entry into the darkened cabin.

Very trusting these folk.

The cottage was no simple fishermen's hut. Tantalus was amazed. Brushing his fingertips across them, he could feel the soft, delicate furnishings and accessories that could only have been the work of a woman. The sitting room had a small fireplace on one side, with a chair covered with a crocheted rug, and fine lace doilies on the arms, sitting beside it. Some unfinished knitting sat in a small basket beside the chair.

A small table with two chairs sat near the kitchen area. It was set for dinner, with two place settings and a full jug of wine in the centre. All were now covered with a thin layer of dust. They had never been used.

Two settings. Company?

The kitchen itself was well stocked, but the meal, never eaten, still lay in the cooking pot, stone cold now that the fire had died in the hearth. The vegetables to accompany the meal had rotted away, lending a sweet, but putrid stench to the place.

She was cooking. Then why did she leave?

Intrigued, Tantalus pushed through the only interior door and found a bedroom. In one corner, a small table sat, in another a free-standing clothes cupboard. The bed, pushed into the far corner, was neatly made but never slept in. A thick layer of dust covered the sheets.

The bed is too neat, even for a fastidious woman. She was expecting someone to use it with her.

Moving to the makeup table, it took Tantalus a moment to decipher the scene. In stark contrast to the rest of the house, this corner was a mess. Several pots of powder were knocked over, the fine dust covering the tabletop and much of the floor. From the marks in the powder on the floor, Tantalus realised that the small three-legged stool had fallen, but then righted. A hairbrush and hand mirror lay in the powder on one side, but it was the dark stain on the floor that drew the warrior's attention.

The powder had drifted across the tiny pool, soaking in, and giving it a dusty appearance. Extending a finger, he touched the stain. It had dried and hardened, but still left a dark reddish-brown smear on his fingertip. He sniffed his finger but could only smell the powder residue.

Must be blood.

Movement nearby caught his eye. Glancing around, all he found were the brush and mirror. Confused, he reached out and picked up the mirror to examine it.

The craftsmanship was exquisite. It was made of silver, with intricate patterns of intertwined vines of ivy and other flowers winding around the frame, handle, and across the back. It was the shape that was most intriguing. Instead of being oval, it was angular, with six sides, but none was the same length. It occurred to Tantalus that the mirror frame looked formed to match the glass, rather than the glass cut to fit the mirror.

It was looking into the mirror's reflection that shocked him to his core. Tantalus was the first to admit to anyone that would listen. Nothing shocked him, but seeing another's reflection looking back at him from within the mirror came close to ending that.

The face in the reflection was a young woman, quite beautiful. She wasn't looking at him, but obviously herself, putting on her makeup and fixing her hair.

In readiness to meet a lover, perhaps?

In the reflection, the woman's face suddenly wrinkled up in agony. As the mirror fell to the floor, there was a blur of motion across the surface. It settled and showed the woman briefly seated on a stool before she slipped from view and revealed the face of her killer. It was a face Tantalus already knew. A man from the Old Goat.

The murderer was her lover, not a thief. If he was innocent, her lover would have raised the alarm when he arrived and found the body. Nobody else has been here for months.

Stepping out from the bedroom, Tantalus realised he still held the mirror. Looking into the glass once more, he saw his own countenance. Placing the mirror on the table, his eyes spied a trail of blood leading to the front door. Exiting onto the porch, he detected further drops on the steps and nearby dirt. The trail led off towards the lake shore.

At the muddy edge, deep footprints led from the shore, with

lighter ones leading away.

Without another thought, Tantalus strode out into the water. Drawing his steel sword, he held it out before him, moving it through the clouds of mud kicked up by his impromptu entrance. After several minutes, the weapon snagged something lying on the lakebed. Prodding the object lightly with the tip, he realised it was large enough to be a body.

Sheathing his blade, Tantalus ducked below the water and grabbed the object, dragging it to the surface. Even prepared for the worst, his stomach tightened at the sight of the woman's body. Her face was bloated, with ragged holes of raw flesh where the lake's denizens had feasted. As her head bobbed on the lake's surface, her clouded eyes seemed to stare at him with accusations, dropping away as he stood to full height.

Wading ashore, Tantalus found a flat spot and gently lay the poor woman's corpse on the ground. Quickly scouting the area, he arranged a pile of dry wood beneath and all around the body. Using his tinder box, he had flames licking at the wet body within moments. Adding more wood, the pyre was soon well aflame.

"You deserve a proper burial, but I need to have you consumed by fire, to send a signal," Tantalus said to the burning corpse.

And then the wraith arrived.

A high-pitched shriek split the silence. Spinning, Tantalus saw the waters in the middle of the lake shimmer with iridescence before the spectre erupted and hovered above the surface. Purple light spilled across the glass-like water as the phantom circled, its claw-like hands opening and closing as its very existence caused it agony.

Finally spying Tantalus, it glided above the water towards him. Its visage was nothing like the beautiful woman in the mirror, or even the bloated corpse pulled from the waters. This was an apparition of hell. A skeletal face bereft of skin. Empty eye sockets filled instead with a burning purple fire. Long, lank wisps of silver hair fell from the skull, trailing out as the spectre flew towards Tantalus, similarly the ragged strips of fabric, which had all the hallmarks of a wedding dress. This was not the woman who had died, but the embodiment of her emotions and pain, and her betrayal at the hands of her lover.

Drawing the silver sword which shone bright blue, a little trick employed by Madragore, Tantalus held it to the side and raised an open hand. "Stop," he called to thespirit . "You hold this woman's spirit in bondage. Let her leave and rest in peace."

The wraith halted, mere yards from the warrior, its flaming eyes staring at him as one would observe the foulest of excrements. A screeching voice cut through the evening. "She was betrayed. I'm here to exact revenge for her. All shall perish until the deceiver is found."

"Why block the river?"

"He farms in the valley beyond. Without water, he shall die."

"So will many others."

"Not my concern."

"They are mine. Begone from this place."

"Never." The wraith's screams filled Tantalus' ears, his head threatening to explode. Darting forward, the spectre caught him off guard. Its talons slashed at him, catching the plated armour and ripping it from his chest.

Tantalus crashed backwards to the dusty ground. Struggling back to his feet, he tore off the loose breastplate and threw it away. Scanning the area to locate the wraith, he realised he was once more alone. A shiver ran up his back. Not knowing was far worse that knowing where his foe was.

A sudden chill behind him warned of the wraith's appearance. Spinning, Tantalus brought up his sword just in time to block an attack as the spectre materialised behind and slashed with its enlarged talons. It disappeared immediately.

Not one to know panic, his chest tightened as he realised the might of the foe he faced. Human, elves, dwarves, all were easy to understand. They were there to hit or be hit. This thing chose its own path.

A purple glow appeared before him, followed by the whistling of the wind. His face erupted in pain as the wraith's nails rent deep wounds across it. Blood ran down into his eyes, clouding his vision. Wiping the blood away, he swayed for a moment, took a deep breath, and peered around.

Suddenly, a line of gashes formed on his unclad chest, as the wraith materialised, attacked, and disappeared within seconds. Tantalus howled in pain. Blood seeped down his front, staining the dirt, to join the unfortunate woman's. A *screeching* sound rang out as sharp nails left deep rents in his right pauldron, slashing halfway through the leather strap. The ghost wasn't just attacking, but strategically removing his armour.

Scanning around for a hint of the wraith's purple light, Tantalus fended off several more attacks, before the spectre struck from behind, severing the leather strap. The now useless pauldron dropped to the ground, leaving Tantalus' shoulder bare. Talons raked across the open flesh, scything through the meat, and virtually disabling the warrior's right arm.

Dropping to his knees, he looked skyward through bleary eyes. His skills as a fighter were of no use against the wraith. His only hope was magic. Fighting the injury to his shoulder, he raised his right arm, pushing his palm outward, and shouted, "Anall nathrach oothvas bethud doe-chiele dienvay," before throwing the hand to the ground. A shimmering purple cage grew around him.

It worked.

His joy was short-lived as the wraith flew towards him, slashing his chest and opening up new bloody wounds. Thrown backwards, Tantalus tumbled from the magic trap and lay sprawled in the dirt. He sucked breath into his ravaged chest, as the shrieks and cries of the trapped phantom echoed across the still lake.

Got to move.

Dragging himself to his feet, he looked at the furious spectre and raised the shimmering silver sword.

"Now to send you back to hell."

Staggering forward, Tantalus used his momentum to swing the weapon in a wide arc. It slashed through the iridescent trap, slicing through the wraith's neck, and launching the head out the other side.

As the head lay smouldering on the cool dirt, a stream of obscenities and screams erupted before it burst into flames and smoke and disappeared from view. The wraith's body collapsed inside the trap and disintegrated in a cloud of ash that blew away on a sudden, strong breeze.

The glittering trap disappeared, throwing Tantalus into the dark of the approaching night. Sign of his victory now only dust on the wind.

Dropping to his knees, he said, "Thank you Alverton, my service is done." Wavering, he collapsed face first into the dirt.

A blurry figure leaned over Tantalus, then disappeared. He blinked, trying to focus as a voice cut through the fog in his mind.

"He's awake, he's awake."

It took Tantalus a moment to realise the voice belonged to Vanessa. Groggily, he tried to rise. He coughed a stream of curses, as a tearing pain in his chest forced him down again.

A darker shape moved from behind Vanessa, stepping close to Tantalus. It was the mage, Madragore. He lifted his right hand, showing Tantalus the odd-shaped mirror. "Well done, warrior," he said.

Tantalus frowned, "How? How did I get here?"

"When the waters returned, and you didn't, the townsfolk realised the monster was gone, and became concerned for you. They raced to the lakefront, seeking you. You were found inside a rundown hovel, unconscious in a pool of your own blood, and holding this mirror."

"I... I don't remember any of that. I killed the wraith, but then nothing."

"You're lucky to be alive." Nodding towards Tantalus, Madragore added, "Those wounds in your chest were very deep. If you weren't such a powerful man, you'd be crow food. I'm sorry I couldn't do much more for your arm. You won't ever get full use back. As to the scars on your face. I don't think you'll keep your title."

Tantalus shook his head. "Thank you for your aid. Looks fade. Mine faster than most, it seems." He frowned with sudden concern. "There was a woman murdered by her lover. I saw his face; in that mirror you're holding."

"Her name was Erin, a former member of the witch council. That is possibly how she came by the mirror."

"What is it?"

"If I'm correct, this was formed from the shard of a cursed mirror, broken many years ago and scattered across the land."

"The woman's murder. I saw it in the glass."

"Yes, and so did I. And many of the villagers."

"Her killer?"

Madragore smiled grimly, "The elders recognised him as Feargal and with very little pressure, he confessed and was banished. He had become besotted with the witch but feared his wife would find out, and so he killed Erin to hide his dalliance. The wife was certain he'd been having an affair during his many hunting trips. When it was revealed, she took to him with a knife. If not for the other villagers, he would be dead. He was last seen heading down river. You've done well, warrior. Your wounds are deep and will require much time to heal. Sleep now, you've earned it."

It took almost a month for Tantalus' wounds to close, and his strength to return to a point where he could leave his bed and join the townsfolk in the main room of the inn. He shuffled in, helped with every step by Vanessa and the people cheered him to a seat set aside for him.

Grimacing with pain as he sat, Tantalus could only smile into the adoring eyes of his nursemaid. Vanessa had forgiven him for his supposed transgressions and now doted on him almost every minute of the day.

She returned with a steaming bowl of the day's stew and a large mug of freshly brewed beer.

"Beer?" he asked.

Vanessa smiled. "Yes, as soon as the waters began to flow, we started a new brew." Glancing across at the dark clad mage in the corner, she added, "Madragore cast a little spell over it to speed up the process, especially for you."

Tantalus noticed all eyes in the room were fixed on him in

anticipation. Smiling, he picked up the mug with his left hand and took a long draw. Smacking his lips, he said, "Just as good as I remember it." He put the mug on the table and gestured at the gathered patrons. "Beer for you all on this glorious day," he yelled.

Tantalus leaned back and drank deeply from his mug once more. He smiled at Vanessa. "I think this shall be the first of many brews that I taste. My wounds are deep. It's going to take many more months before I am fully healed."

Vanessa smiled broadly, her eyes brightening in happiness.

"And by the time my full strength returns, I doubt my wanderlust will have returned. You might have to put up with me for a very long time to come."

"I think we should be able to find something for you to do."

"Good," he said, and took another long drink. Life was going to be much quieter for the man who once held the title of *the Face of Arcadia*.

Children of the Woods

Amber M. Simpson

Knock, knock, knock.

Ruby's eyes snapped open, two deep pools of reflected moonlight as it spilled through the open window. She listened as her mother, Vera, moved through the small house to answer the late-night caller. As low murmurs slipped through the cracks around the bedroom door, Ruby bolted upright in bed at the voice of Matilda Darby.

Matilda Brookson, now, Ruby thought with disgust. What was Jonah's new wife doing here in the middle of the night?

She slid out from beneath her blanket and tiptoed to the door, careful not to step on the few rotten floorboards that creaked loudly. Easing the door open a crack, she peered out into the sitting room, a dim halo of light reaching out from the dying fireplace in the corner. Though she couldn't see her mother and Matilda from this angle, she was able to catch snippets of their hushed conversation, mainly Matilda's voice.

"…know it's late…I've brought payment…desperate for help…"

Her mother's voice was a low growl in response, sending goose prickles up Ruby's arms. Vera Sloan was not known to be a kind woman and most certainly not a kind parent. But it was well known in the village that Vera was a powerful woman—in demeanor and skill—and she served as the closest thing to a doctor the villagers had. And though Ruby never questioned her and was excluded from much, if not all, of Vera's business, she knew that her mother aided the people of Meere beyond the simple realm of medicine.

From what little Vera had shared with Ruby, she knew they descended from the Fae, which was probably why Vera had so much talent in the ways of magic. Ruby had always been interested in learning more about her roots, but whenever she broached the subject, Vera would turn nasty and vicious, refusing to speak of it, so eventually Ruby stopped asking.

"Come," Vera intoned, and Ruby held her breath as the shadowy figures of her mother and Matilda materialized in her range of vision. Vera strode across the room to rummage about in a desk drawer against the wall while Matilda stood waiting, her hands twisting nervously at her abdomen.

Ruby smiled, delighted at the young woman's unease. She couldn't summon even an ounce of sympathy. After all, Matilda had stolen Jonah from her, hadn't she?

Jonah. It still spread a slow trickle of warmth throughout her body at the thought of him. He had been her best friend—her only friend—since she was a young child. Because their home stood on the very outskirts of Meere, surrounded by woods at every angle, Ruby had grown up severely isolated from others. And because Vera had forbidden her from so much as stepping foot off the small secluded property without her permission or attendance, there were few opportunities to make friends.

Ruby had always felt it was the large, garish birthmark that covered the entire left side of her face that caused her mother to keep her so hidden away. Scarlet red, it began at her neck, a series of crooked and twisted lines resembling tree roots. From there it crawled its way up over her cheek and eye—the lashes scarce, the eyelid puffy—before climbing her forehead and vanishing into her hairline. It was her mother's favorite place to strike her when angry, as if she wished to slap the unfortunate mark away.

It wasn't until she had met Jonah—after a particularly traumatic experience at the age of ten—that she felt less ashamed of herself. Ruby had accompanied her mother on a rare venture into the village and was waiting for her outside of the butcher's when a group of cruel children attacked, throwing rocks and calling her *Monster.* Though their words hurt far worse than their rocks, one of them cut a gash in her forehead, releasing a stream of blood into her left eye. With a yelp, Ruby had run from the children as hard as she could, until her legs gave out and she tripped and fell. As she lay in the dirt panting, slow footsteps approached.

"Hello, are you all right?" It was a boy, about Ruby's age, not one from the rock-throwing group. His face looked kind, not cruel. He reached out a hand and pulled her to her feet.

Jonah.

Not wanting him to see her face, she tried to cover it with her hood, but Jonah simply pulled a handkerchief from his pocket and wiped at the blood and dirt, softly pushing her hands away to do so. If the birthmark upset him, he didn't show it in the slightest. It was the smile in his eyes and the gentle touch of his hands that had sent that first trickle of warmth throughout Ruby's body, leaving no room for the cold abyss of self-loathing the cruel children had tried to fill her with.

When she returned to her mother—having *run off* and *filthy*—she didn't feel the sting of the slap across the mark on her face; all she felt was the soft caress of Jonah's handkerchief. And as the weeks turned to months, and the months to years, Ruby harbored in her heart a secret love for the boy who had saved her that day in the village, from what would surely have been a lonesome and torturous existence without him. The friendship they shared had been the only good thing in Ruby's life, so it was a complete and utter devastation when, two years ago, Jonah met and quickly married Matilda Darby from the next village over. Since the wedding, Jonah rarely visited, too busy at home attending to a spoiled, demanding wife.

Now, Ruby glared through the crack in the door at Matilda's shadowy figure. She swallowed hard at the lump of hatred that burned in her throat, sour as rotten milk. It made her sick to think of Jonah's gentle hands touching that abhorrent woman when they should be touching Ruby instead. The thought of Jonah lying in bed beside that wretch each night, when he should be lying beside—

Vera slammed shut the desk drawer, giving a Ruby a start,

and yanking her from her thoughts. Approaching Matilda, Ruby caught the glimmer of the object in her mother's hand twinkling ominously from the dim light of the fireplace: a dagger. Ruby stifled a surprised gasp as she realised the kind of help Matilda had come to Vera for.

Seeing the dagger in Vera's hand, Matilda stumbled back, nearly tripping over the hem of her gown. But Vera was as impatient as she was mean, and she snatched Matilda's hand, slicing the blade across her palm too swiftly for the young woman to do more than cry out in pain. She grabbed a small cup from the rickety table beside them and held it beneath Matilda's bleeding, shaking hand.

Matilda sputtered wildly, obviously dumbfounded by what had just occurred, but Vera cut her off with a snap.

"You want this baby, don't you?"

Matilda shut her mouth then, though Ruby could see the glittering tears continue to slide down her face as Vera filled the cup with blood. With one quick motion, she flung her head back, the cup to her lips, and drained it. Matilda watched, wide-eyed, her injured hand clutched tightly to her chest.

Ruby nodded. She was right. Matilda was having trouble making a baby, and in her desperation, had come to Vera Sloan, known as Fae doctor. For a moment, Ruby was triumphant, reveling in the fact that for once, Matilda had found it difficult to get what she wanted. But that also meant Jonah could not have a baby, and Ruby knew how much he had always wanted to be a father. One of their favorite childhood games had been "Family," in which Jonah played the father, she the mother, and they raised a whole brood of imaginary children.

Ruby ground her teeth. Poor Jonah. He had picked the wrong woman to wed, just as she'd always known.

"Now go," Vera barked, licking her lips and pointing at the front door. "Your hand will heal overnight, and you'll have your baby at the next full moon, not a day before."

Matilda sputtered a thank you and all but ran from the house as Ruby sank back away from the door and dropped to her bed, thinking.. She had seen this part so many times—a woman coming to the house on a full moon begging her mother for help, paying with coin and blood. Afterwards, Vera would disappear to the woods and not return until morning. She would hide herself away in her room until the next full moon, when Ruby would hear her sneak out in the night. Beyond that... Ruby knew nothing. Once, she had tried to follow, hoping to discover the next part of the ritual but had been caught and paid the price: locked in her room and starved for a week.

But that was years ago... and this time it involved Jonah. Ruby had to know how her mother did it—had to know where Jonah's baby was going to come from. So, as her mother prepared to leave, Ruby did as well.

Moving fast, she slid on her boots and threw a cloak over her nightdress. She followed her mother from the house and kept a safe distance as Vera traversed the thick woods that stretched endlessly into the night.

The full moon cast its pale glow through the treetops, scattering in fragmented pieces across the branch and leaf-strewn ground. Ruby had just enough light to trail her mother without losing her, though the longer she spent in the woods, the more her senses heightened, until she could easily distinguish her mother's shape in the dark. The woods were alive with sound; the crickets' song a lullaby, the owls' hoot a cry of welcome. Her feet knew exactly where to step to avoid alerting Vera of her presence as Ruby glided through the woods as smoothly as if through water.

The deeper into the woods she moved, the deeper the sense of tranquility enveloped her. She had never been this far into the woods before, but they were somehow as familiar to her as if she had grown roots there herself. How could that be?

Ahead, her mother's footsteps stopped, and Ruby positioned herself behind a large oak to study the small clearing her mother had entered. Apart from the moonlight, which filled the open space unmolested from densely clumped trees, a large circle of mushrooms basked beneath the full moon's glow. Ruby's eyes widened in wonder. A fairy ring, here, in the woods behind their home? Though Ruby was largely ignorant of the stories of the Fae in her own lineage, she had heard tales of the Fae in general, and of the fairy rings they sometimes used in their magic. It had never occurred to her that her mother may make use of one herself.

Vera stripped away her cloak and gown, her pale flesh shining with a bright luminescence. Naked, she got to her knees and lifted a large rock that rested at one end of the clearing. She dug for a moment with her bare hands before pulling from the dirt a glass crystal hanging from a cord of leather. As she stood and approached the fairy ring with the necklace cord clutched in one hand, the mushrooms swayed from side to side as if beckoning her closer.

Unaware she was even moving, Ruby left the safety of the tree and came closer to the clearing. Vera stepped into the center of the ring and flung her arms out as if to embrace the moon. She spoke in a garbled and unfamiliar tongue. Ruby tried to make out any recognizable words, and though there were a few, she thought she might have glimpsed in Vera's books—always forbidden from her own perusal, of course—she couldn't be sure.

Vera's voice grew louder, stronger, slicing through the night air as sharp as the dagger had sliced through Matilda's palm. The crystal swung erratically from the cord in Vera's hand and lit up from within—a bright effervescent blue. As she brought her hands together preparing to put the necklace on, a shudder passed through her body and dove straight into the ground, lighting the mushrooms up with their own icy blue light.

"And so tonight, I come to thee," Vera spoke clearly, "and ask that you provide a child for the one whose blood I have consumed. I shall act as your vessel and a child shall be made. And I will give to thee as I have always given."

"No!" Ruby's cry rang out through the trees just as Vera was about to slip the necklace over her head. Anger and indignation thrust her forward as she rushed into the clearing and joined her mother in the ring.

"You will *not* give that wicked woman Jonah's baby," Ruby spat, her hatred for Matilda momentarily overriding her fear of her mother. "I won't allow it!" She snatched the necklace from Vera's hands, grabbing it by the crystal. The moment it touched her, Ruby's flesh burned as if on fire, and a violent shudder ran through her—much stronger than the one she'd seen flow through Vera. It coursed down her legs and into the ground, where the very earth shook as if by an earthquake.

"You stupid, selfish cow," Vera hissed as the mushrooms shot up and twisted around her arms and legs, pulling her away. Ruby's anger evaporated as her mother was forced from the ring.

"What's happening?" she cried, dread coiling in her belly like a snake.

"You've interrupted the ritual," Vera spat from outside the circle. "The crystal has made its mark on you. Now *you* must become the vessel!"

"No!" Ruby dropped the necklace in the dirt where the light immediately went out. She tried to run from the ring but was met with resistance—she was trapped. Panicked, she ran along the inner perimeter of the circle, trying desperately to break free.

The woods became deathly silent, and Vera whispered, "He has come." Ruby whipped her head around to find a pair of glowing red eyes watching her from the trees. "You must dance for him," Vera said.

"Dance?" Ruby sputtered, incredulous. Her legs trembled with fear and she was doubtful of their ability to hold her up, let alone lead her in a dance.

"Put the necklace on," Vera barked, her face a mask of fury. "You've brought this on yourself!"

"But, Mother, I—" Ruby began, but Vera had faded back into the trees, leaving Ruby alone in the clearing. She bent to retrieve the necklace, her hands shaking uncontrollably. She hadn't known what to expect when she'd barged in to stop her mother, but it certainly wasn't this.

She slid the leather cord over her head, the crystal resting against her chest. Almost immediately, it lit up once again, this time a glowing red to match the watching eyes. Ruby cried out in surprise as her limbs moved of their own accord, leading her in a frantic dance around the ring. Faster and faster, harder and harder she danced, the glowing red eyes never blinking or moving away from her.

Hours went by, though it seemed more like days, and Ruby

felt she might pass out from exhaustion. But once the moon dipped low behind the trees, making way for the sun to rise, the hold on Ruby's body released her and she fell in a heap to the ground.

In the fetal position, she sobbed into the earth, a mess of pain and fatigue. The fiery-eyed creature finally stepped into the clearing as Ruby's exhaustion carried her off into darkness.

Ruby woke in bed, the covers pulled tight to her chin. Sunlight streamed in through the open window, hammering at her skull. She felt her mother's presence in the room—the air hung heavy with the weight of her wrath.

"You're a damn fool," said the low, deep growl, which never failed to claw its way up Ruby's spine. "You stuck your nose where it didn't belong and now you must bear the burden!"

Without warning, her mother ripped the blankets from Ruby's body, exposing the huge swollen bump at her midsection. Ruby gasped at the impossibly round belly in disbelief, dark purple veins bulging along each side.

"What's happening?" she screamed, a wave of panic washing over her. She pushed at her stomach as if she could force the bulbous horror from her body by sheer will alone.

"You brought this upon yourself," her mother spat, her face twisted in revulsion. "He only gifts his seed once per full moon, and you took it!" Strong, bony hands clamped down on Ruby's forearm, sharp fingernails digging into her flesh. "You're lucky he didn't simply kill you instead! All these years I've kept you out of those woods, protected you from him, kept you safe! I never dreamed you would disobey me this way. How dare you snatch the crystal from me and claim its magic for yourself? You have no idea the power it holds—a power you're not worthy of!"

Ruby realized she was still wearing the necklace. She tried to take it off, but the crystal stayed firmly in place against her chest, attached by some magical force.

"You can't remove it now. You must wear it until the next full moon," Vera fumed. "That's how the magic works."

"What magic?! Where did this come from?!" Even as Ruby

asked, she didn't expect much of a response, so it surprised her when Vera calmly answered.

"That crystal has been in our family for many years, passed down each generation. It was created using a magical bit of glass, though some would say "cursed" is the better word. Though I've learned to harness its power effectively over the years, it can be dangerous in even the most experienced of hands. That's why I prefer to keep it buried deep in the woods, far enough away to do any harm when not in use." Vera eyed the crystal at Ruby's chest, a line deepening between her eyebrows. "Let's hope it takes you to the next full moon."

"What happens then?"

Vera's neutral tone switched back to one of cruelty. "Stupid cow, you're going to give the Darby girl her baby, as I would have done if you hadn't been wandering where you don't belong!"

The crystal flashed hot against Ruby's flesh at the same moment that she felt a sharp kick in her stomach. The anger that had rushed through her the night before returned, and she lurched out of bed.

"You expect me to give that wretched woman this baby?" Vera was mad if she thought Ruby would ever do such a thing, no matter how the child had come into being! Looking down at her distended belly, she found she was holding it, cradling it protectively.

Vera sighed, and for the first time, Ruby was aware of just how old her mother had become. Gone were the vibrant chestnut locks Ruby herself had so long coveted, replaced by wispy strands of gray. Dark bags hung beneath her eyes, and wrinkles crisscrossed her flesh in pale indentations.

"It is naught but a mirror pregnancy. The Darby girl will have woken this morning big with a child herself. It is the magic of the woods, the magic of the crystal… and the demon whose seed you took."

"The demon?" Had she gotten a good look at the being with glowing red eyes before her world turned to black? He had entered the fairy ring, and—

"You shouldn't have been there!" her mother screeched. "Now

look what you've done! Whether or not you like it, you and that girl are connected through this pregnancy; connected through the magic and her blood. If there hadn't been a few drops left in that cup, I've no idea what kind of trouble you'd be in! As it were, I was able to get them down on you while you slept. At the very least, you should thank me, you selfish dolt!"

Ruby gagged, at once aware of the coppery taste of blood in her mouth. Running to the chamber pot in the corner of the room, she fell to her knees and retched a thin stream of vomit.

"What's done is done!" her mother cried from behind her. "At the next full moon, the Darby girl will birth the beautiful baby she's always wanted, and you…" Her voice trailed off and Ruby stood from the chamber pot on shaky legs to face her. "You will return that thing inside you to the woods whence it came."

"I'll do no such thing!" Ruby growled with clenched fists, stepping closer to her mother.

"You will!" Vera bellowed, spittle flying from her lips. "It is a child of the woods and it has no place here! Its very existence is unnatural beyond the confines of the ritual! It's nothing but a monster—an *abominable* monster—like *you*!"

The slap rang out loud and clear, bouncing off the walls and landing like glass in Ruby's ears. Her mouth dropped open in disbelief. Had she really just struck her own mother? The woman she'd been afraid of her entire life? So many times, she had suffered abuse at Vera's hands, but never once had she considered retribution.

Her mother's eyes clouded over before she grabbed Ruby by the hair and yanked hard.

"You wretched little witch!" Vera screamed, hitting the birthmarked side of her face in a flurry of sharp smacks. "I never should've kept you! I should've thrown you out into the woods the moment I had you! All you've done is bring me misery and fear! You stupid, senseless little—" They both froze at the sound of knocking on the front door.

"You are not to be seen!" Vera hissed with one last jerk of Ruby's hair. She left the room with a swishing of skirts and promptly locked Ruby inside. Ear pressed tight to the door,

Ruby could hear Matilda, her voice full of joy. She didn't have to guess why. She ran back to the chamber pot to be sick. So, just like that, Matilda would have her baby with Jonah, yet Ruby was expected to… what? Just throw hers in the woods to be eaten by the first wild animal that happened upon it? To sacrifice it back to the demon who had forced it on her to begin with? It would all seem so absurd and so ridiculously insane if Ruby had grown up as the child of anyone other than the village Fae witch doctor.

Days turned into weeks and Ruby spent them all locked in her room. Her belly was larger each morning when she woke, the veins changing color from purple to black. She tried at various times early on to remove the necklace, but each time, the crystal would not budge. Occasionally it would heat up and burn fiercely—a red-hot sensation that permeated into the very core of her being, keeping her anger ablaze.

She wasn't sure when the next full moon was expected, but she could feel it drawing closer—an eerie sense of impending doom. Each day she felt sicker, stranger. Some nights she felt the baby squirm inside her and on those nights, her dreams were vivid and wild. Dreams of the child in her womb whispering to her, demanding she kill Matilda and the imposter child she grew. As demented as it seemed, Ruby couldn't deny the joy she felt upon waking as she envisioned raising *her* baby with Jonah instead—a true family, at last. The more dreams she had, the more convinced she became; if one was naught but a "mirror pregnancy" why shouldn't it be Matilda's? After all, Matilda wasn't the one who'd been forced to dance and implanted with the magic seed.

One morning as Ruby paced about her room, cradling and crooning to her belly, her mother entered. Ruby was surprised to see that instead of holding her breakfast, she was holding the dagger from her desk drawer—the one she had used to cut Matilda's hand the night of the last full moon.

"The time has come," Vera said, her face cold and expressionless. "Tonight, you will go when the moon is highest and stand within the ring. You'll use this to cut the cord. After."

Cut the cord…cut the cord…

Ruby stared at her mother, her words echoing in her mind. The baby kicked; the crystal grew hot.

"Did you hear me, girl?" Vera spat, stomping closer to push her face into Ruby's. "Have you gone deaf and dumb?"

Cut the cord…cut the cord…

When Ruby continued to stare at her in silence, Vera slapped her birthmarked cheek. The baby kicked fiercely, as if it, too, had felt the blow, and just like in her dreams, Ruby heard it whispering in her head. Without a second thought, she obeyed the voice and snatched the dagger from Vera's hand.

Once, then twice, Ruby plunged the blade into the side of Vera's neck, bright blood spurting wildly from the wounds.

Vera garbled something unintelligible, one hand reaching to cover her neck, the other one groping for Ruby, who laughed and slapped the feeble hand away. Watching her mother slide to the floor, the baby's joy spread from Ruby's womb and radiated throughout her entire body until she was absolutely vibrating with it.

"Your power over me has ended," Ruby whispered, looming over her mother's pathetic, blood-soaked body.

"M-m-mons-ster," Vera muttered. Blood burbled from her mouth to coat her chin, her eyes wide and accusing.

"The only monster here is you." The blade sliced through every inch of flesh it could reach, Ruby panting with her efforts. The baby danced with glee inside her, the crystal burning at her chest. When finally the baby calmed and stilled, Ruby calmed as well. She straightened up from the floor and stared at the bloody mess of torn and mangled flesh that once had been her mother. Her gaze lingered on her face, eyes slashed and oozing in their sockets. They didn't look so accusing anymore.

Ruby tried to remember what it had felt like to fear this woman every day of her life, yet long for her love and affection at the same time. She couldn't seem to conjure up the memory. She felt only a deep well of disgust at herself for allowing this blob of blood and bones to control her entire life.

No more. She had cut the cord, all right.

A small kick in her belly spurred her on. Grabbing a blanket, Ruby threw it over the mess, then went to wash up and dress for the village. She made sure to cover herself appropriately, so as not to reveal the secret at her midsection.

Approaching the Brookson home an hour later, Ruby drew her cloak more tightly around her, hoping Jonah wasn't there. She knew he should be working in town at this time, but the fear of seeing him in this moment twisted her insides. When Matilda answered the door, Ruby nearly gagged at the look of happiness that shone from the girl's pretty face. Rubbing and stroking her own big belly, the girl flaunted her pregnancy as if she'd earned it herself. Ruby struggled to keep her face from betraying what she felt.

"Good morning, Matilda," she said through gritted teeth. "I see my mother has come through for you. Congratulations are in order."

"Oh, yes, your mother is simply brilliant," Matilda gushed. "Please, won't you tell her again how thankful I am? She has truly blessed me and my Jonah!"

Ruby bit down hard at the sound of Jonah's name coming from those wretched lips, and the taste of her own blood coated her tongue.

"So you've told him, then? How the baby came to be?" Jonah knew what her mother was capable of, of course, but Ruby wasn't sure how he'd feel knowing his wife had used Vera's services for such an intimate matter—Ruby's own services, to be exact.

"Well, no," Matilda faltered, her eyes dropping down in embarrassment. "You won't tell him, will you, Ruby?"

"How did you explain the belly, then?" Ruby asked, ignoring the question.

"I did exactly what your mother told me to." Matilda bobbed her head up and down. "She told me I should keep my body well covered at all times, and not to, um, lie with Jonah until the deed was done. Then when I woke with child, I could tell him I'd been keeping it secret, afraid to disappoint him should something go wrong. We've been trying since our wedding, of course, but the pregnancies… they never worked." She hung her head, and for just the tiniest inkling of a moment, Ruby felt something like guilt. The feeling passed, however, as Matilda added, "I know it's deceitful, but we wanted this baby more than anything and now, thanks to your mother, our prayers have been answered!"

"Yes, well, it's my mother who sent me here," Ruby lied, shifting uncomfortably. Her back ached and her feet hurt from the long walk to Matilda's. "The full moon approaches. Tonight, you'll have your baby, but my mother must be there to ensure a safe and healthy delivery. You must come when the moon is highest, so she may assist your birth."

"Yes, yes, I will," Matilda squealed, clapping her hands together in excitement. "Jonah will be so happy to greet his first-born child this night!"

"Jonah mustn't be there!" Ruby snapped, clenching her fists. "My mother was very clear about that. No men are to be present at the birthing, only women. Do you understand?"

The smile on Matilda's lips wilted, but she nodded her head, nonetheless. "Yes, I understand. I only want what's best for the baby. Jonah may greet his child once we've returned home."

"That's right," Ruby nodded, backing away from the door. "Come early—my mother doesn't like to wait." And with that, she turned and fled back to her home in the woods, the baby kicking with echoed anticipation.

Ruby stood between her house and the entrance to the woods, the moon slowly rising as big and full as her own belly. For the dozenth time as she awaited Matilda's arrival, she touched the dagger concealed at her hip to reassure herself of its presence. When at last she spotted Matilda's figure approaching, she breathed a sigh of relief. The baby gave a single, sharp kick.

"Hello, Ruby," Matilda panted, arms crossed over her belly.

"You've not told Jonah, have you?" Ruby demanded, peering around for any sign of him.

"No, of course not. He had a long day at work and fell asleep almost as soon as his head touched the pillow. He knows nothing."

"Good. Come, then. It's almost time." Ruby turned and walked for the woods.

"We're going into the woods?" Matilda questioned, not moving. "Where is your mother?"

"In the woods, of course," Ruby glared back at her. "Giving birth in Mother Nature is part of the process. Now, are you going to keep asking silly questions or do you want to have this baby?"

Matilda said no more but huffed along at Ruby's side as she led her into the woods. Ruby tried to keep her own heavy breathing quiet, the weight of her large belly burdensome. But as before, the deeper she walked into the woods, the easier she found it to navigate. It no longer took a toll on her body as she floated gracefully between the trees, Matilda struggling to catch up.

At the clearing, Ruby led Matilda to the fairy ring and instructed her to lie down, but Matilda hesitated.

"What is this?" she asked, her eyes darting in all directions. "Where's Vera?"

"Don't worry about that!" Ruby barked. She pulled the dagger from its hiding place and the baby bounced with excitement. Matilda's eyes widened, and she stumbled back, clutching her stomach protectively.

"Wh-what are you doing?" she choked. "Why do you have that?"

"It's to cut the umbilical cord, you dumb cow," Ruby hissed, advancing on her. "Now do as I say and lie down!"

But Matilda refused. She continued to back away from Ruby and the ring of mushrooms, her head swiveling from side to side as if searching for an escape route.

"I said *lie down*!" Ruby shouted, as once again the crystal flashed flaming hot. The baby's whispers turned to screams, urging her into action. With a growl, she lunged at Matilda, the dagger pointed forward. Matilda shrieked and ran, but the woods gave Ruby a speed and agility the stupid girl couldn't match. Grabbing her by the hair, Ruby yanked her back, and with one smooth motion, thrust the blade deep into the side of Matilda's round belly.

The high-pitched scream that pierced the night sky bounced off the dense trees and echoed through the woods. Ruby didn't doubt if the moon itself could hear the girl's agonized cries as she stabbed her stomach again and again, soaking them both in blood. When it was done, Ruby dragged her by the ankles to the fairy ring, leaving a trail of dark blood for the earth to drink. She pulled up Matilda's gown and went to work with the dagger, carving the baby right from the womb, her own fetus crying encouragement from inside her. She lay the punctured, bloody mass on Matilda's chest and backed away, heart racing.

Surely, this would be enough for the demon to accept in lieu of Ruby's own offspring. It had to be.

Staring down at mother and child, panting, Ruby realized the necklace was missing from around her neck—it had finally decided to release its hold on her and had dropped off, probably during the scuffle with Matilda. Almost immediately, a horrified, gut-wrenching regret tore through Ruby's body, and she bent over to vomit violently. What had she done? To Matilda and her own mother? Perhaps Vera had been right—Ruby was nothing but a monster.

As she wept beside the mutilated bodies of Matilda and her child, the woods went eerily silent. He had come. Ruby stood, lifted her skirts, and ran.

Exiting the trees near home, she nearly fell over at the sight of Jonah lurching out of the front door. There was blood on his hands and a look of sheer terror on his face.

So he had found her mother.

"Jonah?" she choked, frozen in the shadow of the trees.

"Ruby!" He staggered forward, swaying from side to side like a drunkard. "What's happened here? Your mother, she—"

"Oh, Jonah!" Ruby rushed forward, arms outstretched. With his wide eyes and the look of distress on his handsome face, he looked just like the boy she remembered from childhood—the boy who'd come to her for comfort when his father beat him, or his mother ignored him. All she needed to do was hold him and reassure him all was well, like she used to in the good days before Matilda. She would smooth his hair and scratch his back and tell him everything was going to be all right.

She would make him understand. She *had* to.

Jonah strangled a gasp upon seeing her illuminated in the moonlight, jarring her back to reality. She followed his eyes down her body to see that not only was she covered in blood, but her cloak had slipped off, revealing her large, swollen belly in all its glory.

"What have you done?" Jonah croaked, his body shaking. "Where is my wife? I woke to find a note on the pillow that said she was coming here, but she wasn't inside. Only your mother, and she was—my gods!"

"Jonah, please listen!" Ruby cried, throwing herself at him. "It was the crystal that made me do it! Mother told me it was dangerous, but I had to wear it! For you!" Jonah shoved her aside with no amount of gentleness and she fell to the ground, her stomach thudding painfully against the hard earth.

"Matilda!" he screamed, running into the woods. "Matilda!"

"Jonah, no!" Ruby wailed. He was in there, the demon! She couldn't let him hurt her, Jonah!

Ruby emitted a low moan and struggled to her hands and knees, the baby's relentless kicks like knives to her insides. By the time she got to her feet and stumbled into the woods after Jonah, he was already a good distance ahead. She screamed his name over and over, her voice raspy and raw. What if the demon got him? What if she lost her Jonah forever? But no, there was his voice, far up to her left, calling Matilda's name.

"*Jonah*!" Ruby called again, desperately. She had to stop him before he reached the clearing!

Though Ruby tried to ignore the sharp, stabbing sensation in her abdomen, it slowed her down considerably, even with her strange ability to traverse the woods as if she had lived in them her whole life. It wasn't until she felt the warm trickle of liquid between her thighs that she realized the pain tearing through her stomach wasn't from the baby's kicks at all.

She stumbled against a tree and clutched at it fiercely, her nails chipping off bits of bark as the pain seemed to rip her apart. She fell to her knees and howled, her skirts bunched up in her fists. Her body was a traitor; it pushed without her trying. Moaning, she reached between her legs and felt the soft, sticky head already poking out. It seemed the delivery would go just as fast as the pregnancy itself had.

But no, she didn't want this! Not here. Not now. She sobbed and called once again for Jonah, then collapsed to her back as the explosive pain brought the baby's head down farther.

Approaching footsteps, and she bit her lip to bleeding in order to stop the scream from getting out. Was it the demon? Had he come for her child? But the figure that stepped forward wasn't that of the demon; it was that of Jonah—her sweet, sweet Jonah—returning to her side.

Ruby garbled something resembling a laugh. She knew he had always loved her as she had always loved him. She knew it.

"Ruby?" Jonah stepped closer with apparent apprehension.

"I'm… having the b-baby," Ruby rasped, shaking, teeth clacking together. "Help me, p-please."

He stood at her feet, gazing down between her thighs. Though it was dark, Ruby's heightened eyesight allowed her to read his expression perfectly—fear, yes, but something like awe, too. He dropped to his knees, and she felt his warm, soft hands on her legs.

"I can see the head," he said, his voice hushed.

Ruby howled again as another fierce push rippled through her.

"It's coming!" Jonah cried, and with one great gush of fluid, Ruby felt the baby being pulled from her and into Jonah's arms.

"Our baby," Ruby smiled, shivering. "Look at our beautiful baby." But Jonah was holding it, staring at it in silence.

Ruby's heart seized. "What's wrong?" Jonah slowly handed over the sticky, squirming bundle. A quick peek between its kicking legs confirmed it was a boy, before her eyes slowly scanned up the short length of his body and rested on his face. There, Ruby gasped.

His face was imprinted with the same disfiguring birth mark Ruby had borne all her life—though his covered the entirety of his face, from ear to ear and chin to forehead. And unlike hers, his marks seemed to come from under the skin, raising it like jagged, crisscrossing scars. Ruby gently traced her fingertips along them in wonder.

"He looks like you," Jonah said tersely, standing up. He wiped his hands on his trousers. "Congratulations. Now, where is my wife?" His face was pinched together as if in pain.

"But… don't you see? This is our son, Jonah. We can raise him together. He's ours. Matilda's pregnancy was fake. It was never real. *I* performed the ritual. She did nothing—it wasn't her, it was me, you understand?"

"Where is my wi—?" Jonah's words cut off abruptly as he was snatched from behind and dragged into the dark depths of the trees. Ruby had been so distracted by Jonah and the baby, she hadn't realized *he* was approaching from the sudden silence of the surrounding woods. It happened so quickly: a blur of movement, then Jonah's scream, followed by a sick crunching of bones.

"Jonah!" Ruby cried, struggling to sit up, her baby boy already nestling at her breast. There was movement to her right, and she whipped her head around as a figure emerged from the trees. It shifted from the form of a large beast to that of a tall naked man, his eyes glowing red.

Ruby held her breath as the man-beast moved forward, and for the first time, she could see him clearly. He was covered in blood from head to toe, as if all his skin had been flayed away. More blood dripped from his jaws like the juices of an apple—Jonah's blood, she knew. But what tore the guttural cry from Ruby's throat wasn't the blood or the appearance of flayed skin—it was the birthmark that etched his body beneath the gore, the same birthmark she and her son both shared. The crooked, branch-like marks pulsed like veins across the length of him, glowing red as he came closer. Even his eyes were deeply engraved with the marks, piercing into her soul, filling it with an awful realization. The many times her mother had struck the birthmark on Ruby's face as if wishing it would disappear… perhaps it wasn't because she hated the look of it—but because it exposed her for what she was.

I never should've kept you! Her mother's voice rang through her head. *I should've thrown you out into the woods the moment I had you!*

All you've done is bring me misery and fear!

All the times Vera had forbidden her from entering the woods alone, especially at night. *All these years I've kept you out of those woods, protected you from him, kept you safe!*

The harsh words she had spoken about the mysterious child growing in Ruby's womb. *It is a child of the woods and it has no place here! Its very existence is unnatural beyond the confines of the ritual! It's nothing but a monster—an* abominable *monster—like you!*

Ruby wrenched herself to her feet, nearly dropping her baby in the process. "Please, no," she whispered. But she couldn't deny what she now knew to be true. How had she never seen it before? The magical way she'd been able to navigate the woods, the sense of peace she'd felt, the belonging.

"My children," the demon confirmed. His lips stretched across his face in a grotesque grin, his sharp pointed teeth gleaming in the moonlight. The voice didn't come from his mouth, but from the surrounding earth. It hummed through the trees; it shivered through the ground. In that moment, Ruby longed for her mother, who had once refused to sacrifice her child, just as Ruby had refused to sacrifice her own.

As her father's monstrous smile split his face in two—his mouth stretching wide enough to consume both mother and child whole—Ruby wept, knowing she and her mother had both failed to save their children of the woods.

The Lady of Strangenesse

LEIFE SHALLCROSS

Lune first saw the old woman on the day Lord Livian, Protector of the Northern Marches and Master of Strangenesse, proposed to her. It was at one of her brother's soirees. The ones populated almost entirely by rich peacocks in the market for a pretty, young wife—the kind of men her brother hoped would take her off his hands. Lune was not interested in *them.* Lord Livian, on the other hand, was a military man. Someone who would likely be seeking a partner who could competently manage his estate when he was engaged in defending his coastline from raiders and pirates. Lord Livian was also *not* a peacock. His clothes were fine enough, but he exuded an aura of seriousness. He was—perhaps incongruously for a general of such renown—somewhat shy. Lune had been actively courting him in her own private way for months now.

Tonight, he had wordlessly pushed a small wooden casket inlaid with mother-of-pearl and turquoise into her hands, and turned away, his ears warming red. Lune tucked it into her pocket and escaped the crowded parlour at the first available moment, not wanting to open it where others could see. She went to hide in the kitchen, where she could manufacture a reasonable pretence of needing to attend to some crisis in the unlikely event her brother came searching.

She found a corner out of the way and opened the casket. Despite all her hopes and expectations, her heart still tripped at the sight of a ring set with an *enormous* sea-green sapphire, a star glimmering in its depths.

"Oh," she whispered in awe. She slid it onto her finger.

At almost the same moment, there came a quiet rapping on the door that led out into the kitchen courtyard.

"Rina! Ticky!" bellowed Cook from the stove.

"I'll get it," said Lune hurriedly, given both the maids had just taken trays of appetisers upstairs.

She stumbled across the kitchen in a daze, staring at the gem on her slim, brown finger, her pulse racing so hard she felt dizzy. She opened the door, tearing her eyes from what could only be Livian's betrothal-gift, and stumbled back with a gasp. There, in the nacreous moonlight stood an ancient queen with stars in her hair and her arms piled with small, pearly skulls. Her eyes were wide and milky.

"A flower for your lover?" she rasped.

Lune blinked, swallowing a scream. The vision faded. It was just an old woman with an armful of white roses, the season's first snowflakes melting on her woollen headscarf. Lune took a breath, and then another.

"Come in, mother, and have something warm to drink while I look at your roses," Lune said, snapping the box closed and blinking again to dispel the last of the unsettling vision. "It's so cold out."

"So kind," croaked the old woman.

Cook made faces, but allowed Lune to cajole a bowl of soup and a hunk of bread for the woman to eat.

"We'll sit in the corner," said Lune. "We won't be in your way." She was feeling generous tonight, with all her hopes and dreams now coalesced into the ring making a comfortably heavy weight on the third finger of her left hand.

"So kind!" said the old woman again as Lune gave her three silver pieces and requisitioned her entire bouquet of roses. "Shall I read your fortune, child?"

"Please," said Lune, suddenly curious to see if the cards' thoughts about her future accorded with her own expectations. She tucked her left hand into her pocket and rubbed her thumb over the band around her finger. "I'd like that."

"Well, let's see." The woman extracted a deck of cards out of her own pocket, hand-drawn in watery green ink on pale card. She shuffled them slowly.

"The first card is your immediate past," she said gravely. "And your immediate future. Your first card will tell me how many cards I may draw for you." Lune nodded, and the old woman drew out a card, laying it down between them. "Hmm. Eight of bees. Eight cards for you, then." Lune looked down at the striped insects crawling over their honeycomb.

"Hard work," said the old woman, poking at the card. "But there's wealth as the reward. Sweetness there, too."

Lune thought of all the effort she'd put into wooing the notoriously skittish Lord Livian, and the glorious gem he'd pressed into her hands tonight. She nodded.

"Thank you, mother," she said.

"Now we look ahead. Are you ready child?"

For a moment, her eyes seemed to have turned milky again, but it must have been a trick of the light. Lune nodded and the old woman drew out a second card.

"Ace of trees. There is change in your future," she announced, laying out a card showing a single acorn. She gave Lune a knowing look. Lune curled her fingers into a fist in her pocket. "Hmm." The old woman selected a third: the Crossroads. "And a choice. Interesting." She peered up at Lune again, puzzled this time. "At your age they usually come in the reverse order."

She turned over a fourth card. It showed bones buried under the earth, entangled in the roots of a tree. "The Seven of Bones. That means secrets, my dear." Lune, who was trying to be worldly, shivered anyway. Seven…of Bones. Now that was unfortunate. "You can dig them up or let them lie." The old woman stroked the faded greenish trunk of the tree. A suggestion of a face—or perhaps a skull—showed in the whorls of the bark. "Have a care, though. Even if you've a mind to let them lie, secrets have a way of seeding the ground," she warned.

The fifth card showed a grim-faced man holding a chain and lock in one hand and a key in the other. "Oh, you are an interesting one," the old woman mused, lifting her gaze to Lune once more. "Another choice. The Knight of Chains could mean bondage willingly entered into, or a prison of your own making." The woman tapped her finger on the card thoughtfully. "Just make sure you know who has the key, my dear. It's usually you."

The sixth card was better. "How lovely," said the old woman. "The Twelve of Bones!" Lune blinked. Half of a ribcage took up the entire face of the card, a flower blooming inside it. "You'll capture someone's heart!" trilled the old woman, nodding happily. Lune took a quiet breath, her tightly curled fingers relaxing. Hopefully she already had. The seventh card showed a crescent moon and a single star.

"The Night," said the old woman, nodding thoughtfully. "The refuge of lovers." Lune allowed herself a small smile. "And monsters." Lune's smile vanished. "The Lady Moon and her Sister Stars provide light in the darkness," the woman continued. "They will guide your way. But moonlight and starlight are fey and fickle magics, child. They reveal much and hide more. Things change under the light of the moon."

Lune clenched her teeth and smiled politely. This game was starting to lose its charm.

"Just one more card, mother," she said lightly. "Let's have it, then."

The old woman turned over the eighth card and Lune frowned. She'd had her cards read before. She had played with the family deck many times. But *this* card she did not recognise. An ornate border, like a fancy picture frame, was rendered in the faded green ink. But there was nothing in the frame—just a few jagged lines marring the empty space.

"Ah," said the old woman.

"What is it? What does it mean?" asked Lune, irritation making her voice sharp.

"Why, it's the Shattered Glass, child," said the old woman, laying it down atop the Eight of Bees and arranging the other cards around it.

"I've never heard of it," Lune said impatiently.

"It doesn't often show itself," said the old woman, as though it was possible for a card to just...*hide*.

"What does it mean?" Lune demanded. She withdrew her

hand from her pocket and smoothed her skirts. She had certainly tarried too long in the kitchen. She needed to get back. Livian would likely be thinking he'd offended her.

"It might suggest an opportunity to recreate the way the world sees you," said the old woman, giving Lune a wary look. "Or it could mean a sudden change in the way you see yourself. But, usually it signifies the presence of a—"

Lune stood up abruptly.

"Thank you, mother," she said brusquely. "I really must be getting back to the party." And she left before the old woman could say another word.

Lune was wed to Lord Livian as spring unfurled across the city, dressing all the parks and gardens in bridal finery. They remained there for the first weeks of their marriage, visiting friends, holding parties and attending all the balls, operas and fantasias of the season. But, as spring slowly moved into a headlong tumble towards summer, opening the Northern seaways once again to the Midvorn raiders, Lord Livian's duties called him back his ancestral home in the country. Lune was very ready to see it. He'd painted such an enticing picture, of old stone walls and copper rooftops gone green with age, overlooking the rocky, knockled cliffs of the nearby coast that were riddled with smugglers' caves and the secret harbours of pirates and raiders. And of course, the view out over the mercurial Northern Sea itself, fierce and foaming one minute, calm, sparkling turquoise the next. She was also eager to stretch her wings, now that she'd left the constricting nest of her brother's household, and see how well she could fly on her own. To grasp hold of the future she'd planned for herself. And that began with understanding the domain over which she now held authority: the House of Strangenesse, the Gate of the North and the seat of the Protector of the Northern Marches.

There was only one point on which she felt any unease.

It was something she had thought she'd reconciled herself with before she began to woo Livian. Then that infernal rose-seller had laid it down in front of her with the first card she'd drawn on the very night of Livian's proposal. Lune was Livian's eighth wife.

Of course Lune wondered about those seven other women. Her husband had provided her brother with an account of all their fates. Three lost to childbirth (and their little children with them.) Two to illness—one long and wasting, one short and sudden. Two to regrettable accidents. All above reproach, her brother assured her. Not having much faith that her brother's concern for her welfare outweighed his desire to see her married off, Lune had done what little lay in her own power to verify Livian's blamelessness and she had found nothing amiss.

At least the fortune-teller had offered her some comfort: the eight of bees promised wealth and sweetness as the reward for hard work. Lune thought about this, and not the seven of bones, their secrets seeding the earth. She was young and healthy and clever—a quick study her tutors had always said. And now she was married to one of the greatest military commanders in the realm. A man who had distinguished himself early in his career, somehow wresting victory from impossible chaos and decisively driving the Midvorn raiders from the northern shores. She fully intended to prove her worth to him and convince him she could be his partner and his second in more than just the domestic sphere. It would take time, surely, but…She pictured again the eight of bees: wealth and sweetness. Then, of course, there was also the twelve of bones. A captured heart.

Strangenesse was two days easy travel north and west of the city. They should have arrived there late in the afternoon of the second day, only a horse threw a shoe on the second morning and then the wheel of the carriage caught in a deep rut and broke. So it was that Lune did not get the picturesque view of her new home from afar that her husband had promised. The view from her carriage window was mostly the looming mass of the night-time forest dappled with patches of eerie, shadowy blue-green light. "Wyrdlight", Livian called it, and explained it was caused by certain types of moss and mushroom.

When they were not travelling through forest, Lune caught the occasional glimpse of distant bonfires.

"But bonfire night was last week!" she exclaimed, the first time she saw the flickering silhouettes of people dancing against the gold. Indeed, she'd begged Livian to postpone their travel until after the traditional festival to call up the start of summer, given it was her favourite. And this year, now she was married, she'd been able to indulge in what was whispered to be the *true* way to summon the sun and celebrate the coming season, once all the dancing was done. Livian had been very obliging.

"Ah," said Livian, his smile suggesting he remembered the night as happily as she did. "But we are in the country now, love. The city runs on schedules or it would all fall to chaos. Out here, though, the villagers wait for the signs to tell them when to light the fires."

"Signs?" Lune was a child of the city through and through.

"New growth on certain ancient trees," he explained, "or the habits of local birds and animals. The movements of the stars. The dates of our festivals are a little less fixed out here, my love. But these people's livelihoods follow the seasons closely, they must take their cues as they come."

"Does this mean," asked Lune, allowing mischief to lower her tone, "that we will be celebrating bonfire night again tonight?"

Livian laughed.

"Indeed," he said, catching her hand and running his fingers caressingly over her knuckles. Then he made a face. "Although, one of our traditions is that all the household fires are doused at sunset and relit from embers brought from the bonfires. So it may not be quite as comfortable at home tonight as I might have liked."

"Well then, surely we must huddle together for warmth?" she returned.

It was, even absent a fire in her bedroom grate, a very satisfactory evening. Given the unexpectedly late hour of their arrival, they postponed all the usual activities Lune, as the new Mistress of Strangenesse, might have engaged in on her arrival to her new home. So Lune and Lord Livian were left alone to partake their supper in Lune's bedchamber and then partake of each other as

Lune had teased her husband in the carriage.

Yet, despite the satiation such activities usually bring, as well as the weariness of two days of travel, Lune could not sleep. Perhaps it was all the little anxieties that came with arriving at her new home and wishing to make a good impression, but now that Livian was breathing gently in the darkness beside her, Lune was wide awake. Around her, the unfamiliar night-time quiet was like a vault, waiting to be unpacked. All the noises she was used to from the city—cats fighting, dogs barking, distant tavern noises, the cry of the watchman on his beat—were absent. In their place were new noises, not yet known to her.

A slice of moonlight lay across the floor, brilliant in the unlit room. It was so bright she fancied she could see dust motes floating in it, as though it were a sunbeam. Softly, so she did not rouse her slumbering husband, Lune twitched back the covers and left her bed. She had heard the stars shone brighter in the countryside, marking a trail across the sky like a long splash of spilled milk. She padded across the room and drew back her drapes…and let out a shriek of fright.

There, in the branches of the tree outside her window, crouched an old woman. *The* old woman, the rose seller. She glared at Lune from behind a cage of twisted branches, tears frozen on her face as though they had been cast in molten silver.

A hand landed on her shoulder and she jumped and spun around, but it was just Livian.

"It is only an owl," he said soothingly. "Did it frighten you, love?"

"No, it's—" Lune twisted in his arms to look back out the window and saw there was indeed a huge, snowy owl perched in the tree. It glared back at them with eyes that shone green as a cat's, then spread its wings and was gone, a ghostly shadow fleeing into the dark.

"But—" said Lune, feeling herself go weak and limp in his arms. "I saw…" She trailed off, not wanting to sound ridiculous.

"Something else?" Livian asked, a note of humour entering his voice. "They say on bonfire night, the veil between the mortal realm and Faerie grows thin, love. Perhaps you did see something."

She turned her face into the soft warmth of his nightshirt, not wanting to be teased for what was surely a city reaction to everyday country occurrences.

"Come back to bed," Livian urged, so she did. But even when she did eventually fall asleep, her dreams were haunted by her vision of the old woman, dappled in a motely of silvery-green moonlight and deep black shadows, her expression bleak and bitter as midwinter. Only in the dream, the old woman was reaching between the branches imprisoning her, snatching at something Lune held. In the way of dreams, Lune could not seem to see clearly the object in her own hands. She turned her head this way and that trying to glimpse it, but the moonlight danced and her vision flickered and all she could see was a shard of twisted silver.

The next day, Lune took possession of the keys to Strangenesse.

"This is your domain now, my love," Livian said, taking them from his desk drawer. He handed her the heavy iron ring, dozens of keys hanging from it in all shapes, sizes and metals. Nothing in twisted silver, though she could not explain why she had expected to see such a key. "There is nowhere here you may not go. Only—" He hesitated, shadows suddenly darkening his eyes and he looked away. "There is a walled garden below the north tower." His voice was rough. "I built it for my first wife, Lady Celara. Now, it is become something of a memorial place. It has grown rather full," he added bitterly.

"Ah," said Lune softly.

"It is a private space," Livian said. "I do not visit it often, and I only allow the gardeners in three times a year. I would rather you did not—" He broke off.

"Of course not," Lune hurried to assure him. "I would not dream of intruding."

He held out his hand to her and she went to him. Surprisingly, he pulled her into his lap and buried his head in the crook of her neck.

"Do not leave me, my love," he whispered hoarsely.

"I won't," she promised, putting her hands into his hair and kissing the crown of his head, touched this thought could bring him so undone.

It was a matter of mere days between when they arrived and when word came that Midvorn raiders had been sighted in the Northern Sea. Of course Livian was called away to ensure they were deterred and Lune was left alone. She had plenty to do—she was still familiarising herself with the running of Strangenesse, huge and old as it was, part keep and part grand house. Her staff were competent, but—she was surprised to learn—none of them were local. Not one had been in the area above three years and none of them had ever met Livian's last wife, the one who'd died after a fall from her horse. There were also no portraits anywhere of the seven women who had gone before her. This she found a little odd, especially regarding his first wife, the one who had died of a wasting illness, to whom Livian had been married for almost ten years.

There was only one remaining tangible connection to the seven dead women at Strangenesse. So of course Lune went to find the garden. She discovered the path down the cliff where the grounds ran a little wild. The path led to a door, but it was locked, the keyhole bright silver and oddly untarnished for something only used a handful of times in a year. When she laid a fingertip on it, the metal was ice cold. A fretful breeze sprang up, but she stood there for a little while, frowning as it plucked at her skirts and tossed her dark curls. She could not deny it bothered her that the hidden memorial garden was the only reminder Livian's other wives had once existed.

You can dig them up or let them lie, but secrets have a way of seeding the ground.

Did she want to dig them up?

If I died, she thought, *I would not want all record of my life erased from the world, save in a little, wild garden only visited three times a year.*

Once back inside, Lune called for a tea tray while she thought about the matter of Livian's departed wives. She felt no immediate threat to her own safety. Livian had been nothing but tender towards her. He did not seem a man given to violent rages. If anything, he was far more tender than she'd anticipated. But she was, after all, his eighth wife and that, in itself, was reason enough to seek out a little knowledge of what had gone before. To understand if there was, indeed, some hidden threat lurking somewhere in Strangenesse.

The maid brought the tray and Lune sent her away, wanting to be alone to think. She picked up the teapot, but as she poured, it gave a little jump in her hand, splashing a brown stain speckled with stray tealeaves across the linen cloth on the tray. Lune stared down at the mess, the hairs on the back of her neck all a-prickle. The scattered tealeaves had somehow formed the words *Refuse the Lock*.

Lune set the pot down quickly, her hand shaking.

The words began to appear everywhere Lune looked. Sewing threads would loop themselves into letters where they lay across her lap as she embroidered a kerchief. A crumpled laundry list dropped by a maid was creased in such a way the writing formed the phrase. She knocked over a stack of books in the library, and when she picked them back up, she found she'd unwittingly piled them in such a way the letters in the titles on the spines had aligned to exhort her, once again, to *refuse the lock*.

She was determined not to be frightened—her person was not being threatened, after all, and the odd message seemed to be some kind of warning. But there was only one conclusion her mind could settle upon. What could this be, if not a restless spirit? And whose spirit, if not one of Livian's lost wives?

When Livian returned the next day, she playfully asked him over supper if there were any ghosts in Strangenesse. She was unprepared for the flash of genuine fear that darkened his eyes.

"No!" he said after a moment. "Did any of the servants say anything?"

"Not at all," she assured him, trying to sound unconcerned. Had his face turned pale? Her husband who faced down brigands and raiders? "I merely wondered if there were any stories in a house so old."

He shook his head. "No," he said again, "there are no ghosts in this house." But his fingers tapped restlessly against the table and when he picked up his glass, the wine splashed about inside as though his hand trembled.

With Livian returned, the haunting messages stopped—something Lune noted with interest. But after his reaction to her mention of a ghost, she decided not to tell him. This latest skirmish with the Midvorns had been fierce and cost him some good soldiers. Worse, he told her grimly, it seemed the wards set in place to guard the northern coastline were weakening, and no one could tell him why. It was the first time Lune had seen him in such a sombre mood. To raise the subject of his dead wives now seemed particularly egregious. Instead she encouraged him to tell her about the battle, what had gone wrong and how he had countered it, comparing his stories to the military histories she was reading.

Afterwards she let him bury himself in her. He clutched her close under the covers of their bed, murmuring "Stay with me, stay with me, my love," into her hair.

"Always," she whispered, pressing her hand against his chest, feeling his heart beat under his ribs.

Privately, Lune began to conduct her own investigation of her predecessors. It was an exercise in amassing a collection of scraps. She hunted for anything that might have been left behind, unnoticed. She meticulously went through each book in the not-inconsiderable library, looking for forgotten bookmarks or folded corners that might indicate the reading habits of one of Livian's lost ladies. She found several that looked likely in books of recipes, herbal remedies, animal husbandry and local crafts. But the most intriguing were references to a local story Lune found marked in a collection of folklore: Eleusine's Well had once been a place of blessings, until the Fairy Eleusine was vanquished by a wicked sorcerer. An illustration of the languishing fairy well depicted it at the foot of a cliff with a familiar castle looming above. The note printed beneath confirmed Lune's burgeoning suspicion: *Eleusine's Well is located on the Estate of the Lord of Strangenesse.* Lune contemplated the tower on the cliff above a pool surrounding the figure of a woman with her arms raised, and wondered.

The next time Livian went away, Lune once more began to receive uncanny messages via impossible means. Dewdrops on a cobweb outside her window, a momentary configuration of dust sweepings as a servant paused in her work to let Lune pass. Still, she hesitated to tell Livian about them. He had so much on his mind. The Midvorn raiders were becoming worryingly rapacious, and he spent more and more time away from Strangenesse.

Then one night, Lune and Livian were roused from their bed in the small hours by the arrival of an exhausted, muddy woman on horseback, carrying ill news from further north. An entire fleet of ships had been sighted by the coast guard. The raiders were several days from landfall, but Livian's own forces would be hard pressed to repel them alone. Lune threw a dressing gown over her nightclothes and sent servants to rouse couriers, then helped Livian write the dispatches to the capital requesting urgent support.

Less than an hour later Livian himself was ready to leave and ride back north with the watchwoman and those of his lieutenants stationed locally.

"I want to help," Lune begged him as he pulled her into his arms.

"My heart," he said, his voice rough. "There is likely to be fierce fighting. You must prepare yourself."

"I will have people and supplies ready to manage the casualties by dawn," she said. "You can rely on me, my lord. I will come myself once I have done all I can here. Don't think me afraid!"

"No," he said gently, "I mean for the possibility of my death."

Lune went cold.

"If that comes about, they will all look to you," he went on. "You will be mistress here in your own right."

Lune closed her eyes, grateful her face was hidden against his shoulder. Now was not a time for tears. She felt him fumbling at his belt, then he pressed a leather purse into her hand.

"Keep these for me," he whispered into her hair. Then his voice cracked. "Don't leave me!"

"It's you who are leaving!" she admonished him. "Come back to me!"

She waited until he had left to look inside. It contained half a dozen keys. Most were small and intricate, clearly to open Livian's personal and official lockboxes. But one made the bottom of her stomach drop all over again. She drew it out and stared at it. It rested cold and bright against her palm, a key fashioned from a shard of twisted silver.

The next few days were frantic, sleepless and tense. Strangenesse became the point of coordination for all further military dispatches, news from the north and offers of assistance, and Lune was its linchpin. Two days after Livian left came the news that the Midvorn fleet had attempted a landing at Oxcliff, but had been repelled, only for Livian's forces to discover a day later a second landing had been effected with greater success slightly to the south in Saltern Cove. Much of that village had been plundered and put to the torch; the lists of casualties were grim.

A force of Midvorn warriors was pushing inland in numbers never before seen, and for the first time in living history there seemed to be some doubt as to whether the North's forces were equal to repelling them. The initial flurry of activity eased, but then Lune found herself in charge of the logistics of getting building materials, food, medical and other supplies out to the affected villages and finding places for refugees to shelter, tasks no less urgent than the initial deployment of militia had been.

So, Lune did not notice exactly when the ghostly messages changed.

On the evening after the day they had received the sobering report about the burning of Saltern Cove, Lune was readying herself for bed. She unwound the braid she'd worn for the last three days, and half-heartedly dragged a comb through her hair. She was so tired her eyes ached. She looked down at her dresser and saw a handful of fallen strands of hair spelling out words on the polished wood.

Restore the key.

A spatter of raindrops against the dark stone of a windowsill. The loops of laces on a set of discarded stays. Tealeaves again, this time in an empty cup.

Restore the key.

Lune knew which key. But what did it mean? How? And she still didn't understand the first haunting message.

The missives from her husband were far more comprehensible. His return was still far away. He wrote to her about protecting the coast, the brutality of the raiders and the tactics he was using to thwart them. And he wrote about how he missed her, how he longed to be by her side again, how he could not do without her, and how they belonged together, like a hand in a glove, a fiddle and a bow, a lock and a key. *Wait for me,* he begged her at the end of every letter.

Then, two weeks after his abrupt departure, a new message arrived, not in her husband's familiar hand, but his lieutenant's. It contained the dire news that Lord Livian had been gravely injured.

Turqin promised her Livian was receiving the best care possible and would be brought to Strangenesse as soon as possible, but this was little comfort when he was so far away. For the next seven days, Lune barely slept. The mysterious words that had plagued her could have been painted in blood on the very walls and she would not have noticed, as desperately busy as she was.

On the eighth day, Lune received two messages that gave her equal measures of relief. The first came from Lieutenant Turqin, notifying her that the Southern reinforcements had turned the tide and the battle was won. There were pockets of raiders left to clean up, but the main force of the invasion was defeated. The second came from Livian's physician to tell her Livian's wound-fever had broken at last. He needed a few days to rest and build his strength before travelling, but they would be back in Strangenesse before the week was out.

Lune went to her room and collapsed upon the floor, sobbing. She was bone-tired and so weary of standing at the top of the north tower searching the horizon for sails in one direction and smoke in the other.

Eventually she cried herself out and opened her eyes. From where she was crumpled upon the floor, she could see under her bed where dust and dead moths had gathered during the weeks Strangenesse's resources had been dedicated to packing boxes of bandages and brewing tonics to stop wounds festering instead of simple tasks like dusting. Their faded wings and desiccated carcases spelled out the words *Refuse the lock. Restore the key.* Lune closed her eyes again too tired to care.

She ordered a bath. She slept for four hours. Then she rose and dressed and told her maid she was going for a walk outside to clear her head.

Once she reached the door at the end of the path beneath the north tower, Lune put the key in the lock and turned it. The door swung smoothly open. She stepped through, pulling it silently closed, and looked around. She could no longer hear the sounds of the sea—that was the first thing she noticed. Instead, the wind sobbed and soughed mournfully against the pocked walls of the cliffs and a high keening, which must have been birds, came and went. And it was cold, her arms prickling into gooseflesh with the drop in temperature. The colours were also strangely muted—too blue and cool, as though nothing bright was permitted to bloom here. The central part of the garden was a smooth lawn scattered with statuary and the wall at the back natural rock, the cliff below where the north tower jutted. The black rock glistened with water, which fed a pool, glimmering darkly in the deep shadow at the foot of the cliff.

Cautiously, Lune made her way across the lawn towards the nearest statue. She had only taken a few steps when she realised the lawn was not in fact grass, but some kind of dense, plush moss. To her delight, each step she took set off a little puddle of faint glimmers in the grey-green velvet and she wondered if at night it might glow. The plinth of the closest statue had a collection of pale mushrooms sprouting around it, fuelling her fancy. But as Lune lifted her eyes to see what stood on the marble pedestal, she gasped and took a step back.. Instead of a flattering portrait of a young woman cut down in her prime, Lune confronted a carved stone creature that, while recognisably feminine, was shockingly insect-like. Strange spikes thrust up from her back, almost as though she were about to burst out of her skin, Her face was alien and avaricious and she crouched over a clutch of stone eggs. One had cracked apart and whatever was emerging looked…larval. Lune backed away quickly.

The next statue was hardly better. It was of a woman seated, facing away from Lune, but turning a little, one hand lifted, as though to catch Lune's attention. She was swathed about in what look like grave-cloths, with a veil clinging to her face, giving the impression she had crawled out of her resting place and was lying in wait for a visitor. Lune's belly filled with an unpleasant, curdled sensation.

Why would Livian choose to remember them like this?

She hardly wanted to look at the others, until she realised she could only see five statues. She turned a slow circle. Each of the other three statues was just as disturbing in its own way as the two she'd already viewed. But why only five?

Towards the back of the garden was a white marble mausoleum. She started towards it, but after a few steps she stumbled over something embedded in the moss. Looking down she nearly shrieked to see an upturned, anguished stone face and a single hand protruding from the ground as though the woman was being slowly, excruciatingly smothered by the moss.

Lune closed her eyes for a moment, clutching the silver key and trying to calm her ragged breath. This garden was *horrible* and she *didn't* understand why Livian had created it. Steeling her nerves, she stepped over the sunken statue and walked resolutely to the mausoleum. As she drew close she spied the remains of another statue, on the other side of the pond at the foot of the cliff. Was it the final wife? It seemed wrong, somehow, lumpish and crude and for the briefest of moments recalled to Lune's mind the image of a hunched old woman, her arms full of roses.

Lune ignored the chill prickle of sweat on the back of her neck and forged past the mausoleum to better see the last statue.

The pond was no lovelier close up than it had been from across the garden. The water was a deep, sullen turquoise, almost black, and may as well have been bottomless. There was a faint, dank mist hovering over the unnaturally still surface and the only plants at its edge were strange, sere clumps of leafless thorns. The statue looked much older than any of the others, as if it had been hewn straight from the cliff, instead of grey marble like the others. It was broken now, a headless torso, and either very worn or had never been carved in detail, more the suggestion of a female form. But the toppled head, now lying half-submerged in the strings of thorns at its feet, was strange enough to match the rest of the garden—the worn features vulpine, with a pointed muzzle and ears. The straggling brambles growing over it made it appear as though it still wore the remains of a desiccated flower crown.

Lune stepped back from the eerie pond, determined to brave the mausoleum.

There was another lock on the heavy wooden door, bright silver as the one on the gate. She put the key in and turned it, leaning inside as the door swung open. The sun seeping in behind her was the only source of light in the windowless room. It illuminated little other than a large slab-like plinth on which reclined a stone woman, entirely covered by a shroud. Even through the obscuring folds of carved fabric Lune could tell she was emaciated. This must be the memorial of Livian's first wife.

At least this one was closer to the accepted mode of remembrance statuary, even if the outlines of her ribs and eye sockets were a little too grim to be truly tasteful. Lune stepped closer, twitching at her skirts to fan a little breath of cool air from outside into the thick atmosphere. The shroud over the stone woman shivered. Lune blinked.

It was not a carved stone shroud. It was real fabric draped over the statue.

Lune went up to the plinth. She hesitated a moment, then drew back the shroud, curious as to why Livian had been moved to create such a grotesque memorial of Lady Celara, only to cover it.

Her knees buckled and she sat down in a heap, before scrambling backwards towards the door.

It was not a statue.

She sat in the cold sunlight, half in and half out of the dank mausoleum, gasping in fright and staring at Lady Celara's desiccated corpse. It took her a minute or two before she could breathe properly again and another minute more to feel her legs might sustain her. She clutched the silver key to her chest, knowing she could not simply run. She had to at least replace the shroud before she left. But as her eyes adjusted to the crepuscular light of the tomb, the wall behind Lady Celara came into focus. It was not flat, but contained a series of large, vertical, rectangular niches, and in each niche stood a corpse.

Surely they cannot stand on their own, Lune thought in something close to hysteria. *Did he hang them there? Will he hang me?*

She dragged herself up using the doorframe and made herself cross the floor back to Lady Celara. She put out a shaking hand to draw the shroud back up into place, and stopped.

There, in the centre of Lady Celara's chest, just above the neckline of her rotting silk gown, was a silver keyhole. It glimmered amidst the flaking, parchment-like remains of Lady Celara's decolletage. It looked like it was set directly into her breastbone.

Refuse the lock.

Lune looked down at the silver key in her hand, gleaming brightly in the gloom. Did this go in the keyhole? The lock was the same bright, pale metal as both the key and the keyhole at the garden door. What would happen if she tried the key in it?

She couldn't try the key. She didn't have the courage.

It felt as though all the air was being squeezed out of her lungs again. She was starting to feel dizzy. Perhaps the air in here was bad? The sound of Lune's hitching breath filled the chamber and it suddenly seemed as though the sobbing wind outside was louder here. With trembling fingers she drew up the shroud to cover Lady Celara's face again, tweaking it carefully into place. As she backed away, she looked up at the eerie figures, standing in the niches in their burial clothes. Her eyes had sharpened again and she saw a bright, gleaming keyhole in the breastbone of every mummified corpse.

She fumbled the door of the mausoleum closed and all but ran through the garden, one thought filling her mind.

What has Livian done?

This thought occupied her all evening and late into the night as she tossed and turned, chasing sleep that wouldn't come. By the next morning, however, she had discovered a new thought to worry her.

What must I do?

Pretend she had never visited the garden? Confront him about it? Make him tell her what it meant? What it meant for *her?*

What must I do?

Her hands shook as she brushed out her braid and she bumped a vase of flowers on her dresser. Petals cascaded down and her heart pounded to see they had fallen to form new words.

Release me.

I am the Lady of Strangenesse, Lune told herself as she made her way down the narrow path again in the bright morning sunlight.

I am the Lady of Strangeness, she repeated as she took out the silver key and opened the garden door.

I am the Lady of Strangenesse, she told the broken statue where it stood on the other side of the dank pool, its arms reaching out as if to plead some favour from her. Lune clutched at the key like a talisman. It was easily the brightest thing in this bleak place. She repeated her mantra again and again as she unlocked the door of the mausoleum and stepped inside, holding up the key like the Knight of Chains.

"*I* am the Lady of Strangenesse," she said to the relics of Lady Celara as the wind sobbed and keened and she drew down the shroud. The key shone bright as a moonbeam in her hand.

"I am the *only* Lady of Strangenesse," she said, and set the key into the lock in Lady Celara's breastbone.

When Livian's carriage rolled through the gateway of Strangenesse the next day, Lune was the first person at the foot of the carriage steps. He managed to walk the short distance to the entrance gripping her hand and leaning on Dr Cyrene's arm, but had to be carried upstairs to the chamber Lune had prepared for him. He looked terrible. Far too pale and thin and clearly still heavily favouring the side where his thigh had been pierced. Once settled, he barely had the energy to kiss her hand before falling into an exhausted sleep.

"This is good," Dr Cyrene assured her. "The travel has been hard for him—he was better than this before we left. But he was desperate to get back to you and I think he will heal faster now he's here."

Lune couldn't sit by him all the time. There was still so much to do and people she needed to speak with, hour in, hour out, and she couldn't do this by her husband's bedside without disturbing him. Every time she returned, he clutched at her hand. It was worrying. He had always cherished her, but in his infirmity he had grown clingy and anxious. Dr Cyrene was right, however, and the following day, after almost eighteen straight hours of sleep, he was much restored. Over breakfast he asked her for his keys and she only hesitated for a moment before taking them from her pocket and handing them over.

Something in her balked at the idea of relinquishing the silver key now she'd held it in her possession. But she had no right to withhold it, and now was not the time to have the conversation about what the garden meant. Already there were couriers outside waiting for dispatches to carry back to the battle grounds and a contingent of wagons was due to arrive mid-morning to collect a consignment of supplies. And—Lune looked into Livian's face as she placed the leather pouch back in his hands—her husband still looked so ill. His cheeks were sunken and his eyes deeply shadowed, a good measure of the strength she was used to seeing there leached away.

"Why don't you spend some time out in the gardens this morning?" she suggested. Even though summer was grown late, it was still warm.

"I am not grown so old and decrepit yet," he grumbled, but there was a shadow in his eyes that gave her pause.

"If you will rest but one day, tomorrow I will put you to work on the dispatches," she told him. "This work needs doing and I am glad to do it, but I would rather do it by your side. But you *must* get your strength back."

He took her hand and kissed it, then waved her out of the room. She went and busied herself while her husband rested, but her hand kept straying to her empty pocket all morning.

Livian continued to prove Dr Cyrene right, and before the week was out his colour had returned and he was able to walk on his own, if slowly and with the use of a cane. His mood improved as well, until one evening when, over dinner, it became apparent he had fallen into a dark mood. When Lune tried to draw him out, his answers were curt and sullen. It was the first time he had ever spoken to her in displeasure. Eventually, when the table was cleared, Lune asked him what was amiss.

"You visited Celara's garden," Livian said, his voice thick with bitterness. "Even though I asked you not to. Did you like what you found?"

"I—" began Lune, an automatic denial springing to her lips. Then she forced herself to stop. "No," she said quietly. "I do not understand why—"

He cut her off with a broken-sounding laugh.

"I don't expect you do."

"How did you know?" she asked.

He gave her a bitter, sideways glare.

"Come," he said, pushing his chair back from the table and limping off, leaning heavily on his cane.

He ignored all her protestations about the dark and showed no inclination to wait for her while she went to find a lantern and cloaks for them both. Fortunately he moved slowly, so it was little trouble to catch him up.

"You won't need it," he said when she reached him at the base of the north tower.

Afterwards, Lune was inclined to think he was being stubborn. They might not have needed it *in* Celara's garden, as he called it, but it certainly helped her find her way there in the dark. Arguably, it even helped Livian find the lock in the door and fit the silver key to it. But when he pushed it open, Lune gasped.

Pale blue wyrdlight, brighter than her lantern, spilled out through the doorway. Lune followed him inside. The garden that seemed so sparse and sere by day had come alive under the stars. The pale mushrooms sprouting at the bases of the statues glowed limpid green, the tangles of thorns a thready violet. Growths on walls she'd not even noticed before made bright dots in shades from indigo to turquoise. The grey velvet moss she'd crossed to inspect the statuary glowed with brilliant cyan light in the dark. And tracking across it, this way and that, were Lune-sized footprints, little lightless blots against the blue.

"I see," she said, unable to suppress her wonder at the luminescent garden. "But Livian, the statues—"

"Grief is an ugly thing," he said bitterly and turned away from her. "Why *did* you disobey my one request of you?" His voice could not have been bleaker.

She was about to respond, to tell him about the ghost, when he lifted his head, as though something had caught his attention. He whirled back around, staggering on his bad leg.

"What have you done?" he demanded wildly. Without warning he took off, limping across the iridescent carpet, the moss flaring into incandescence where his feet fell, then sinking back into new puddles of darkness. She stared after him in shock. Had he guessed? *How?* She took a deep breath, steadying her resolve, and set off after him.

He was always going to find out, she reminded herself, as she followed him through the unnervingly silent garden. Even the sobbing wind that filled it during the day had fallen away and the only sound she could hear apart from her own breath was the far-off keening of birds.

She did not hurry. She knew he would need a moment when he saw what she'd done. All that was left of his wives' remains now were little more than piles of dust and scraps of rotting fabric. When she reached the door of the mausoleum, Livian was standing over Lady Celara's bier, his head bowed. His arms hung limply at his side, but the key—still clutched in his hand—was shining more brightly even than the lantern she carried. Lune stayed by the door, hardly daring to breathe.

"They're gone," croaked Livian, his voice echoing strangely in the empty hall.

"I released them," whispered Lune. "It is what they wanted."

"And they left," he said brokenly. "They all left me."

"I'm here," she reminded him. "I won't leave unless you send me away."

He turned his head then, to look at hear, and in the strange light from the key she saw tear tracks coursing down his face like molten silver.

"Why?" he whispered.

Lune swallowed. She wasn't sorry she'd done it, but—confronted by his grief-shadowed face—she *was* sorry she'd hurt him.

"They were so unhappy," she said. "They left me messages writ out in cobweb and tealeaves. They begged me to release them."

He gave a bitter laugh.

"I doubt it was them," he said. "It was more likely *her*."

"Her?"

"What did they say, these messages?" he pressed.

"Refuse the lock," Lune recited. "Restore the key. Release me. Livian, what do you mean, *her?* Who else could it be if not Celara? Or one of the other wives?"

He shook his head and turned back towards the doorway. Lune backed away as he stepped out into the wyrdlight.

"*Her,*" he said, gesturing with the hand holding the key towards the cliff…and the pool…and the broken statue.

Only it did not look so broken now. In a strange pastel rainbow of wyrdlight cast over the still black water, the statue was whole, standing tall with her arms outstretched towards them. Her foxish face was crowned with nacreous blooms of softly-glowing fungi and the muted keening of night-birds grew suddenly louder and more urgent.

"Eleusine," whispered Lune.

Livian opened his hand, the key on his palm emitting a brilliant azure light.

"It holds part of her soul," he said. "She wants it back."

"But why do you have it?" asked Lune. She hardly dared raise her voice above breathing with the fae statue so potent a presence across a mere few feet of water.

"It's a powerful charm, a fragment of a fairy's soul," said Livian. His voice was barely a thread of a whisper in the uncanny dark. "The stories say the dark mage that vanquished her trapped her soul in an enchanted mirror. The glass was shattered when the sorcerer was defeated, but the shards still hold the souls of the fae he enslaved. And the mirror itself was infused with formidable magic, vestiges of which still remain."

"What?" Lune's knees went weak, visions of a green-inked card on a kitchen table rising from her memory.

"I needed something to help me prevail against the raiders," said Livian. "When I was given my commission the situation was dire. I sought out every means by which I could glean an advantage, including magical ones. When this came into my hands I didn't know how closely it was connected with Strangenesse. But I have searched out its history and I'm certain the soul trapped in it is Eleusine's."

"What does it do?" asked Lune, awed.

"It helps you achieve your greatest desires, nothing less," said Livian.

"I see," said Lune. She looked at it glittering in his hands and had to once again suppress the urge to snatch it back.

"And mine was holding the North against the Midvorns. There is a price of course." Livian's voice turned suddenly dark.

Lune's breath froze in her throat.

"Celara?" she croaked. "The others?"

He swiped at his face with the back of his wrist and gave her a look of such bitter despair her heart lurched.

"I did not *kill* them, Lune," he rasped. "I used their deaths and tethered their souls to the key, but I *did not* kill them!"

"What do you mean *tethered their souls*?" she pressed.

His shoulders slumped. "She fought me. But with another soul tethered to the key—one loyal to me—its magic became more biddable. When each of them died, I—" He turned a devastated gaze upon her. "And now you have released them."

The enormity of her actions crashed over Lune and she stumbled back a step, visions rising in her mind of the horizon crowded with rust-red sails, the coastline shrouded in smoke from villages put to the torch. Then a realisation dawned.

"No!" she said. "It was failing before. I only unlocked them the day before you arrived. The Midvorns began to invade weeks ago."

To her shock, Livian sank to his knees, covering his face with his hands.

"Of course!" he rasped.

"What happened?" she begged. "What changed?"

Livian gave a hopeless-sounding laugh. "Oh, Lune," he said. "I fell in love with you."

He held out his hand, the key resting in it like a fallen star.

"I am no longer fit to hold the Gate of the North against the Midvorn raiders."

Lune itched to snatch it off him, but she held herself still.

"Take it!" he demanded.

"Livian!" she whispered.

He reached out his other hand to her and she stepped forward and took it.

"You are the Lady of Strangenesse," he said. "While you held the key, we prevailed." Gently he uncurled her fingers and tipped the key into her cupped hand.

Instantly, the night sky above them filled with a terrible shrieking, as if all those far-off birds Lune kept hearing had suddenly turned upon them. At the same moment, the stone fae erupted into pale flames, her arms reaching out to them across the water.

Give it to me! cried an awful voice in Lune 's head. *Restore what was stolen from me!* She felt an almost unbearable urge to step towards the pond.

"Livian!" gasped Lune, falling to her knees beside her husband. "Eleusine! She wants it back!" The unnatural mist began to thicken and rise off the pool, flickering with sallow lights. Lune clutched at Livian, terrified she would break from him and throw herself into the water.

"Ah…" he breathed, putting his arms around her. "Resist her, Lune!"

Lune tugged at his grip, trying to rise.

"We should go," she said, trying to sound firm, as though she wouldn't run into the mist the moment he let go.

Please! cried the fairy in her head in a voice equal parts rage and pain. *Give it back! Release me!*

Lune cried out as she was flooded with all the fairy's agony of having her soul shattered and captured, a piece trapped in silver like a butterfly flattened under a book

"What happens if I restore it to her?" she whispered.

Livian turned a pale face towards her.

"The wards in the North will fail entirely," he said bleakly. "There will be nothing to stop the Midvorn raiders other than our own steel."

"How do I resist her? Livian?"

Lune was beginning to panic. The leprous luminescence was licking at the shores of the pool now and she knew she could not run from it.

"You must tether another soul to the key," he said grimly.

"How? Who?" cried Lune, twisting in his arms.

Was the statue moving? It seemed larger, its head wreathed with pale flames.

"Like this," said Livian.

He closed his hand around hers, crushing the shaft of the key in her grasp, and yanked it towards his chest. She felt it connect, then there was a sudden flash of bitter cold and Livian collapsed with a horrible wheezing gasp.

No! screamed the fairy in Lune's head. It seemed as though every night bird for a hundred miles had gathered in the sky above them and was screaming too.

Lune fell back down beside Livian. He had gone very, very still. She looked down to where her hand had connected with his chest. The key had sunk a good three inches deep in his flesh. Not in the centre of his chest, like his poor dead wives, but about two inches to the left. *What had he done?*

"Livian!" she whispered, afraid to pull out the key in case she hurt him more. She was expecting a torrent of blood any moment, but none came. "Livian?"

"Dear heart," he whispered, his voice hoarse. "Forgive me. It is done."

She looked down at the wound she had made. Beneath the hole in his shirt, she saw the glimmer of silver surrounding the place where the key pierced his skin.

"Oh no," she gasped.

She reached out to grasp the key and pull it from him again, but he closed his hand over hers, holding it in place.

"Livian!" she gasped, but he gripped her hand harder, then twisted the key. She heard a *click*, a tumbler falling into place. All the tension left his body and he finally let go of her. She tugged her hand back, silver key in her grasp.

Immediately, the luminous mist began to roll back across the pool, faster and faster. The shrieking in Lune's head rose in pitch until she cried out herself, throwing her hands over her head. Then it cut off abruptly. When Lune cautiously opened her eyes again, the pool had gone quiet and Eleusine's statue was nothing more than a worn and shattered stub of stone again.

"Livian," whispered Lune, leaning down, fearing the worst.

But he moved his hand to wrap his fingers around hers again. His hands were cold, but he was alive.

"My love," he said, his voice rough. "You see. Now you hold

the key to my heart and all the North. You truly are the Lady of Strangenesse."

Contributor Biographies

Kirstyn McDermott is an Australian author of two award-winning novels, *Madigan Mine* and *Perfections*, along with numerous pieces of short fiction and poetry. Her most recent works are *Hard Places*, a collection of short fiction, and the *Never Afters* series of retold fairy tales. She produces and co-hosts a literary discussion podcast, *The Writer and the Critic*, and holds a PhD in creative writing with a research focus on re-visioned fairy tales. Kirstyn lives in Ballarat, Australia, with fellow writer Jason Nahrung and two distinctly non-literary felines. www.kirstynmcdermott.com

Leanbh Pearson (she/her) lives on Ngunnawal Country in Canberra, Australia. An award-winning LGBTQI and disability author of horror and dark fantasy, her writing is inspired by folklore, fairytales, myth, history and climate. She's judged the Australian Shadows Awards, Aurealis Awards, is an invited panelist and member of the HWA and SFWA. Leanbh's alter-ego is an academic in archaeology, evolution and prehistory. Follow her at https://www.leanbhpearson.com | Twitter, Facebook & Instagram @leanbhpearson

Mendel Mire enjoys writing sci-fi, horror, dark fantasy and designs speculative ecosystems and scientifically plausible creatures for kicks. He is an academic researcher living in Adelaide. He has a PhD in comparative anatomy and studies animal biology while assisting with dissections and mentoring university students. He can be found on Twitter @MendelMire

Leife Shallcross is a hopeless fairy tale tragic. Ever since she can remember, she has been fascinated by stories about canny fairy godmothers, heroic goose girls and handsome princes disguised as bears. She's the author of the novel *The Beast's Heart*, a shamelessly romantic retelling of Beauty and the Beast. She's also written a bunch of short fiction: *Pretty Jenny Greenteeth*, a nasty story about how little girls deal with monsters, won the 2016 Aurealis Award for Best YA Short Story. In cahoots with Chris Large she co-edited the 2018 Canberra Speculative Fiction Guild anthology of short Australian science fiction, fantasy and horror stories, *A Hand of Knaves*. She is always working on more new novels, just probably not the ones she should be working on.

K.B. Elijah is a fantasy author living in Brisbane, Australia with her husband, daughter, and three cockatiels. A lawyer by day, K.B. has written for various international anthologies, and her work features in dozens of collections about the mysterious, the magical and the macabre.

Clare Rhoden is an author, editor and reviewer who started writing young, and hasn't stopped. She lives in Melbourne, Australia with her husband and super smart poodle-cross. She enjoys reruns of old *Dr Who* and *Star Trek*, but who doesn't? Her dystopian trilogy *The Chronicles of the Pale* tells of intelligent canines living alongside human tribes on the ruined land. Her WWI historical novel is *The Stars in the Night*, and her latest book is a fantasy called *How to Survive Your Magical Family* (2022). You can find Clare's short fiction in several publications, and she has edited a handful of anthologies including *From the Waste Land: stories inspired by TS Eliot* (2022). Clare's stories derive from culture, legends and history. See more at https://clarerhoden.com

McKenzie Richardson lives in Milwaukee, WI. A lifelong explorer of the dark corners of imagined worlds, she's spent the past few years chronicling her findings. Her work can be found in publications from Iron Faerie Publishing, Eerie River Publishing, Black Ink Fiction, and Nordic Press. McKenzie currently works as a librarian, doing her best not to be buried beneath an ever-growing TBR list. When not writing, she can usually be found in her book hoard, armed with coffee and a good read. You'll find her on Facebook & Instagram @mckenzielrichardson

Amber M. Simpson is a poet and fiction writer who pens primarily in the horror and dark fantasy realms. Her work has been published in multiple anthologies and online. For a time, she worked as assistant editor for an indie publisher where she was able to work with many talented authors from all over the world. Currently, she is focused on getting her first novel, Wolves Hollow, completed, along with putting together a collection of her short stories (some already published, others brand new) into a book of its own for publication. Aside from writing, Amber enjoys crafting, traveling, collecting books, attending concerts, genealogy, chess, and all things mystical. She lives in Northern Kentucky with her husband/best friend, Brandon, her two sons, Max and Liam (who keep her feet on the ground even while her head is in the clouds), and her two dog children, Odie and Callie. To check out Amber's other publications: https://www.amazon.com/author/ambermsimpson

Stephen Herczeg is an IT Geek, writer, actor, filmmaker and Taekwondo Black Belt from Canberra, Australia, who has been writing for well over twenty years, with sixteen completed feature length screenplays, and numerous short and micro-fiction stories. Stephen's scripts, *TITAN, Dark are the Woods, Control* and *Death Spores* have found success in international screenwriting competitions with a win, two runner-up and two top ten finishes. He has had over two hundred short stories and micro-fiction drabbles published. He has also published a collection of stories *The Curious Cases of Sherlock Holmes* (2021) and two novellas *After the Fall Part 1 and 2* (2021) He lives by the creed *Just Finish It,* and his Mum is his biggest fan. More on Facebook @stephenherczegauthor | Twitter @HerczegStephen

Louise Pieper has a lot of opinions, a lot of black clothes, and a house full of books. Once, that would have been enough to see her burned as a witch but in these happier times she is largely left alone to read, rant, and write. Her published short stories have won an Aurealis Award and been shortlisted for an Australian Shadows Award. You can find out more about her obsession with weird words and her stories at www.louisepieper.com

Nikky Lee is an award-winning author who grew up as a barefoot 90s kid in Perth, Western Australia on Whadjuk Noongar Country. She now lives in Aotearoa New Zealand with a husband, a dog, and a couch potato cat. In her free time, she writes speculative fiction, often burning the candle at both ends to explore fantastic worlds, mine asteroids and meet wizards. She's had over two dozen stories published in magazines, anthologies and on the radio.

Her short fiction has been shortlisted six times in the Aurealis Awards with her novelette *Dingo & Sister* winning the Best Young Adult Short Story and the Best Fantasy Novella categories in 2020. In 2021, she received a Ditmar Award for Best New Talent. Her debut novel, *The Rarkyn's Familiar* won the 2023 Sir Julius Vogel Award for Best Youth Novel, three Indie Ink Awards, and Bronze in Young Adult Fiction at the 2022 Foreward INDIES Book of the Year Awards.